REAPER'S KEEPERS

ACCIDENTAL REAPER SERIES, BOOK 2

MISTY EVANS

Beach Path Publishing

Reaper's Keepers, The Accidental Reaper Mystery Series, Book 2

©2022 Misty Evans

ISBN: 978-1-948686-55-6

Print ISBN:

Cover Art by Fanderclai Design

Formatting by Beach Path Publishing, LLC

Editing by Elizabeth Neal, Patricia Essex

Please Note

ONE

"Come on, Andy." I checked my watch. The plastic face caught the red and green blinking lights strung around an overhead window of the apartment I'd been staking out for the past hour. "I have to be at work in an hour."

The noncompliant shifter, whose soul I was supposed to reap, spread his hands in supplication. "Can't we let this slide?" The bag of stolen presents hanging off his shoulder suggested he'd made quite the haul. "It's Christmas. A time for goodwill toward men and all that."

The hem of my black robes fluttered in the breeze. I tended to leave them at home for most jobs, but it was the coldest December in this part of Louisiana in decades, and a scattering of snow coated the ground. I needed the extra layer to stay warm. "First of all, you're not supposed to be here, as in alive and breathing, and secondly, you're a wolf shifter, not full-on human. Oh, and also? You're a thief. You've more than used up any goodwill that may have been allotted to you."

He waggled a finger in the frosty air. A light sprinkling of snowflakes were stuck in his reddish beard and thick, wavy locks. "I was given a second chance. Cured by a healer. I deserve to be here as much as you do."

Warming to his speech, he took a step toward me. Ghost, my dog and psychopomp, twitched her ears and growled, interrupting him. He glanced at the five-pound Papillion mix, with long hair and satellite dishes for ears, and snickered.

Kill, my death blade whispered in my ears.

"Yeah, yeah," I muttered. I lifted my hood and tucked my braid under it. My ears were freezing. "I'm getting to that."

"Who are you talking to?" Andy asked.

My palm itched to hold the magical scythe strapped on my back. It was compact, light, and deadly, and most folks couldn't see it until I was coming for them. Even then, they didn't necessarily see the weapon itself, but something far more enticing.

The skull and bones tattoo on my chest tickled, warming my skin. Too bad it couldn't warm the rest of me. "Soul Management Group doesn't give second chances." This was a lie, as attested by the fact I'd negotiated the terms of several peoples' contracts with Death himself to allow them more time. The noncompliant didn't need to know that. "You've violated the terms of your agreement. I'm sorry, but this is the end."

Andy didn't come any closer—the only smart thing he'd done tonight. "I'm not hurting anyone," he argued. "I'm your friendly, werewolf Robin Hood—I take from the rich and give to the poor."

His faulty morals aside, I had to reap him or SMG

would send Death to reprimand me. *Again.* My neck was on the chopping block with this job.

While I moved folks across the divide to the Great Beyond on a regular basis, the embodiment of death still scared my socks off. I did not want him showing up because of Andy.

Enough small talk. I was cold and tired, and I needed to change clothes before my shift at The Smoking Bean. The first thing I'd have to do was make myself a triple-shot espresso. "Take a look at this." I removed the scythe slowly from its new holder. It had been a gift from my mentor, a master vampire named Killion Reveux, after I'd solved my first case. SMG had made us partners to investigate mysteries and other strange goings-on in the supernatural world. The blinking lights danced across the well-polished steel blade. "Tell me what you see."

My tool could be used to slice and dice, but during reapings, it usually took the appearance of an item that soothed my quarry. A bargaining chip, so to speak, to alleviate their fear of dying and smooth the transition to the other side.

His attention landed on the slightly curved blade and his expression softened. "Mac and cheese."

What was it with food? In the six weeks since I'd accidentally killed Grim Reaper 281 and was forced to step into his robes for the coming year, nine out of ten souls saw comfort food when they stared at my weapon. "That's right." My teeth chattered and I stomped my feet to try and warm them inside my boots. "Piping hot and delicious. It's yours, so why don't you have a bite?"

With glazed eyes, he advanced, and this time Ghost, knowing the drill, panted and wagged her tail. "My grandma always made it for me when I was growing up," he said. "It was my favorite."

I could work with that. "She made this bowl especially for you. You've had a rough time and she wants you to come be with her. You can have her homemade macaroni and cheese any time you want. She'll take care of you."

Another step. My fingers twitched to take a swing and get this over with, but I wanted his compliance. It was his time to go, and yes, this was my job, but I didn't like the guilt of harvesting a soul who was scared.

He licked his lips. Although I still only saw the scythe, I could almost smell the food. It was certainly a better odor than those emanating from the alley.

"I sure have missed her cooking something fierce." The bag of stolen booty slid from his shoulder and rested on the ground. The garbage bag containing the gifts would keep them dry, and hopefully, stink free. "When I was going through those awful treatments, I was so miserable. All I wanted was to hear her voice, have a bowl of this"—he reached his hands out as if to wrap them around the imaginary food—"amazing treat."

I almost felt sorry for him. Most supernaturals never succumbed to human ailments, and cancer was the worst. However, Andy was truly a noncompliant soul, and the part where he'd paid a "healer" to remove his cancer, had consequences. The healer had apparently only transferred the disease to someone else—an innocent woman who might be facing her last Christmas this lifetime.

Andy's healer wasn't on my reap list, but 'accidents' did happen. "Take a bite," I encouraged him. "Grandma's waiting."

My cell rang, *Graveyard* by Halsey echoing off the brick walls. The glazed eyes snapped to my face, clearing away his desire for the temptation. "You're trying to trick me!"

Indignation, rage, and self-righteousness mixed in his expression. "I thought we were friends!"

At no time had I suggested that. I fumbled with chilled fingers to shut off the ringer, noting it was Killion. Odd, since most of the time he preferred to text. "Sorry." I slid the phone inside the interior pocket of the robes. "Now, where were we?"

Andy's eyes flashed orange and he snarled. The top of a paw tattoo peeked out from the edge of his turtleneck, his throat muscles tensing. It seemed to flash a warning as well, alerting me that his werewolf was riled up. Ghost, with her hair-trigger, morphed instantly into her psychopomp version and snarled back.

"Good dog." I patted her between the ears, her head at my eye level. Even if Andy were to shift, he'd be on the losing end. She'd devour him in three chomps.

"No eating the noncompliant," I reminded her. Andy shot me a terrified look. "We're working on her manners," I explained. "She's had some accidents. It was only two, really, but it's important that I train her on proper procedure."

The phone vibrated against my thigh. My mentor was persistent tonight.

"You're sick." He backed away and reached for the stolen gifts. "Death must be desperate to hire someone like you."

He knew my boss? Interesting. Humans couldn't see him, but certain supernaturals could. "Hey, I'll have you know... *Wait!*"

Too late. Faster than I could breathe, he grabbed the bag, shifted into his wolf form, and raced from the scene. The yellow drawstrings were clamped securely in his mouth, while his haul bumped along the ground, spraying snow.

Death was definitely going to be paying me a visit. I sighed dramatically and shook the blade at the starry sky overhead. "I don't have time for this," I yelled.

The handle seared hot in my palm, angry at being denied. Ghost whined, drool dripping from her fangs. A sticky plop landed on my arm and I made a face and shook it off. "Go," I told her, "but only stop him. Do. Not. Eat. Him."

She streaked away in a flash and I slid the scythe into the carrier. I hated running, but I followed at a decent pace, tracking the prints in the snow.

When I reached them, she'd cornered Andy at the park, and had him pinned down on the soccer field, dormant this time of year. He was in human form once more, naked from the waist up, and covered in her drool. "She ate my shirt!" He wiggled under her massive paws and tried to shove her away. "Call her off."

His screams could have awakened the dead. Out of breath, I stopped on the sidewalk and glanced around, needing to bend forward, hands on knees to catch my breath. Killion was right, I needed to work out more.

Luckily, no one was out in the cold at this time of the morning, except for the garbage truck moving at a snail's pace a block over. I wished I could toss this moron in it and be done with him.

Dante's Grove boasted approximately twenty-thousand people. Some, like Andy, were a mix of mundane and magical, and others were full-on supes. The hardcore lived off the grid, yet moved in the shadows of our tiny city, nicknamed Hell's Rejects, which was trying desperately to be the next top ten tourist destination in the state. Competing with New Orleans was laughable, but we had our fair share of actual magic users, along with those who wanted to profit off the idea of it.

Yet again, my phone rang, and having repositioned itself during the run, gave me a tiny thrill when it vibrated. To say I was hard-up in the relationship department was like saying Death was cute. "For grim's sake," I groused, as I drew it out and fired off a message to Killion.

Me: *Busy!*

Pocketing it once more, I made my way to Andy and held out the scythe. "Last chance to do this the easy way. Eat the food."

"No," he snarled. "I want to live!"

It wasn't my call. "No free passes."

I raised the blade overhead and he waved his hands, shrinking back. "She healed me. It's not my fault."

"Your time's up, and there's nothing I can do to change that."

My heart skipped a beat and my blood warmed unnaturally, causing me to pause. I knew what that meant, and it had nothing to do with the soul I was about to harvest. There was a master vampire within range.

No, no, no. Not now!

I made to bring the blade down when a sleek black limo crawled up next to us at the curb. The warmth in my veins spread like maple syrup through my system, making me shiver with its intensity. It magnetized me to the Undead male inside.

The rear passenger window slid down and Killion's violet eyes glinted under the streetlight, looking like purple heaven. Wavy locks of dark hair fell over his forehead. "Forget the shifter. Come."

I flicked my gaze to Andy and kept the scythe raised.

"One second." I hated that it sounded like a plea. "I really have to—"

"Now." The cold power of the command made my head pound and my arms lowered involuntarily. He had that effect on me, and I resented it. "I need you, Chloe," he said. "This can't wait."

TWO

The plush interior of the limo was quiet and dark, a few streetlights reflecting off the vamp master's handsome, if stoic, face in repeating stripes.

I adjusted my robes and removed the leather sheath. "What's got your undies in a bunch?"

Ghost was puppy sized between us, making herself comfy after showering Killion with kisses. He absentmindedly stroked her fur. "You will see when we arrive at our destination."

I'd expected coffee for sure, maybe even doughnuts or a scone. Killion was always feeding me, and rarely missed an opportunity to try and show me what a good guy he was, regardless of his fangs and haughty attitude.

He gazed out the window with unseeing eyes. His demeanor was normally cool and detached, but at the moment, the absolute control he was using to keep a lid on his emotions made him practically vibrate. I'd only seen this reaction once—when I'd asked if he'd ever been married in his three-hundred-plus years. He had. She'd been human, and she, along with their son, had died.

I suspected the only thing that could cause his current state pertained to his Undead family. His *nest*, as he referred to them. Why would he need me if he was dealing with a vamp issue? I tried again to draw him out, get a hint. "Are you okay?"

He clamped his jaw, making a muscle jump. "My welfare is not in question."

I glanced at the passing landscape, the yards becoming bigger and more spaced out. Normal three-bed, two-bath houses became mansions. Ritzy holiday decorations replaced cheap ones. "I hate to sound insensitive to whatever has you upset, but I have to be at work in"—I checked my watch—"forty-six minutes."

"If you would quit your menial labor jobs, this would cease to be an issue." He continued avoiding my eyes, and stopped petting Ghost. "As I've told you repeatedly, your grim duties come first."

A worn out argument we'd circled dozens of times in the past month. I gritted my teeth as it once more rubbed like sandpaper on my skin. Vampires, especially the one next to me, had no worries about money or the future. I, however, was human. An unusual one, granted, but still. My initial reaper case had landed me a nice bonus, paid off my school loans, and aided me in the financial department with my continuing semesters at the local university to become a veterinarian, but I needed a lot more to buy the building my parents had owned before their untimely deaths in a car accident.

I'd spent all my free time at their clinic when I was younger, helping them and the animals they'd treated. It was my dream to reopen the place and that required a degree, along with that building.

Balancing multiple jobs, school, and grim hours was like

juggling flaming knives. I was getting better at it, but had a long way to go before I stopped dropping one or another.

I was just as likely to get burnt by them at this pace. Hence, my lack of sleep, no social life, and falling GPA.

Luckily, I was on Christmas break from classes and planned to catch up on my zzzs. I'd also squeezed in two training sessions, although my conditioning was still subpar. Killion insisted I needed more, but getting routinely beat up by a favorite vampire minion of his, Katarina, wasn't my jam. I'd recently heard him refer to her as his "punisher." The moniker was apt.

I definitely needed to get more comfortable with using my scythe, and although I had enhanced strength when needed and healed quickly when injured, my stamina was for the dogs. I relied on caffeine and fear of failure to keep me running.

Reaching over to sink my hand into Ghost's silky fur, I let his grumpiness slide off. As the blocks continued to whip by at high speed, I thought about another strategy to lasso Andy. I still had today, but needed to reap that werewolf by midnight or face Death.

Always a thrilling prospect.

Killion rubbed his eyes in a weary gesture. "My short temper is regrettable. I am, as you say, upset. The situation is...concerning."

Killion Reveux concerned? Hmm. That meant he couldn't control whatever this was. "How exactly do you think I can help?"

The limo slowed and took a turn. Ghost sat up, alert. A gated community loomed ahead, with a welcome sign boldly declaring with its artsy font that *Tremont Village* was pricey and exclusive.

"I believe you have the skills to get to the bottom of this

for me." He met and held my eyes, now. "I will have one of my people at the coffee shop at five to prep for the morning rush in your place. Everything will be ready and you will arrive before opening time."

"One of your *people?* You mean a vampire? Absolutely not! They don't know what to do, and what if my boss shows up and some stranger with fangs is running around?"

"Mason is not a stranger, and he was trained by you."

"*Mason?*" My jaw dropped. "He's one of yours?" The high school nerd had been working for us for the past six months. I'd never have guessed he was anything but human, and our training had consisted of a whole hour tutorial on how to run the espresso machine and clean dirty tables. We'd barely spoken beyond yelling orders to each other. "You turned a kid? Killion!"

His glare went icy. "I would never. He was born to a vampire female, an extremely rare occurrence, as you and I have discussed. His father was human, but Mason has vampire traits."

And yet, holds a 'menial' job. I bit my tongue. Now was not the time to dive into that. "Did you know who I was before the incident in the alley at Halloween?"

"Mason is dear to me. I watch over him carefully, and when he decided to get a job, I asked Simone to make sure he had a decent one."

The Bean was good enough for him, but not for me? Worse, it seemed Simone, Killion's right hand vampire, had known about me for a long time. She and I were not fans of each other. Also, he wasn't answering my question—an annoying trait of his. "Nita handles the newbies. Did you arrange for me to train him?"

"Would it bother you if I had?"

"So you *did* know who I was that night when I killed

Gustafson." That didn't sit well. "I thought I made it clear about being forthcoming with important information."

"Mason requested to learn from you." He sighed, suggesting I was as vexing to him as what had happened to his nest. "I had nothing to do with that. In truth, I did not realize you were the Chloe he spoke so highly of when I happened upon you that night."

"But you knew Darcy." She was a fellow university student, and the one Gustafson, the rogue reaper I'd killed, had originally been after. "You telepathically told me her name."

"She had been reckless around town for some time, and I knew she was a prime candidate for Gustafson to prey on, so yes, I knew who she was."

Ah. Now, I understood. He'd been watching her for a good reason. I relaxed. "Sorry to be suspicious. I'm running low on, well, everything right now."

In a rare show of patience, he patted my leg. "I hope that one day you will trust me fully."

I hoped that, too.

The tall iron gate slid open as we approached and the limo eased through. I focused on the tasteful but expensive houses of the quiet neighborhood, some decorated for the holidays, others not. My blood did a slow slide again in my veins, but with more grit. Like it was flowing over honey-covered barbs.

Or perhaps, more accurately, *fangs*. I was now surrounded by the Undead.

The subdivision contained four large, well-appointed blocks, each ending in a cul-de-sac that snugged up to a community center, golf course, and swimming pool. Trees were decorated with white lights, an LED community sign in an island of gardenia and hibiscus flashed messages about holiday changes to the normal garbage day pickup, a fundraiser for a community garden, and reminders of a holiday party at the golf club.

So...human-like.

Two streets over, we pulled into the winding drive of a modern two-story with dark shutters and not a single holiday decoration. An interior light was on downstairs, but no one greeted us when we stepped up to the front door and Killion walked in like he owned the place.

Maybe he did. My mentor was not only the master of the local nest, he owned multiple businesses in town, including his own financial investment company.

Dread crept along my spine and my tattoo itched when I scented the home's owner. My inner survivor yelled at me to run as we passed through a clean, neat foyer with black and white checkerboard tiles and dark paneling. The crystal chandelier was off but the large windows to the east let in the fading moonlight. A single bouquet of blood red flowers on a side table under a mirror was the only splash of color.

I smelled her before I saw her—Simone.

The tang of copper pennies—or old blood, in this case—was mixed with her lilies and grave dirt scent. Killion and I entered a sitting area off the foyer and found her in a chair facing a white brick fireplace. No logs burned in it, and only the illumination from a shaded floor lamp provided my non-vamp sight with enough light to see properly.

"Simone." Killion's voice held a gentleness I'd rarely heard. "I've returned with help."

She rose slowly, head bowed. "Master."

I paused mid-step. The beautiful, arrogant vampire was in a state of disarray. Her dark hair was matted with an oily, muddy substance, an eye blackened and swelled. Fresh bruises decorated her jawline and throat.

Killion took one of her hands and used his other to lift her chin. She looked at me with defiant eyes and I found I was relieved the fire hadn't gone out of them.

Her clothes were smeared with the same substance as her hair. I'd learned in the past few months never to ask a vampire if they were all right, although I continued to forget when it was the most natural thing to say. Their pride kept them from admitting anything was wrong, so it was usually a moot point. "What happened?" I inquired instead.

She lifted her free hand to touch her face and brush back her bangs. Three of the nails were broken, dried blood coating her skin. The lamplight on her hair now made the mats appear bloody as well. "I was attacked."

"By what?"

"That's the question." Killion guided her toward the back door as he spoke to me. "Come with us."

"I told you what it was," she murmured. "You saw it."

He squeezed her arm.

I had to admit, I didn't like him touching her, but I sensed her fear as I followed them. Was I jealous? The thought made me cringe. *Of course not.* I simply didn't like her, although I felt guilty about the fact at this moment, seeing her current state.

The house was beautiful, but stark, like a magazine spread. There was no personality to it, and I wondered how much time she actually spent here. Killion owned the famous Beaumont Hotel downtown, and many of his nest lived there. When not working, he spent time there, too.

He retrieved a flashlight from a kitchen drawer and handed it to me. The vampires didn't need one to see in the dark, but I did. I wondered why Simone had it. Again, the humanness of it stood out to me.

Stepping outside, it took my vision a few seconds to adjust and I flicked on the beam. We were on a screened-in deck that lead to an open patio. As inside, the furniture was high-end but sparse.

A built-in fire pit graced a corner of the patio, chairs placed around it. There was an expensive outdoor kitchen under an overhang. Vampires rarely ate food and I wondered if she ever used it. Most likely, she kept up the appearance of being human, even when surrounded by others of her kind. And maybe, in this swanky subdivision, it came standard with the property.

I followed them down the steps and out into the yard, the grass still green and lush, blades poking through the dusting of snow. Had to be magic, or one incredible lawn service, since most yards in Dante's Grove were feeling the effects of the short winter days and cold nights.

A white fence enclosed the space for privacy and Simone had her own in-ground pool. A long rectangular thing lined with sculpted evergreens, it was currently covered with a tarp. Did she even swim? Again, it might have been standard fare here.

Killion led us to the north side of the patio, darker here due to the house's shadow. A blob lay in the yard next to the bushes, and it wasn't until my light rolled across the end that I realized what was there. The breeze engulfed me in a stench that made me gag. "Holy reapers," I muttered, seeing bare, dirty feet and ankles. There were long, narrow claw-like nails sprouting from the toes.

Simone stopped, refusing to go farther, even while Killion urged me on. The pungent odor of rotting corpses filled my nostrils. Covering my mouth and nose with my free hand wasn't enough—I had to hold my breath as I let the beam rise higher.

A simple, brown garment covered the man's hips, marred with more blood and soil. The oily substance stuck to his hands and slender fingers. His nails again reminding me of claws. His arms and thighs were generously muscled, but he never stood a chance against the vampire. His chest was bare, and had been scored from Simone's nails. The flayed skin showed gray, rather than red, though, and I thought for a moment it was a trick of the light.

My focus continued up to his head and I stumbled back at the sight. Then I leaned forward once more. "What the...?"

He wore a mask, so lifelike, curiosity made me step closer to get a better view. It was a canine head, but not dog or wolf. I choked and gagged again. Even with my hand over my nose and holding my breath, the smell was unbearable. Pivoting, I speed-walked away to a section of hibernating roses around an inactive water fountain and sucked in clean, fresh air.

When I glanced back, Simone had her head turned, refusing to look in the direction of the body. Killion stood expressionless next to it, staring at me as he waited for me to return.

Why he thought I could help with this situation—whatever it was—was beyond me. I stayed where I was. "Who, or what, is that?" I called softly.

With his acute senses, I didn't need to raise my voice for him to hear me. He cocked his chin at me and spoke to Simone. "Tell her," he commanded.

She shifted into the shadows, nearly disappearing. "I saw him hanging around a few nights ago, over there." A trembling finger pointed toward the golf course green in the distance. "I thought he was a drunk frat boy. We get those once in a while when they sneak over the gate. But he showed up here tonight. Not drunk. Not a frat boy. I confronted him and he attacked me."

Stick to the facts. It was one of my Uncle Morty's rules at the morgue. Usually I appreciated a succinct analysis, but this was...odd. Throughout the speech, she was detached, although her voice hitched here and there. I couldn't get a read on whether she was in shock or simply wrestling with her emotions to keep her vampire demeanor in check. I glanced at the body. "Did he say why?"

"I didn't have time to ask. He was on me before I could think. Incredibly strong, and I..."

"Killed him," I supplied when she trailed off into silence. "It was self-defense."

"No." Her eyes flashed in the shadows, red and eerie. My tattoo grew hot—a warning. "We fought and I made it back into the house. I called Killion and he rushed over."

The red gaze flicked to her master and he took up the story. "Once I made sure she was all right, I came out here to check if he'd gone and if not, confront him myself." He indicated the body. "I found him like this."

I glanced between them, searching for subterfuge or maybe a punchline. I pinned my gaze on Simone. "He simply dropped dead after your altercation?"

She nodded.

Riiight. Because that happened all the time. Placing my hands on my hips, I debated moving closer. No way I believed that...thing...had attacked her for no reason, then died. Had those scratches been the cause? Even at this distance, I could smell that horrible odor, and I stayed where I was. "You must have some idea why he would attack you, and why he ended up dead."

She stepped from the shadows, fists clenched. Her magic slapped at me and all my warning bells went haywire. "He was alive when I ran into the house. He tried to get in the door." Indignation rolled off her as she pointed to the back entrance.

I flashed the beam over it and saw scratch marks in the

wooden trim. Along with those, there was an indent in the door the size of a meaty fist.

"I'm going inside," she told Killion, but waited for his nod before she stomped off.

While we'd been out here, the swelling around her eye had gone down, but her movements were jerky, indicating she was in pain and favoring her left side. I watched her stride to the steps, my mind reviewing what she'd claimed, but also considering the time it had taken for Killion to come and get me and bring me back. "Why aren't your injuries healing more quickly?" I called.

She sneered over her shoulder. "You try being assaulted by an Egyptian god and see how fast you heal."

The door banged shut behind her. I took a step toward Killion, but another whiff of the dead guy made me stop. "Egyptian god?"

"With the jackal head, he resembles Anubis, the god of death." He said it so reasonably, I did a double take. This was a joke, right? But then he added, "We're dealing with ancient, very dark magic here."

For a heartbeat, everything went surreal. "You think that guy"—I pointed—"is a god?" Exhaustion was hitting me hard, and I felt jittery. I stumbled to a pool chair and sank into it. "Look, I don't know who he is, but you have to call the police."

Killion strode to me, fierce and intense. "I need to know how it's possible this being is here and why he attacked her. Since he's dead, that becomes more difficult, and that's where you come in."

"Me?" I shook my head. "He's a guy in a costume. His strength could be due to drugs."

Killion gripped one of my hands and tugged me to my feet. "Try to remove what you believe is the mask."

I bristled and jerked out of his grip. "I'm not touching him."

"Fine." He returned to the body, grabbed the muzzle, and gave a hard tug. The head moved, but the mask stayed put. It was either a well-made costume, or Killion wasn't kidding.

Before ending up a grim, I couldn't have imagined such a creature, but I had come to believe in a lot of things I'd only read about in books or seen in movies. "Fine. Move." I motioned my mentor out of the way, held my breath, and reluctantly, but determinedly, attempted to rip it off.

It wouldn't budge. I stumbled away once more, my legs giving out. My knees sank into the snow-kissed lawn and I gulped air, trying not to heave.

Killion was by my side in an instant, a hand on my back. I thought it was concern, until he said, "I need you to autopsy the body."

I whipped my head around to stare at him. "Are you nuts? Hard pass."

He knelt beside me, stroking my back and shoulders. "The only clue I have is this body. I need to know if it's truly an old god come to life, or something else."

Like a god wasn't bad enough, but the way he said *something else* sent pure fear into my bones. The knees of my pants grew wet, right through the robes. Distant sounds of cars on the road buzzed too loudly in my ears. The town was waking up, and even in a vampire community, I suspected a dead body on the lawn was frowned upon.

"What kind of something else?" I could barely whisper.

His eyes shone black in the creeping dawn. "The kind we don't want running around among humans." He took my elbow and lifted me to my feet. "I need to know what killed him in the event there are others like him being resurrected and sent after us."

This was certainly more than I had bargained for, and me without coffee.

Without warning, Ghost barreled into the yard, Moss on her heels. "Sorry, boss," the limo driver said. "She was going crazy in the car."

The dog ran like a greyhound in circles around the yard, stopped once to relieve herself in the rose garden, and then did another lap. Panting, she raced up to me and launched herself into my arms. The girl had spring.

If Killion hadn't still had hold of me, I would have toppled over. She licked my face with gusto, as if we'd been apart for years, rather than minutes.

"Okay, okay." My anxiety diminished at the feel of her in my arms. I hugged her and put her on the ground. "She has a small bladder," I said to Moss, by way of apology. "When a girl's gotta go, a girl's gotta go."

He looked slightly embarrassed. "Should I return her to the car?" The question was directed at Killion, rather than me.

Ghost growled and Moss, all two hundred and fifty pounds of badass vampire, backed up. "Leave her," Killion said. He walked to the form. "Get a body bag. I need you to take this to the morgue."

"The what?" I followed him and put out a hand to stop Moss' advance. "I can't autopsy that...thing, and you can't take it to The Pit." That was the nickname we used for the hospital morgue where I worked part-time. "Mary Lynn, Dwayne, my uncle," I continued, "they'll see it. And smell it. God, that's just atrocious."

Killion took my hand when Moss bent to pick up the

body. "I will glamour it. No one but you and I will be able to see him."

"What about the smell?"

"It will be contained. We can go there now."

"Do I want to know why you have body bags in your car?"

Moss pressed his lips together and became suddenly interested in the sky overhead.

"They can be invaluable when investigating," Killion said. A calm was sliding through my mind and body. He was working his mojo on me. It pissed me off, since he claimed he never did.

Maybe he didn't. Not intentionally. And all right, maybe I wanted him to. I told myself to pull away, but it felt warm and comforting. "I have work, remember?"

His steady gaze bore into mine. He was fighting his annoyance, but I wouldn't be swayed. My stubbornness was a match for his, and realizing he was getting nowhere, he gave a conciliatory nod. "Very well. What time does your shift end? Ten, correct?"

The fact he knew my schedule was slightly unnerving. I tugged my hand from his. "Even if I could perform an autopsy, this one is out of my league."

"I know very well that you can, and have, in fact, as a vet student. You've also observed dozens performed by your uncle. I will be there to assist if anything appears unnatural."

A crazy sounding laughter bubbled out of me. "Unnatural? Like all of this isn't? And two. I've performed an autopsy on all of *two animals*, not to discover what killed them, but to grasp the placement of organs. It's not like I grab a bowl of popcorn and watch when Uncle Morty is doing them, either. Gross!"

"Uh, boss?" Moss called. He'd hefted the jackal-man over his shoulder and now pointed at a lump on the ground underneath where the guy had lain. "Do you want that, too?"

Killion and I moved as one to stare at the spot. A mass of black feathers lay there, my flashlight showing me what appeared to be a dead raven.

"Eww," I muttered and corralled Ghost from getting too close. "No."

"Yes," Killion contradicted. "Take that, too."

FOUR

It took three shampoos to get the smell out of my hair. I was twenty minutes late for work.

Mason greeted me at the rear entrance with an iced caramel mocha and a fresh blueberry muffin, warm from the oven. "Killion said you needed food and caffeine."

He was a cute kid, hair down to his shoulders, dark eyes, like Killion's. He stood about my height and had a dimple when he smiled.

I accepted the offering and continued to my tiny locker. The coffee shop was empty, save for the two of us, the scents of beans and vanilla welcoming and comforting after my night. "We are going to talk about you being a vampire," I told him, sipping the drink, "but not today."

"You seem upset about it." He grabbed a twenty-pound bag of custom-roasted beans to take out front and fill the machine, hoisting it onto his shoulder. "It's not like you're a hundred percent human."

I stowed my backpack and coat, donning an apron and wishing I'd had time to dry my hair. I was shivering. "I am, in fact, just a plain old mortal, short on sleep and patience."

He gave me a knowing wink. "Sure you are, boss."

Every time I thought about what Killion wanted me to do later, I felt clammy. I stayed focused on grinding beans, tamping out grounds, and baking between rushes, for the next five hours. Mason didn't say any more about supernatural stuff and I was glad my bestie, Nita, didn't come to work until my shift was ending.

"You're pale as a ghost," she said, strapping on an apron. We were both in the back room. Mason was working a double shift. "You didn't braid your hair. Are you sick?"

I sure felt like it. "Too much sugar. Not enough sleep." I replied. "Heading home to collapse."

She walked me to the exit. "Call me later if you're feeling better. I've got shopping to do for my par—uh, family."

My parents had been gone for twenty months. I kept count. Holidays were bittersweet, and Nita danced around the topic, sensitive to my grief. "Sure, sounds fun."

Mason waved at me over her head. "See you, Grave Girl."

Ugh, the nickname the supernaturals loved to tag me with. Seemed it had spread from Death and his minion, Tinder, and then to the Undead Nation.

Nita shot me a questioning glance. I glared at Mason and shrugged at her, acting like I had no clue what he was talking about.

Moss and the limo waited a block down. He jumped out to open the door for me. "Everything is ready for you."

"Oh, goodie." Surprisingly, the back seat was empty and seemed much larger without Killion's presence. "Where is he?" I asked.

"Already at the morgue."

I leaned against the cool leather and closed my eyes.

The soft acceleration of the vehicle instantly eased me into a cushy half-sleep and I wondered if a five-minute nap was worth it. Dreamland called to my tired body, so ready to drift away.

Sidewalk carols blasted from the street speakers but barely penetrated the interior, creating a sort of background white noise.

I had nearly succumbed when Moss slammed on the brakes, jerking me awake. My eyes flew open as my body nearly catapulted into the divider between us.

"Sorry, Grave Girl," he called.

"Not you, too."

Two women jaywalked in front of us, both on their phones and paying no attention to traffic. A horn blared and still they continued on oblivious, heavy bags swinging from their free hands.

"What do you want to bet I'll be meeting one or both of them up close and personal one of these days?" I grumbled.

Moss snorted. "Humans." It was said with derision, and no concern for my feelings.

Of course, I did have a leg up on the garden variety mundanes, those with no supernatural qualities. Killion had resurrected me with a few drops of his blood when I took out the original Grim 281. Now, the robes and scythe added a layer of Jason Bourne to my repertoire. Might be time I acknowledged I *was* a bit different.

My eyes gravitated to the store fronts and my heart pinched. I finger-combed my hair and began braiding it. Frosty Paws sat closed and empty, the ghosts of yesterday looking back at me from the window.

Not real ones, thank goodness, but memories... They could be just as haunting.

When we were once more on our way, I shifted

forward, staring at the place. It had the only windows on the block that didn't have lights or decorations, a single plastic dog staring out forlornly. The sun had bleached him to nearly white, his once black eyes now washed gray.

Another ghost. That gaze seemed to follow me, begging for my return.

I placed a hand on the chilly window, craning my neck. "Soon," I promised him. I just had to hope the company who now owned the building didn't find a tenant before I could buy it back.

Fresh dread settled heavy in my belly when we reached the morgue. The hospital and the police station bookended the small building and both had attempted holiday cheer. From the faces of those coming and going from each, they'd failed.

Our security guard, Dwayne, was missing from the front desk when I badged in. The attendant that helped Uncle Morty with postmortems, Mary Lynn, was MIA as well. The work log showed no active cases, so no autopsies today.

Except for the jackal. Just the thought of seeing him again nearly made me gag.

The skip of my pulse and race of my blood told me Killion was inside, but I didn't seek him out initially, going through my normal routine and walking past The Pit, as we called it, without so much as a glance through the glass.

We speak for the dead. Respect and honor them.

Stick to the facts, and do not suppose you know what their life was like.

In the end, we are all the same—
none of us gets out of this world alive.

My uncle's sign taunted me. I definitely didn't know

what kind of life the creature on the steel table had experienced, and I had no idea what to expect. *Stick to the facts.*

In the pint sized office, Ghost greeted me. I smiled at her display, her tiny tail wagging so hard it knocked her off balance. She had a plastic bone twice her size on her dog bed and I knew Killion was a softie when it came to my psychopomp.

Dropping my bag near her, I mentally readied myself for the inevitable. I thought about saying no and suggesting we ask Death or someone at SMG for help. That would never fly, unfortunately, since Killion and Death were always at odds with each other, and SMG would no doubt declare it a vampire issue and order me to keep my hands off.

Which might be the excuse I needed, come to think of it. If Simone's injuries and the fear in her eyes hadn't been on repeat in my mind all morning, I might have actually taken that option.

But I owed Killion, and the whole incident bugged me. Curiosity might kill the cat, but it wouldn't me.

I hoped.

The master vampire stood guard over the body and greeted me when I entered The Pit with a solemn nod. A smaller body bag was off to one side—the bird. "I wish to state how much I appreciate your assistance."

My gaze flicked to him. I tried to look away, but only Killion could look drop dead handsome in such a place, those violet eyes compelling me to answer.

Focus. At least the place smelled normal—no carrion odor coming from the sheeted body. "We need to be quick about this. A full autopsy takes hours and we don't have that kind of time." I took an apron and face shield from the storage locker and slipped them on. "First, we'll check for obvious injuries and I'll run a few tests. Because of his... unusual anatomy, I may not catch anomalies, so I can't offer definitives."

He stepped to my side with a nod. "How may I assist?"

I pointed to the computer station on the counter. "Turn on the recorder."

"You're going to video the session?"

It was protocol, and also simply a good idea. "Yes, always. We may want to review it later. You'll need to wipe the hard drive after I make a copy on a USB, and any trace of the tests from the hospital system, so I don't get in trouble for this, but we do this by the book."

A solemn tilt of his head. "I understand."

Taking a deep breath, I grabbed a wheeled metal tray covered with a cloth and guided it to the slab. Mary Lynn had a set of tools cleaned and ready for the next body. I snapped on a pair of gloves and concentrated on the steps I had to take and not who or what waited under that thin sheet.

"Okay, then." I gave myself a mental and emotional nudge. I could do this. "Let's get started."

FIVE

I told myself I would not be grossed out, freaked out, or upset by anything I discovered.

No gold stars today. I failed and did so big time.

Drawing blood made my jaws tight and my empty stomach heave, the black oily substance nothing like a human's. Testing it seemed pointless, so I skipped that, but the skin was an unusual texture and ashen gray under the bright lights, so I scraped cells from the arm to place on a slide and examine. They were as dead and non-cell-like as anything I'd ever witnessed. They didn't appear to be canine, either, and I was stumped.

Returning to the body, I examined it in more detail. One of Simone's dagger nails was buried in the skin near the clavicle and I extracted it, the tissue making an odd tearing noise. There was no bruising or dried blood from the injury—another mystifying anomaly.

Time to dig in. Using a scalpel, I started with the chest and made a Y incision. Slicing through the claw marks Simone had left, I had to put more effort than anticipated into opening the incision. Past the epidermis, dermis, and tissue, I sawed, rather than sliced, the odor again overpowering and rotten, even with the magical deodorizer trying to contain it. I lowered the blade, the incision incomplete, and stepped away, stomach roiling.

Killion said nothing, and I appreciated it. I paced The Pit a few times, cleared my mind, and got back to business. While the body was all kinds of gross, it was also...fascinating. If only Uncle Morty could see me right now.

Good thing he couldn't.

When I returned, I inspected the hands, rather than diving into the organs. There was dried blood and a few scratches. One of Simone's long, dark tresses was stuck under a fingernail.

I'd never used rib cutters and didn't relish the thought of this being my first time. Through the cavity, the heart appeared as gray as the skin and encased in strips of cloth. Confused, I left it, moving to examine the organs.

Like the heart, they were wrapped in some type of rough fabric. I glanced up and exchanged a look with my mentor. He seemed as surprised and confused as I was.

"I believe the organs have been mummified." I couldn't quite process it. "How was this guy alive and functioning?"

A muscle in his jaw jumped. "Magic," he replied.

I removed the liver and cut through the cloth. I could detect no living tissue in it. Next, I checked the intestines, which weren't mummified, but shrunken and nonfunctioning. By sheer will, I held myself together, weighing and noting the measurements of each specimen and taking slivers of samples as I went.

Still avoiding the ribs and heart, I examined the neck and cranium. There were no marks indicating it had been attached in some manner. My mind could not fathom that it seemed to be...natural. As if a man had grown a jackal head. It simply was part of him.

Yet, this was no man.

Was he?

An inspection of the eyes showed petechial hemorrhaging, suggesting he'd been smothered or choked. I checked the neck again, but it showed no sign of bruising or other trauma. When I opened the long snout to inspect the throat, I had to stop, back away, and steady myself. In all my work with dogs—and corpses—I'd never smelled anything like this.

Determined to get through this, I shone a penlight into the interior of the mouth and the beam illuminated what resembled the edge of wet burlap. "What's this?"

As Killion watched silently, I grabbed forceps and motioned for him to hold the massive jaws open. "Have you discovered the cause of death?"

"There's something in his throat." It was lodged good. I wiggled, adjusted the grip, tugged harder. "He shows signs of choking, although there's so much oddness about him, it's hard to say that's what he died from."

When I couldn't dislodge it, Killion stayed my hand. "Let me."

We switched positions and within seconds, he yanked the wad free. Vampire strength—hard to beat. A bag, tied with a string, dripped with saliva.

"Gross," I muttered, quite familiar with drool, thanks to my psychopomp, if unsure of the reason our jackal-man had burlap stuffed down his throat. I grabbed a stainless steel pan and held it out for Killion to drop the item in to. "That's the same material, I think, as the cloth used to mummify the organs. Do you know what it is?"

His furrowed brow suggested he was wracking his brain. "A hex bag?"

Placing the pan on the counter, I began untying the string. "What's that?"

Killion grabbed my hand. "Witchcraft that you do not want to touch. Hex bags are created to harm an enemy, but"—he glanced back at the body—"that thing is not human, and to shove the bag into its throat would be quite challenging, one would think."

"There's something inside it." I poked at the burlap with the forceps. "We need to see what it is."

He studied the soggy lump. "If it is a hex bag, the material should be inert to anyone but the person it was intended to harm. Still, do not risk it."

"Maybe Jackal was delivering it to Simone. She was the target. He accidentally swallowed it and choked to death." I hoped it might be that simple. "Mystery solved."

The vampire narrowed his eyes. "He could have easily removed it himself."

There *was* that. "It was really stuck," I said in defense. "Maybe he was carrying it in his mouth, then accidentally swallowed it while they fought. It became lodged and did him in before he could yank it out."

"You saw the damage he did to Simone. This is a supernatural creature with extreme strength." He seemed completely confounded. Which unnerved me—were there creatures stronger than a vampire? "Why would he carry such a thing in his mouth? He has human hands. Further, if he were delivering it for a witch, all he needed to do was place it on Simone's property, not attack her."

"Superhuman strength aside, I think you can rule out her assumption that he's a god."

Lost in his thoughts, he didn't reply.

I grabbed a pair of scissors and snipped the tie.

"Wait," he ordered.

"We need to see what's inside." The burlap unfolded and I pushed the edges back.

Bad move. A tingling sensation tickled my skin. My eyes teared from the wave of rot that emanated from the contents. I coughed, even as my eyes were riveted on what it contained.

Several finger bones, two canines, a small white feather, and a piece of parchment with a weird symbol on it. All were jumbled together with slender slices of what resembled meat. They were pinkish, suggesting they were fresh. "I'm going to be sick," I muttered, turning away.

"Witches," Killion spat. He took the forceps from me and examined the sigil. The combination of blood on them, and saliva from Jackal's mouth, had caused the ink to blur. "This is evil business."

I knew what I had to do, my gut already telling me what I'd find, but I relished it about as much as I had cutting open the corpse in the first place. With due diligence, I tested the strips of flesh and the samples taken from the organs. Killion, thankfully, remained quiet over the next hour, watching as I worked. Once when I glanced at him, he seemed pale, but I brushed away my worry. I probably looked like death warmed over, too.

Eventually, I'd done as much as I could. Or would. "Heart, lung, stomach." I pointed to the lined up segments on the counter, both the mummified ones, as well as the fresh. I'd viewed each under the microscope and tested them, identifying them to the best of my ability. "Lower intestines, pancreas, and finally, liver." Returning to the body, I pointed at our creature. "The fresher tissues don't match the mummified versions."

"They came from someone else?"

I nodded. "The cross-sample is missing a brain, and it's going to stay that way. I suspect our guy here has one, although possibly mummified like his organs."

"This is dark, dark, magic," Killion stated. He gripped the edge of the counter as if to steady himself. "I do not like it."

"Yeah, well..." I glanced at the clock. It was nearing two a.m., and I was beyond exhausted. I needed carbs or sleep, probably both, before my shaky limbs gave out. "We need to clean this up. We'll have to figure out the rest later." I reached for the body bag to close it up. No sense sewing Jackal back together.

Killion held up a hand to stop me. "I need you to look at the bird."

While I was certainly more at home dealing with an animal, I was in need of fresh air and a mental brain wipe. I snapped off a glove. "What's the bird going to tell you that we haven't already figured out? Simone pissed off a powerful, dark witch, who sent Frankenstein's monster after her. He choked on his own juju bag and killed himself."

"I'm afraid it is not that straightforward." His thumb raked across the inner skin of my wrist as he took my hand. The muscle in his jaw twinged again. "This is necromantic magic."

Okay, maybe he did know more than I did. "Wait. You mean, raising the dead?" An involuntary shiver raced down my spine. "Wouldn't it be simpler to hex Simone than go through all of this to create a...monster to take her out? And not a very bright one at that. Why do this to the organs?" I pointed to the heart. "I'm not ignorant. I've seen movies and read books, but those are fiction. No one can take pieces and parts from people"—I glanced at the head—"and animals, and form a whole being."

"Can't they?" His hand was still warm on my wrist, as though he were checking my pulse. "Organ transplant is real, is it not?"

"Sure, *human*-to-human transplants. Xenotransplantation is still in its infancy."

"Yes, of course, but it *has* been done, and science continues to work at making it a viable option."

"There are no signs the head was attached to the body. It honestly looks as if he grew it. Like, he's some type of hybrid." I glanced at Killion. "Similar to you and Mason."

"Me?"

"You're half-human and half-vampire. I've seen your monster." *And it's not pretty.* "However, you're a good deal more handsome, in general, and no doubt considerably more intelligent."

He lost the incredulousness and considered it. "A hybrid. You make a compelling argument."

I wanted to pull away, but the feel of his hand encircling my wrist grounded me. Part of me wanted to stay like this, staring into his beautiful violet eyes and knowing that no matter how bad this was? I could count on him to help me figure it out. "And even human-to-human transplants require living tissues and experts to perform the surgery."

"Magic makes many things possible." His thumb stroked across my pulse point again. I knew he was trying to slow my heart rate, calm my nerves. "I know this is out of your comfort zone, but it has indeed happened. This is no fictional horror story, and necromancy does exist."

"Like vampires and werewolves," I said crossly, tugging against his grip. He let go and I stalked to the table where the smaller bag rested. I didn't bother putting my glove on again or starting a fresh video. "Fine. I'll look at the bird, but no promises."

The moment my hand touched the black fabric, it moved. The formerly stationary lump began gyrating. "What the...?"

"Caw! Caw!" The cry was muffled, but still sent icy fingers shooting over my skin.

I jumped back, watching in renewed horror. At my side, Killion did the same.

The raven was alive.

SIX

"Out!" came a muffled screech from inside the body bag. The whole thing tumbled over. "Out, out!"

"Holy reapers." I was screeching, too. "It's alive, and it's speaking!"

"Ravens can mimic human speech," Killion stated.

"I know, but—" The imprisoned bird was struggling so hard, it was about to topple off the table. I lunged for it and Killion grabbed my hand.

"Don't touch it."

"It's trapped. I have to get it outside and set it free."

He wouldn't let go. "You did this."

"Did what?"

"Out!" the bird demanded.

"Resurrected it." Killion's voice was low, wary, and his grip on me was tight.

I tugged hard and broke free. "I'm a grim. I kill things, not"—I waved at the bag—"raise them."

His gaze flew to the corpse, then to the trapped raven. This time when my hand shot out to stop the bird from ending up on the floor, he didn't stop me. "The damage is already done."

The bird jerked when I lifted him from the table. "I'm taking it outside. The dumb thing was just stunned, that's all. I need to make sure it doesn't have any injuries, and if it can fly, I'll release it."

Ghost meandered in, either drawn by the squawking bird or my raised voice. She eyed the thing in my hand, then backed up a step as I started for the door.

In a literal heartbeat, the vampire was in front of me, blocking my path. "The raven is the witch's familiar. It will report back what has happened."

The bird had to weigh ten pounds and my already strained arm muscles were starting to burn from trying to keep hold of it while it fought against its prison. "And that's a bad thing?"

He looked almost sick. "He or she is a necromancer and it seems some of their power has been transferred to you."

The raven pecked at my hand through the fabric. "Ouch," I grunted. At the same time, it cried, "Out!"

I gave him a shake. "Enough."

The fight stopped, the bird falling silent.

"That's better." I glanced at Killion and saw the tiniest hint of surprise cross his face. "This is ridiculous. I'm not a necromancer."

"You raised it from the dead." He took a step back. "You can command the witch's familiar."

It was part horrified statement, part shocked question. The surprise turned to something I'd never seen in his eyes —fear.

"Scared I'll resurrect *you*?" I joked.

He didn't reply and kept his distance.

"Oh, for heaven's sake. Grab that towel. When I open

the bag, throw it over the raven's head and wrap him in it so I can examine him."

Killion's posture stiffened. "We are not releasing it."

"Then what? Are you looking for a new pet?"

Eyes turning hard as flint, he said nothing. He didn't need to—I knew instantly what he planned to do.

"Absolutely not." I held the bag close. "Witch's familiar or not, I'm not killing it."

"It was already dead," he argued. "This can only end poorly."

I marched to the counter and grabbed the towel. "I'm going to examine him." I set it and the bird on the table. "Are you going to help?"

Scowling, he snatched up the towel. "I will iterate, this is a bad idea."

I motioned at the corpse—thank goodness, that thing hadn't reanimated. "What part of this hasn't been?"

Jaw set, he watched warily as I unzipped the bag. A dark, glossy head poked out, one beady eye circling around and around, while its matching one fixed on me.

I peeled the fabric back. "Take it easy, little fellow. We aren't going to hurt you."

Killion moved toward it with the towel. "Speak for yourself."

The bird cocked his head sideways, the normal eye locking on the vampire. His wings fluttered, releasing several damaged feathers. There was a piece of rawhide leather sticking from his beak. It fell when he opened it. "Kill!" he snarled and lunged for Killion's neck.

One of the wings flapped but the other was damaged, sending him into a lopsided freefall. Killion moved with lightning speed, catching him and winding him up in the terrycloth.

Only the bird's head poked out, the wild eye continuing to whirl. "Careful," I told Killion, and then to the bird, "Looks like you've been through the wringer."

His head and beak seemed normal, outside of his wandering eye. It wasn't bulging, red, or inflamed. Loosening Killion's grip, my fingers brushed his, and I felt the unease radiating off him.

Focus, I reminded myself again. "Head, neck, and chest appear within normal limits," I recited as I reviewed them. "Let's have a look at that wing."

The raven chittered and shuffled between his two claws as much as possible with the vampire still restricting his freedom. The left wing appeared normal other than the missing feathers. The right however... "This is nasty." A deep gash oozed blood and I spotted bone as I gently pressed my fingers and thumb around it. "There appears to be a break. I need an x-ray."

Killion was impatient as I made him don an apron in the x-ray room. "I am a vampire," he reminded me. "Radiation at such low doses will not harm me."

"Good to know. Set him there." I pointed to the table under the machine and swung the overheard arm into place. As Killion pressed the bird onto his back, the raven's claws pedaling in the air, I gingerly drew the wing out to its full span. "Now, hold this."

Begrudgingly, he did, and I ran back to the computer to activate the machine. A few minutes later, the bird cocooned in the towel once more, I stared at the gray and white image. "The joint where the ulna, radial, and humerus bones meet is busted." I sighed. "He may never fly again."

"Too bad." The statement was more calculating than sympathetic.

I shot the vampire a glare. "He needs surgery and a bird sanctuary."

"Hmm." I didn't like the cold way he sized up our patient. "What is your name?" he asked it. I knew he thought to command it with the designation.

The crazy eye stopped spinning. As the normal one peered at Killion, the other focused on me. "Kill," the bird whispered.

"Aww, that's sweet." I sent a copy of the image to my email and deleted the one on the computer. "You share the same name."

Killion didn't find my sarcasm amusing. "Who are you to kill?"

Silence. I continued cleaning up. "Look, we really need to get out of here. Leave him be—he's not going anywhere—and help me."

He ignored me. "Who is your master?"

Another silence, but this one became heavier. I glanced over to see both of them staring at me. "What?"

Killion took the bird and shifted him around so he couldn't see me. "Who is your master?"

The raven swiveled to face me once more.

As the realization sunk in, my stomach clenched. "Oh no." I waggled a finger in their general direction. "I have a dog and a one-pet max at the apartment. I'll call the bird sanctuary and drop him off there, and that's the end of it."

"We need to get the bird to lead us to the witch. You can command him to do so."

I stripped off my shield and apron. "He's not leading us anywhere. He's injured."

After removing his own apron, Killion followed me to the office, the bird under his arm. "I will take care of the cleanup." He moved closer, concern evident as he studied my face. "You are beyond exhausted. Moss will take you home so you can rest. We train tonight."

"Send a copy of the autopsy video to my email before you wipe the drive. Tonight, I'm sleeping for at least ten hours after I reap the werewolf." I dropped the strap of my bag over my head and grabbed my jacket. Ghost danced at my feet. "You know, the noncompliant you cost me? He's two weeks overdue on getting his ticket punched, and Death will be coming for me if I don't take care of him."

Killion set the raven on the floor and tossed the towel aside. The dog sniffed the air in the bird's direction, then danced on her hind legs, wanting me to pick her up. The raven hobble-walked to get to us, and I lifted Ghost into my arms.

"I'll take care of the familiar," the vampire said.

The bird stared up at me, his crazy eye on Killion. "Go," he squawked, and hopped to hide behind me.

"He doesn't trust you anymore than I do," I joked.

Killion speared me a look. "Fine, I'll remove the corpse and erase our time here from all the logs, but leaving that thing,"—he pointed to the raven peeking out from my leg—"at the sanctuary is unwise. Care for it the best you can and keep it with you for now."

"He needs surgery."

The vamp waved a hand at the room. "Then perform it."

My blood sang with the command. His vampires had to bend a knee and do what he said, but I didn't. "This is a morgue, not a surgical unit, and besides that, I don't have the training."

"You wish to be a vet? Dive in and figure it out."

Incensed, I huffed. "I've never set a bird wing before. It most likely needs multiple pins and who knows what else. I can give shots, draw blood, and handle minor injuries, not surgery."

"YouTube," the raven croaked.

We both glanced at him.

Killion held out a hand. "There you go. Problem solved."

Ghost squirmed, ready to go, and I shook my head. "Killion, this is nuts." I glanced at the cadaver, the chest still lying open from the Y incision. An idea struck. "Blood." I glanced at the vampire once more, setting Ghost down. "Give me your arm."

He didn't move, watching me as I put down my jacket and bag and went for a clean scalpel. "Whatever are you thinking?"

He knew what I was thinking. I didn't hesitate, latching onto his hand and pushing up his sleeve. "Your blood can heal."

Vampires have incredible strength, along with supreme self-preservation instincts. When he jerked from my grip, I nearly fell over from the force of it. "Absolutely not."

Ghost and the raven following me, I went to the cabinet and searched for a rubber tourniquet. "Roll up your sleeve."

"I will not have that thing bound to me."

I whirled. "Wait? I'm *bound* to you?" Sure I could sense him when he was around, but... "What does that mean exactly?"

He purposefully relaxed his posture. "You have free will. A dumb beast does not."

"Kill!" The bird lunged at his leg.

"*Christosul!*" He jumped back when it pecked at him, swearing in his native Romanian tongue. "How dare—"

I laughed and grabbed a syringe. "Look, your blood is already part of me, and the bird has attached itself to me already. You're connected to him, whether you like it or not. This is the best option."

"That's not how it works."

"I did you a solid here. Time to return the favor. Which reminds me, I think this should earn me the right to know your real name."

It wasn't easy to surprise a vampire. Killion looked like he might choke. "I don't see the relevance."

"No, you just don't want to share. I thought we were friends. This is what friends do—they share their real names."

The paleness I'd noticed earlier returned. "I have not identified with that name for over a century. It is not who I am."

"Why are you being stubborn about this?" I'd been on a mission to figure this out, and no amount of internet searches had revealed anything about his former life in Romania. Unless, he truly was related to Vlad Dracula... "I just want to know."

"It could put your life in danger. I will not tell you."

"Danger, as in someone might torture me for it?"

He nodded. He'd once told me that giving your true name to another in the supernatural community made you vulnerable. They could use it to control you.

He looked rather tipsy again. Or maybe that was me. My vision was fuzzy around the edges. Could it be from the lack of sleep? The nightmare I'd just put myself through?

"Fine." I ripped open the bag with the needle. *But I will find out.* "Hold out your arm, and quit being such a wuss."

The criticism worked. The master flashed his fangs, both as warning, and as a tool. "That isn't necessary. I can open a vein myself."

"Now you're just showing off. By the way, intimidation

isn't your best look." I ignored the parts of my anatomy that tingled at the sight of those sharp teeth. Guess I was too exhausted to feel scared. "He won't drink from your wrist, so put those things away. I need to draw the blood from you and inject it into him."

He snarled and a dark shiver raised gooseflesh on my skin. Our eyes met and held. My tired limbs flooded with adrenaline and...anticipation. Whether it was my fight or flight instinct kicking in, or my very female parts, I wasn't sure. Probably both.

I saw his nostrils flare and he whirled away, seeming to have to collect himself for a moment. That made two of us. While he did, he rolled up his unbuttoned sleeve to expose his skin. Once completed, he propped his elbow on the counter, avoiding my eyes. "Don't make me regret this."

Doing my best to breathe normally, I adjusted his position and wrapped the rubber strip around his arm. "Make a fist." I hated that my voice came out low and breathy.

His muscle bulged as he did my bidding and his eyes glittered at my obvious response to his power play. I brushed his skin with an alcohol wipe, knowing it was unnecessary, before I tapped a prominent vein with my finger.

"You smell...delightful."

Heat from embarrassment crept up my neck and into my face. I knew exactly what he was referring to. I had no idea what good, old-fashioned lust smelled like, but his vampire senses were highly attuned to it.

Forcing my fingers not to shake, I sunk the needle into his flesh. His grunt told me my touch was heavy-handed, and I found that gratifying. "Did that hurt? I'm so sorry."

The fangs flashed again at my insolence. The black

depths of his pupils expanded to shade his violet irises. "I welcome the pain and anything more you wish to do to me."

My breath caught. I held onto his forearm longer than I needed to. He was hot under my touch and I didn't want to let go.

I swallowed hard, forcing myself to release the rubber knot. I filled the syringe and attempted not to squirm. "I'm not into rough stuff."

"Too bad," he murmured.

Another swipe with the pad and a bandage later, I had his blood. I stared at it for a long moment, licking my lips. He saw the action and our eyes caught. The air sizzled between us.

I needed to get out of here. Away from him. I broke eye contact and searched for a fresh syringe.

Ripping off the dressing, he rolled down his sleeve. The moment was over. "Command the creature to be still so I can hold him."

While issuing orders came easy to him, it didn't to me. I smiled at the raven and showed him the syringe. "This will help you heal. You need to let me inject you with it."

As expected, he darted away, sensing there might be pain involved. "Out, out, out," he chanted, running into the door.

Killion rolled his eyes. "I will kill you, if you don't obey."

The raven squawked, beating his one good wing at the exit. Ghost watched with her head tilted to one side.

"There, there," I said, scooping him up. "Don't be afraid of the bossy vampire. I won't let him hurt you." I glanced at Killion, who flashed his fangs at me again, but it was more playful this time. "Can you get the corn chips from my bag?"

"Whatever for?"

"Please?"

He shook his head, going to the office and emerging a moment later. "Now, who's bossy?"

The chips did the trick. As Killion distracted our injured fellow with them, I injected the blood into the tender breast muscle under his wing.

Ghost whined, and got a couple chips as well. "How long before it takes effect?" I asked.

Killion shrugged. "With humans, it's approximately a minute."

Carefully, I unwound the stabilizing wrap from the bird's wing. The open skin was knitting itself back together and I had to assume the bones underneath were, too. "Cool. See?" I nearly jumped up and down. "I told you it would work. No surgery or YouTube necessary."

Killion watched me, a different look in his gaze now. "Well done," he said, sounding somewhat reluctant about it as he tossed the empty bag in the garbage can. "Now, we can find the witch."

SEVEN

On the ride to my place, I used nearly an entire container of hand wipes to remove the worst of the smell that had seeped into my hair and skin. Moss was unnerved by the bird and kept making the sign of the cross. You could ex-communicate the vampire from the Catholic Church, but you couldn't take the Church out of the vampire.

Unfortunately, when I called the sanctuary, I was told they were full. They couldn't take the raven, even though he seemed to be healing nicely. "It's only me here," Gus, the owner told me, "and I don't have any cages or places left to put all these birds." His voice was slow and drawn out. "If the bugger can fly, turn him loose."

I had no choice but to take the raven to the backyard and set him on the bistro table my landlady Vera had placed under an oak tree. She'd hung a wreath on the gate door, and a lighted plastic Santa, half my height, waved from the screened in porch. Ghost sat on the lowest step and watched us. "Okay, my friend," I told him, "fly."

The raven's unnerving eye whirled and he turned his

black head to spear me with his good one. He fluttered his wings and the injured one actually spread out.

"Good," I praised him. "Now, flap it."

He watched when I mimicked what he should do. His feathers ruffled and he beat the wing against the tabletop. He didn't lift off. Instead, he took a couple steps and hopped down to the ground. He cocked his head and stared up at me.

"Fly." I put more steel in to the command, channeling Killion. If I didn't get this bird to embrace his freedom, I feared he'd end up at the master vampire's mercy.

The raven toddled around at my feet. *"Reste,"* he said with a trace of an accent.

"No, we're not resting. You need to leave, skedaddle, vamoose. Understand?"

"Chloe?" Vera emerged on the back porch, her cat, Miss Pickles, in her arms. She squinted through the screen, adjusting her glasses. "Are you talking to a bird?"

"Reste," he cawed, and then ducked behind me.

The cat hissed and Vera flinched. "Miss Pickles, that hurts. Retract those claws, young lady."

The cat was at least thirteen. She didn't act it, and her owner didn't acknowledge that either of them were getting up there. At least I'd bought Vera ten more years by negotiating her contract at Halloween. "He injured his wing," I told her, "but he's healing and I'm trying to get him to use it."

Vera returned the cat to the house, then joined me. "What's wrong with his eye?"

"Not sure." Since the vampire blood hadn't cured it—yet—it might have been genetic or a birth defect. "Maybe that's why he won't fly. His vision is wonky."

He rubbed his head against my calf. *"Reste."*

Vera bent to get a better look at him. "You speak! *Tres bien!*"

The bird peeked at her. "*Bien.*"

"That's your problem," she told me. "He's French."

I stared at her in disbelief. "He's a bird."

"*Vole,*" she said to him.

I would swear the thing shook his head.

"What does that mean?" I asked.

"Fly. Soar. Use your wings. He was probably a pet and his owner spoke French. Who knows what other languages he might know." She scrutinized him. "Seems he's attached to you. You do have a way with animals."

The only other language I spoke was that of coffee. French Roast was as *le français* as I got. But being in this part of Louisiana with plenty of people who did speak it, I mimicked my best accent. "*Vole,*" I commanded, stepping away from him and making a fly motion with my hand.

He did that side-eye thing again and hobbled over my feet, extending his good wing like he was attempting to hug me. "*Necare! Mortifera!*"

"Latin, too!" Vera clapped. "You're a renaissance man."

He was something. "Why me?" I grumbled.

Vera headed for the house. "Do you have food?"

The weight of everything hit me hard. This was not what I needed on top of my already heavy load, yet I felt the tug to take care of him. My mom and dad would have.

I sighed, turning to follow her. "Not for a bird."

"Come on." She waved a chubby hand for me to follow. "I've got a few things."

Her sister, Velma, ran Helping Paws, a dog rescue. She often ended up with other animals, too, from gerbils to parakeets. Vera had adopted a parrot not long ago and had an extra bedroom full of items folks had donated and Velma didn't need. Most of the bird items went to Petey, but she had extras. We didn't find a big enough bird cage, since the raven stood as tall as my kneecap, but a dog kennel would at least corral him when I was gone.

While I cleaned the dust off the wires and snapped the sides together, she gathered a cuttlebone, spray bath mist, and a few toys, all still in their original packaging. I brought in a sturdy tree branch we'd been saving for the outdoor fire pit and secured it between the metal bars to act like a perch.

"What do you think he eats?" Vera asked. "Would he like Petey's food?"

"Corvidae are scavengers, so pretty much anything." I grabbed my phone and did a quick search. "Says here they like nuts, meat, fruit, and dog and cat food."

Her eyes lit up. "We have plenty of all those." She trundled off.

Hauling the cage upstairs to my apartment, Ghost and the bird followed. Ghost ran effortlessly; the raven bounded on his feet.

"This is temporary," I told him, as if he could understand. Maybe he did. His species was one of the smartest in the bird kingdom.

He refused to get in the cage, even when we offered various edibles. Vera and I started with dog food, then tried canned tuna, nuts, Petey's preferred chow, and finally, Vera pulled out the big guns. She brought him some of her prized meatballs. Even that didn't interest him. She huffed, clearly put out about it, but I happily accepted the snack and thanked her.

"Like all animals, he'll eat when he's hungry," she declared and disappeared downstairs to watch her favorite talk show.

I wanted to fall into my bed, but I showered quickly,

leaving the dog and raven in an uneasy alliance in my bedroom. Toweling off, I heard the *peck, peck, peck* of a beak on the wooden door. "Out," the bird called through it. "Master."

Peck, peck, peck.

With only the towel wrapped around me, I jerked open the door. "Do not destroy this wood or I'll have to pay for it. And I'm not your master."

After throwing on a t-shirt and shorts, I attempted to get him in the kennel. He refused and I warned him, "You better not mess up anything."

Then I climbed under the covers and fell into an exhausted sleep.

EIGHT

I woke to someone shaking my arm. "Chloe, get up."

I jerked upright and shoved the offender off the edge of the bed. Reflexes 1; visitor 0.

"Whoa, whoa, whoa." A hand grabbed the edge and a face peeked over it. "It's me, girl. Get a grip."

"Nita?" I blinked and rubbed my eyes. The room was shadowed, the shade down. "What time is it?"

"Time to go shopping. You didn't answer my text, so Vera let me in. " She stood, brushing off her tight black pants. Her trusty rose-colored trench hung over them, and she'd left her purple hair down, the naturally curly ends brushing her shoulders. She glanced at the blankets behind me. "Is that a bird?"

Ghost was sprawled on her back, legs in the air and head cocked to the side. So much for being a guard dog. The raven, mimicking her, was in the same position, his wandering eye doing circles. I rubbed a hand over my face. "He's injured and the sanctuary couldn't take him."

She raised the shade, allowing soft afternoon light in. "Looks like Ghost has an admirer."

"Kill?" the raven said, though it sounded like a question.

"No," I huffed. "No killing."

Nita startled, her pink lips puckering. "It talks?"

"I assume his owner taught him." I left out the part that it was most likely a witch. "He has to be a lost pet."

"Did he get hit by a car or something?"

Umm. "Or something." *Like a two hundred-pound jackal-man who might be an Egyptian god.*

"We can put a listing on the local lost and found sites." She whipped out her phone.

As she reached out and tickled the raven's belly, snapping a picture, I considered the idea. *Maybe I can get the witch to come to me.* "Okay, but do it anonymously."

She exaggerated a sigh and then showed me the photos. "Which one should I use?"

The raven looked like a cartoon character who'd been dropped off a cliff. Every angle she'd snapped, he was either lopsided, wild eyed, or lying on his back like a corpse with his twig legs hoisted in the air. "None of them?"

She feigned offense. "You question my skills? He's adorable."

"If by that you mean odd, quirky, and homely as sin, sure."

Her fingers hustled over the keypad. "Go brush your hair and get dressed. I'll have this done in no time and we can go."

Sure enough, it only took minutes for me to pull my hair into a ponytail and switch out my sleep attire for jeans and a sweater, but she had created an alternate email for me and several social media accounts for it.

"Sent you the passwords," she said, still typing. "*Lost raven seeks owner.* Where did you find him, by the way?"

I gave her the general area of Simone's, but not the address or subdivision name, while I shook food into bowls.

"What were you doing in that part of town?"

Both animals downed the kibble, and I almost broke out my Rocky fists-in-the-air dance. Whether he was continuing to mimic Ghost, or had grown hungry enough, the bird was fed. I wondered if I could coax him into the kennel. "I was with Killion."

Her head snapped up. "House shopping?"

"Hardly." One of these days, the pretense of him being my boyfriend was going to bite me. And not in the *sexy vampire at my neck* kind of way. "Just visiting a friend of his."

Her face fell. "Oh."

"Kill," the raven said, wobbling toward me.

"His lexicon is limited, isn't it?" She eyed him. "Should I mention he can talk?"

"No, we'll use that fact to verify the owner's identity, if and when they claim him."

"Right." She returned to typing. "Good plan."

A final press of her thumb and she nodded, satisfied. "It's on Pet Finder and I'll copy and paste to the other sites after shopping."

I herded the bird into the bathroom and put the kennel with his water and toys inside. He attempted to follow me back out, but I maneuvered around him. Ghost looked at me expectantly, wagging her tail. "Gotta run the dog out," I told Nita.

Before Ghost and I got to the back entrance, the bird begin hammering on the bathroom door with his beak. "Out!" He squawked. "Kill!"

Nita laughed. "Miss Vera's gonna love that."

"You take Ghost. I'll handle this." I was not giving up a

few minutes of normalcy for this bird. The raven was going in the kennel.

Inside the room, I grabbed a towel and squared off with the wacky-eyed thing. "Look, I respect the rebellious vibe you've got going, but you can't destroy property, and pecking at that old wooden door could hurt your beak." Reasoning seemed like a good approach. I shook the towel like a matador. "I'll only be gone an hour or so, I promise. Get. In. The. Kennel."

He stared at the towel and cocked his head. In one deft motion, I tossed it over him and grabbed his wiggling body. Then promptly tripped when I stepped on the corner of the fraying terrycloth.

By some miracle, he ended up inside the cage, but I managed to clock my lower lip on the corner. It split, I yelped, and the bird cried, as though I'd broken one of his legs.

"Everything okay in there?" Nita called, having returned with the dog.

The cut stung and my eyes watered. I dabbed blood from my lip. The raven shook off the towel and rushed the open end of the kennel. "Fine," I called, slamming the door into place.

Since my near-death experience in October, my reflexes are super-charged. I'm not quick like the vampire who resurrected me, but I slid the tiny bolt into place before the raven could whirl his cuckoo eye.

After years of working with animals, I knew not to underestimate his potential Houdini abilities when it came to releasing himself from a cage. Ravens were intelligent and crafty. I grabbed a carbine and snapped it into place as an extra measure.

Unhappy, the raven fluttered around and squawked. I

doctored my bleeding lip. The cut was not deep, but boy, did it sting. I spit blood into the sink and rinsed my mouth.

"Oh, my stars," Nita said when I emerged. "Did it attack you?

"I'm fine. Ready?" I grabbed my crossbody bag. Along with my reflexes and improved strength, I healed lightning fast. The cut would be gone in the next few minutes. I didn't wait for her to answer. "Let's go Christmas shopping!"

We *chutchutchut-ed* through town and out to the highway, Anita's old stick shift a far cry from Killion's limo. We sang along to Christmas carols she had on a playlist and she gave me the low down on her latest dating app experience. "I think I'm going to try women," she said, taking the left toward a set of specialty shops decked out in holiday trimmings. "Expand my horizons."

I'd heard this before. She was just annoyed that Officer Pete Rogan had turned her down last week when she asked him to the coffee shop's Christmas party. "Except you're not gay," I reminded her.

"I might be." The parking lot was full, a popup tree lot taking up space in one corner. There were booths selling homemade treats, hot chocolate, and poinsettias. "I could give it a try."

As we waited for a mom and kids to cross in front of us, she waggled her brows at me. "Oh no." I raised my hands to ward her off. "I fully support your mission, and don't take this the wrong way, but I'm not interested."

She shrugged. "Your loss." We inch-wormed forward, scanning for anyone exiting a space. "The dating pool is so limited here."

"There are hundreds of eligible guys at school alone."

"If you like immature, beer-obsessed, sex maniacs, sure. I want someone sophisticated. Older and mature."

"With a fat bank account and muscles," I added. She made a face at me and I chuckled. "I'm just saying. You want a lot. Guys our age don't usually have all the boxes checked. They need fine-tuning."

"Does Killion have any brothers?"

I actually had no idea, but even if he did, she didn't need one. Up ahead, a white SUV's brake lights flickered, the reverse lights coming on. "There!" I pointed.

She shifted and revved the motor. "Hang on!"

We managed to squeak in before a blue truck coming from the opposite direction could make the turn, cheering as we came to a sudden stop in the spot. Her car seemed to sigh with relief when she put it in park.

The place was crawling with shoppers, most of them women, their hands full of bags. Over the next two hours, we hit all five of the specialty shops and were loaded down with some ourselves when we finished. I hadn't thought about work—at The Smoking Bean, morgue, or for Soul Management Group—and I hadn't worried about the bird, dog, or Killion and Simone's issues.

My life had been messy before the reaper gig. It certainly hadn't become easier or more organized since. These stolen moments were few and far between and I was grateful for Nita's presence in my life. We'd been friends since grade school when I'd punched Julie Jensen in the nose after she'd made Nita cry.

"Let's get a cocoa for the road." She pointed to a food truck behind the tree lot. There was a white sandwich board announcing their Jingle Bells special — cocoa, whipped cream, and peppermint candy shavings on top. "I could use the sugar boost."

Not one to deny myself, I led the way, anticipating the deliciousness.

Professor O'Leary, a teacher at our college, was in line, his salt and pepper hair less salty today. Was it me, or had he dyed it? It was subtle, but made him look younger. He smiled at our approach, his light blue eyes crinkling at the corners. "Hello, ladies."

"Professor," we chorused in unison.

He had a sparkling gift bag under one arm, and turned to pay the older woman selling the drinks. She handed him two beverages, steam rising from slits in the to-go cups' lids.

Several birds circled overhead. One of them cawed.

"Finishing up your Christmas shopping?" I asked, ignoring them. It was winter; birds moved around town in groups hunting for food. *Nothing to worry about.*

He glanced at the bag and his expression flickered. He thanked her and moved aside for the next customer. "I needed something special for my daughter. This time of the year is hard on her."

The sky overhead darkened with more birds. They were big with large wingspans.

Ravens.

"Sorry to hear that," Nita said. We walked a few steps away. Nita pointed at the second cup. "Is she here with you?"

"Oh no, this is for my...friend." The professor lifted his chin to point at a woman across the way. Dressed head-to-toe in a red wool coat, hat, and gloves, her eyes were hid behind sunglasses and her lipstick matched the shade of her attire. Her lips moved in a forced smile and she mimicked checking out a store and signaling she needed another minute. He raised a cup and called, "Take your time!"

She ducked inside.

"How nice," Nita said. "Is she from around here?"

"Oh no." His face brightened. "Ms. Leon is from Cairo. A fellow doctor with a similar specialty in genetics, only her focus is human, where mine was... You two don't care about that. Anyway, I'm working on a ground breaking research project and she's been instrumental in it."

Nita gave him an impressed face. "Egypt, wow. It's on my bucket list."

He smiled. "My daughter's as well."

I was more curious about his research project than his friend, but the birds were distracting me. Nobody else seemed to notice them. It was too much of a coincidence that I had one of their kind back at my place and now they were everywhere.

Did the witch know I had her familiar? Had she sent these ravens to bring him home?

My gut clenched and the palm of my hand began to warm. Tingles ran down my fingers. *Oh no. Not now.* Omen birds and witches forgotten, I glanced around at the crowd —someone here was on my list.

Wasn't that a cheery thought for the holidays?

The woman emerged from the shop. "Well, I should be going." O'Leary offered a smile to us, but his attention was on her. Totally smitten, it seemed. "I haven't seen class lists for the new year. Do I have either of you next semester?"

"Me." I raised my tingling hand, determined to ignore it and the forewarning about an impending death that settled in my chest. "Microbiology."

His face brightened. He seemed to truly like me, and that made me happy. "Very good. You're nearly there, Chloe. Keep at it."

"That's the plan."

"Enjoy your break." He stepped off the curb and raised a drink. "See you soon."

As he crossed through the parked cars, making his way to the woman, Nita sighed and turned me around, marching us back to the ever-growing line. "If only he were a few years younger."

The ravens disappeared. I felt ill. Previously, I'd only been assigned noncompliant supernaturals—not humans, but with my recent promotion came expanded duties. Frowning, I glanced over my shoulder at O'Leary; he was gone. My hand stopped tingling. "No, not him."

If my guess was correct, Professor O'Leary didn't have long to live.

NINE

"What's wrong with older guys?" Nita put her arm through mine. "I mean, he's probably pushing fifty, but he's super smart. He's still a vet, you know, he just doesn't like being called doctor. I feel bad for him."

A breeze kicked up and I shivered. Continuing to scan the folks milling around, I hoped I was wrong about our professor's impending date with death. I absentmindedly said, "Uh huh," but her words sunk in. "Why do you feel bad for him?"

"About his wife." When I gave her a blank look, she rolled her eyes. The line moved forward and she dragged me a step. "You need to get out more."

I noticed a rather tattered squirrel over at the tree lot. It looked dazed and misshaped, and—holy reapers—had one of his eyes just gone spinning? I jerked my gaze away and focused on the sandwich board. I no longer felt like a cocoa. "What happened to her?"

"She died of breast cancer a couple of years ago. Their daughter was only thirteen at the time. He stopped his vet practice, and Megan went off the deep end."

My heart sunk farther. "That's terrible." I felt for all of them, especially because the young girl lost her mom. At least I'd been an adult when mine had died nearly two years ago.

Not that that made it easier, but I did have more memories. Having experienced a near death experience and becoming a grim, I'd connected with my mom's spirit twice. Death claimed I was a "tweener"—someone who could walk on both sides of the veil. Linking to her hadn't filled the horrible void in my chest, but I now knew without a doubt there was an afterlife.

I'd experienced it during several reapings. Soul transference, it was called. While Killion insisted it was dangerous, allowing a soul to carry me to that plane was the most blissful thing I'd ever encountered. My parents were in that space now and that made the emotional void of their deaths easier to handle.

I supposed that was what mediums could do—offer some peace to a person stuck here after their loved one had passed. The thought settled my stomach.

Once we had our drinks and a giant gingerbread cookie to split on the way home, I glanced over and saw the squirrel had hobbled to the curb and was staring at me. At least his good eye was. His entire right side was still flat, and that eye swirled one direction, then another. "Is the professor in good health?" I narrowed my eyes at the animal and mentally shooed it away.

"Why?"

Cutting across the lot, we made it to Nita's car. A mom in a minivan stopped on a dime, and motioned at us to hurry. She wanted the spot. "Just curious."

We loaded our packages into the backseat. Glancing toward the curb, I could no longer see my new animal friend and breathed a sigh of relief. Surely he hadn't been...dead. I hadn't somehow...

No, the idea was preposterous. This was Killion's fault for planting the idea in my head.

Giving our spot to the minivan owner, Nita finagled us out of the lot. As she drove down the street with one hand and ate pieces of the cookie that I slipped her with the other, she hummed along with her playlist. "As far as I know, Professor O'Leary is fine. In fact, he seems as healthy as ever. Better than he did before break even. Don't you think?"

He did. I chewed a piece of cookie, not really tasting it. "Dyeing his hair to make him look younger didn't hurt."

"Bet his friend from Cairo has something to do with it."

"He deserves to be happy." I sipped my drink, and considered the future. Whatever was going to happen to him, it was going to be soon. Since he appeared healthy, that could mean an accident. "Poor guy."

"I don't know if I could handle a suicidal teenager," Nita shifted and made a turn. "No wonder he had so many gray hairs already."

I shot her a look. "Suicidal?"

She finished chewing and reached for her cup when we stopped at a traffic light. A raven landed on the pole to my right. "Megan's attempted it two, maybe three times? I don't remember, but it's pretty nasty."

I leaned my head on the chilled window, the cold pane doing nothing to cool my burning worries. The raven stared down at me, and I stuck my tongue out at him. I could only imagine what Megan might do if she lost her dad, too.

"Chloe?" We lurched forward again, leaving the bird behind. Nita divided her focus between the street and me. She reached over and patted my arm. "You okay?"

I forced a smile and nodded. My facial muscles were too tight, and I knew she could see right through the fake smile. Licking whip off my cup, I worked at regaining some of our earlier cheer. "I'm good," I said around a sip. It looked as though I'd be making a deal with Death soon. Better reap Andy and any other noncompliant on my list, and fast, to make myself look better. Death really hated it when I negotiated, but I couldn't leave O'Leary's daughter parentless. Decision made. "Thanks for today. I needed it."

My newfound cheerfulness earned me a flicker of a smile from her. "You're going to have a great Christmas," she insisted, squeezing my hand. "You have Killion and Ghost this year."

I almost spit out my drink, but the thought did bring on a chuckle. I wondered if Killion and his 'family' celebrated the holidays. I bet Moss did.

Nita had no idea how far from great I was, but she didn't need to know. Our friendship was one of the few normal things I had left. With ten months remaining on my employment contract with SMG, I could hang in there. Then, I would be done with reaping and I could get back to my real life. "It's going to be fantastic," I told her.

My conviction faded as we pulled up to Vera's. Death was waiting for me.

TEN

Thankfully, Nita couldn't see him and his six-foot-seven Adonis figure. If she had, I would have been in trouble as he looked up from scrolling on his phone and waved.

My insides shook, not due to his blinding smile or handsome face, but because I knew what he was here for, and it wasn't to wish me a Merry Christmas.

My friend put the car in park to let it idle. "You working at the bone house tonight, Morticia?"

I glanced at Death. I might be *in* the morgue at this rate. "Nope. It's me and sappy holiday movies with my landlady."

Death stood, pocketing his phone and giving me a *hurry up* gesture. I exited the vehicle and reached into the backseat to pull out my shopping bags, trying to juggle them with my nearly empty cup. I almost wished I was heading back to the smelly, depressing, but mostly quiet morgue for real. Hopefully, Killion had kept his word and cleaned up the earlier mess.

Nita got out, too, and peered at me over the roof. "Need

help?" When I shook my head, she glanced at the cheerily decorated front lawn and yard. Vera had done a great job of turning it in to a Louisiana version of a winter wonderland. "Wish I could hang out with you guys, but I have duty tonight. The holiday hours are going to kill me, but the extra tips are so needed."

A shadow cut across us. A raven flew over our heads. Good thing my hands were full. I couldn't flip him off. "Thanks again for the shopping trip." I strode for the house. "Talk later, Gomez."

My outside entrance was at the rear, and I needed to avoid Vera if possible. I ignored Death as I approached, but cocked my head to the side of the house where the sidewalk would take us around back.

"Don't forget the holiday party," Nita called. "Want me to pick you up?"

I mumbled a frustrated curse, because I had indeed forgotten it and I didn't want to go. But Uncle Morty would insist I be there since the hospital was hosting it, and he thought I needed the socialization. Instead of getting a date, I'd invited Nita, like I always did for these things. Glancing over my shoulder, I put on my happy face. "Sounds good. Can't wait."

Death fell into stride with me while she drove away. He followed me up the stairs without saying a word, more birds landing on the railing and fence. I continued to ignore him and the birds, and I could sense how it annoyed him.

Finally, he broke his silence. "Enjoy yourself today, love?"

"Chloe, remember? Not love. And yes, up until now." I made him hold the cup so I could wrestle my keys from my messenger bag, hoping he meant the shopping trip and not what occurred earlier with the jackal. He didn't always know everything that happened in the world, but he often knew more than I was comfortable with when it came to my business.

"The wolf shifter is still loose."

Ahh. I slid the key into the lock and let us in. Ghost was at the door, and she jumped up and down in greeting. "Hey, girl," I said, skirting her and dumping the purchases on my sofa. I petted her and said to Death, "I'm working on it."

He filled my apartment with his physique and over-whelming presence. He sent the cup into the trash and I felt his 'death' glare on the back of my neck. "Oh, I can see that." His Aussie accent was in full force. When I glanced at him, he motioned to the pile of gifts, then picked up Ghost and let her lick his face. "You seem to be very focused on everything but reaping Andy."

"Curtain," I ordered, making a twirling motion with my finger.

Since my landlady had once been a floor monitor years ago at an all-girls school, she had a strict "no men in the apartment" rule. If she heard or saw one up here, I could be evicted.

Death snapped his fingers and the soundproof bubble of his magic enveloped us.

I slung the messenger bag onto the floor near my tiny desk. "It's Christmas. I have things to do that don't involve being a grim. I know you're angry, but I *will* get him. Just give me another twenty-four hours."

"There's something different about you." He sniffed the air and scrutinized me, then reached out and plucked some-thing from near my left shoulder. As he drew it away, I felt a tugging sensation and saw a strand of what looked like a black, wiggling worm. He held it up, evaluating it. "Who have you been hanging out with?"

"What is that?"

A sudden thud sounded against the bathroom door. The raven called out, "Kill!"

Death raised an eyebrow. "New addition to the menagerie?"

"A rescue." I pointed at the thing. "That was attached to me? Why didn't I see it?"

"A magical leech." He balled it between his hands, and when he opened them, it was gone. "I haven't seen one of those since..." He shook his head. "It's probably been five thousand years or more. That's some dark, ancient magic there, Chloe."

Another bang came from the bathroom and he opened the door. The raven hopped out, glanced up at him, and was immediately bowled over by Ghost. At the dog's enthusiastic greeting, he listed sideways, then toppled, causing him to squawk and flap madly before he regained his footing. He gave Death a wide berth to hurry to me, hiding behind my legs.

Dark, ancient magic—one guess where that had originated from. "Do I have anything else on me?"

Death's eyes went cold. "Besides the stink of vampire?"

"Can you be civil? Just answer my question." I brushed at my shoulders. "I feel as if I have cooties."

"You sound like a five-year-old."

Patience deserted me. I had to filter my next words. "And you sound like a jealous boyfriend."

He glanced away—a concession. "What has he exposed you to?"

"What can you tell me about necromantic witches?"

His gaze jerked to mine and he made a face, waving a hand under his nose. "They smell terrible." His eyes dropped to the bird, rose back to mine. "Oh, hell and brimstone. That's what it is."

A raven flew past my window, sending a shadow over the floor. "What *what* is?"

The bird behind me pressed himself against my legs and trembled. I automatically reached down to pat his head and reassure him.

"The *cooties*." He ran a hand over his face. "You're infected. How did that happen?"

My mind flashed back to the morgue and the bag; the bird who had been dead now at my feet. The squirrel at the tree lot. I hated to admit it, but Killion was right—I could raise the dead.

Animals, at least.

Choosing my words carefully, I explained about the bag I'd found during an autopsy, leaving off details about the jackal. "How do I get rid of it? This magic?"

There was a long, tense pause while he gave me the stink eye. "That's not exactly my area of expertise."

I'd heard that before. "Be serious. You're king of the dead, so to speak."

"Grave girl, we're talking about necromancy. I may deal in death, but I don't *raise the dead*. What's dead should stay that way."

"I respect your stance on the subject, but if that were the case, I wouldn't be here, so you'll excuse my opposite point of view." I knew he was, in truth, lecturing me about the Undead. I didn't need to hear that song and dance again. What I needed was information. "I just need to know how to fix this."

"I'll have to get back to you. For now, you need to find Andy and take care of him."

I hadn't so much as glanced at the squirrel before it had

resurrected. "What if I harvest Andy and he comes back to life? So far, it's only been animals, but what if I start inadvertently raising humans?"

A long, exasperated breath left his full lips while he considered this. "Quite the quandary. We don't want a bunch of zombies running around. That gets ugly."

It shouldn't have surprised me, but I still had to ask. "They're real?"

He rolled his eyes. "You have no way to control it? To turn it off?"

I shook my head, the implications overwhelming. I certainly had to stay away from the morgue until this was resolved. What an excuse to not go to the holiday party, right?

His sharp gaze rested on the raven, still cowering behind my legs. "There must be a way to reverse the hex. I know someone who might be able to help. Let me check with her and see what she recommends."

Without an answer, he vanished, my mouth still open and ready to ask another question. Frustrated, I raised a hand. "Okay then, see ya." I slumped into my chair as the raven ran circles in the middle of the room and shouted, "Kill!"

"We have to expand your vocabulary." I eyed a bag of candies sitting on my desk. "Try this: jelly bean."

He didn't stop pacing and flapping. I finally corralled him and set him on the bathroom vanity. "Let's have a look at your injury."

I examined it carefully and he let me, staring mesmerized at his reflection in the mirror. The once broken wing appeared normal, not a sign of any injury left. He still seemed unable to fly, though, or maybe simply unwilling.

"Okay." Death appeared in the doorway, making me

and the bird jump. He handed me a folded piece of paper. "My resource says you have to destroy the hex bag and perform this ritual while you do it."

Heart hammering, I accepted the note and unfolded it. "This is in another language. How am I supposed to read it?"

"You can't read Latin?" He shook his head in disgust. "What are they teaching kids these days?"

I narrowed my eyes at him. "Can *you* read it?"

"Of course, but I've got to run. Death is a twenty-four/seven business, you know. Get your friendly vampire to help you and harvest my noncompliant shifter. Tonight. No more excuses."

"Wait." I scrambled after him as he strode away. "I need a favor."

He whirled on me and chucked my chin. "I just did you one, love."

I balled the paper in my hand. I'd been so caught up in my own problems, I'd nearly forgotten about the O'Learys. "I have a teacher—Jamison O'Leary. I think he's scheduled to die. He has a teenage daughter who lost her mom not long ago. She's emotionally traumatized and needs her dad."

Death held up a finger in warning. "No extensions. I already agreed to your terms with the gal downstairs. You can't save every person you like or feel sorry for, Chloe. If this O'Leary character is scheduled to die, then so be it. There's karma, life lessons, and all that other mumbo jumbo surrounding birth, death, rebirth cycles. You mess with that and you throw off the precious balance of the world."

We'd had this discussion before, and I was still undaunted in saving those I cared for. "Please. There has to be something I can do to buy him a little more time—six months? A year? In the grand scheme of things, that's nothing. A blink of an eye to you."

His face remained impassive. "No."

"Hey, I've been covering the Grim 1st and 2nd Class duties since Halloween, thanks to the vacancy left by Jacqueline. I appreciate the promotion, but it's getting to be too much. I deserve compensation, and this is what I want."

"About that." He rubbed his jawline. "We'll have a replacement for the 2nd class position soon. Smudgy appreciates your dedication, and understands the pressure you've been under. Once you harvest Andy, your schedule should be clear for Christmas. Enjoy the time off."

Smudgy is what he'd nicknamed SMG. While time off was great, I was annoyed that he was quoting the company line to me. He dematerialized before I could blink.

The raven peeked his head out of the bathroom. "Jelly bean?"

I patted his head. "You're a quick learner." Maybe I could teach him more. I stared at the writing on the paper, sagging onto the sofa, still full of bags. Two fell off and both dog and bird climbed on with me, crumpling those that were left.

While I longed for a quiet night in, that was a pipe dream. After petting the animals and praising the raven for his new word choice, I pulled out my phone and texted my mentor.

ELEVEN

"After we do this," I told the master vampire, "I want to talk to Simone."

Night was falling when we made our way to a long-ago abandoned Catholic church in a different part of town. I'd given up hope of sleeping tonight, and I rather looked forward to getting rid of whatever magic had invaded my system.

The church was considered a place out of time—a different dimension, if you believed in that sort of thing. The stones and spires certainly looked like they'd come from the medieval era, and the magical glow it emanated confirmed it was otherworldly.

"The resurrections have only occurred with animals?" Killion frowned at the screen divider between us and Moss. "No humans, correct?"

"Not that I'm aware of. I didn't run to the nearest cemetery to test the theory. I also seem to be attracting a lot of live birds, mostly ravens."

"Some consider them omens of death or misfortune."

"Awesome."

"Others believe they are a sign of luck. Either way, I regard them as links to the other side. Like you." The limo rocked as we drove into the weed infested lot next to the church. "Why do you wish to speak to Simone?"

Ravens were tweeners, too. Hmm. "Did you ask her about our witch theory?"

He nodded. "She claims she doesn't know any."

I highly doubted that. Ghost wagged her tail as we came to a stop. Killion had insisted I cage the raven and leave it behind. No easy task, but I'd managed it, feeling guilty when the bird cried forlornly when I left. "Yet, she managed to piss off one enough that he or she sent Jackal after her?"

The glow of the magical church enveloped us and made my skin tingle. The last time I'd been here Jacqueline Vermouth had tried to kill me and nearly succeeded. It was only due to the vampire next to me that I was still alive. "I have interrogated her in-depth. I can find no connection to any witch or necromancer."

While that seemed like a dead end, I wondered if Simone was holding back information from him. I doubted she'd be more forthcoming with me, but it wouldn't hurt to try.

I scanned the landscape, zeroing in on the cemetery next to the church. I could only see part of it, since it wrapped around the side of the building, but from all indications, Katarina's pets were absent. The caretaker of the church had them guarding the property, and I didn't quite know what the grotesque creatures were, but she loved them.

After putting the vehicle in park, Moss opened my door and Ghost jumped down. "Okay," I said. "Let's get this over with. I have a soul to reap."

Our Holy Virgin Mother had been righted since my last visit; her serene expression formed by the plaster mold seemingly unfazed by her surroundings. The beads she'd worn at Halloween had been replaced with red and green twinkling lights strung around her neck and single upraised hand. We passed by her patch of overgrown grass and started up the crumbling concrete steps.

I was on the third when Ghost's hair stood on end. Killion was at the set of heavy wooden doors, ready to use the metal knocker, when I heard a low snarl behind us.

The cemetery's guardians, with their red eyes and elongated muzzles, bared their teeth from the cracked sidewalk. Ghost growled back, morphing into her psychopomp version.

The beasts were in no way intimidated.

"I thought Ghost killed one of those last time we were here," I said to Killion, easing backward up the steps.

"Katarina?" he called to the caretaker. "Open up." He glanced at me. "They're already dead."

"Right, duh. So while Ghost decapitated one, it simply... what? Regenerated?"

A series of clanks and clicks from the other side cut through the growling. Killion nodded and reached for my hand. The big, bad vamp wasn't afraid of much, but he did seem nervous around the guardians.

They're already dead. "Oh, snap."

As one of the church doors shifted open, squeaking on its ancient hinges, Ghost leaped from her stance. At the same time, a creature bounded toward us. The two collided in midair, a tangle of snarling hair and menace.

I jumped aside. "Stop," I yelled, worried Ghost might lose this round. I appreciated her protective streak, but it would be her undoing someday.

They landed, tumbling over each other. "Get inside," Killion ordered, grabbing me and shoving me toward the entrance.

Katarina stood in the opening, watching the fight with wide eyes. "Your dog better not"—she was cut off by an ear-splitting yelp.

The second guardian had joined the fray.

"Hey!" Two against one wasn't fair, regardless of Ghost's abilities. I broke free from Killion's hold and barreled down the stairs. "Break it up!"

Looking for an opportunity to grab Ghost's collar, I ignored both his and Katarina's protests. Overhead, the cry of a bird rent the air, the last rays of the setting sun turning the scene an odd lavender shade. The magical glow of the church's energy rippled in white hot flashes around us.

I felt it in my bones, that flash.

The raven landed like a drunken college boy a few feet away, a wing fully extended and flapping at Ghost and the creatures. The other made it about half out and dragged a bit on the ground. Everything, including those fighting and the bird, seemed electrified for a heartbeat when my feet touched the ground. They all froze.

The electric jolt hit my chest, a familiar, yet uncomfortable tugging at my rib cage. "Oh no," I muttered, and yep, before my eyes, Katarina's pets popped like fireworks. The next thing I knew, she was swearing at me and Ghost looked perplexed.

Gone were the undead beasts. In their place were a black lab and golden retriever, looking confused.

"What have you done?" she shrieked, shoving me aside. Her thick, black boots thumped on the steps and her piercings flashed in the purple haze. She fell to her bare knees, her pleated schoolgirl skirt fluttering out around her. She drew the Labrador into an embrace. "Mommy's so sorry! That bad woman did an awful thing to you."

My sigh echoed around the area, nearly as loud as the golden retriever's whine. "I didn't mean to, Katarina."

She snarled, showing me her fangs. "You're a menace."

"Why are you mad I brought your dogs back to life?" The golden wagged his tail. "Most folks would be delighted to have a beloved pet returned to them."

She whirled on me, irises glowing red. "What kind of magic is this?" She pointed at the two dogs. "Undo it."

Killion moved to my side. "Chloe's not to blame. It is my fault. There is a necromancer after one of ours, and her hex bag somehow managed to pass its abilities onto Chloe when I needed her assistance."

Ghost sniffed at the dogs, and they put their tails between their legs and tried to avoid her. The raven flapped his wings, still off balance, stirring up dust and crying, "Jelly bean!"

The master cut his gaze to me. "You taught it a new phrase"

Katarina dipped her chin to Killion, but glared at me. "You turned my ferocious guardians into everyday canines."

You'd think that was the worst thing ever by the glare in her eyes. She could give Death a run for his money with that.

The voice in my head told me to take a step back from her anger—and her fangs—but I wasn't about to apologize. Or let her see any weakness. "It wasn't intentional. Trust me, I don't want this ability and that's why we're here—to break the hex."

She pointed at the mild-mannered dogs and Ghost sidled up to me. "Reap them."

Was she serious? "You want me to kill your pets? What kind of psycho are you?"

A quick step put her in front of my face and she glared into my eyes. She was the taller of us and had on four-inch heels. I had to admit, it was totally intimidating. "What's dead should stay dead."

"You and my boss should get together."

She snarled.

I didn't back away. "I get it. I've read Stephen King." Once. One chapter. Way too scary for me. "I'm not re-killing those two innocent dogs."

Re-killing? Was that a word?

In the Chloe-universe it was.

Killion tugged at my sleeve. "Let's take this inside."

Katarina gnashed her fangs at me when she passed, but she followed, the dogs seeming lost until she ordered them to come. Along with Ghost, they bounded up the steps and entered the church, tails wagging.

Dozens of lit candles and statues of praying saints greeted us. Shadows danced and the cloying smell of incense lay like a blanket over the underlying scent of death and devotion.

Here, death was a layer cake of guilt, torment, holy water, and flowers. Regardless that this place was magical, it had once been an actual church. Thousands of humans had worshipped in it. Babies had been baptized, mourners had cried at funerals, and candles had been lit for the souls on the other side. Hail Marys and Our Fathers still echoed in the stones. Some long buried DNA passed down from thousands of ancestors made me want to act like Moss and cross myself.

Katarina took her usual post at the nearby desk. "Besides breaking a hex, are we training?"

I could see she was hoping for that, and the possibility she would be in charge. Anything to get her hands on me.

Her dogs sniffed at the edges of the room, while Ghost stayed by my side, watching them as though they were an alien species. Maybe I wasn't the only one who needed to socialize. "Just the hex breaking."

Her eyes flicked to Killion.

He passed both of us, heading to the hall that led to the nave. "Collect the items on Chloe's list and bring them to us."

The vamp pursed her lips in distaste when I held out the paper. Reluctantly, she took it, her brow furrowing as she read. "What kind of weird magic is this?"

I shrugged and trotted after Killion.

"You're responsible for my pets," she called after me.

The nave was back to its normal self. Even the giant statue of Saint Anne had been repaired. I moved past the various torture devices and down the aisle to study her more closely. My previous visit had ended with the statue exploding and her cross embedded in Killion's back. Seeing her returned to her previous glory was both reassuring and somewhat creepy. There wasn't even a hairline crack to suggest she'd ever lain in a hundred pieces on the floor. "That must be some kind of super glue," I said, noting her solemn eyes following me when I moved to one side.

Killion opened a cabinet in the shadowed corner and removed chalk and a bag. He handed the items to me, and then used his supernatural strength to move a chair that looked like the kind dentists used out of the way. I hadn't noticed the dark stains on the floor around the pedestal until the brighter section was revealed. A lot of blood had been spilled here and it made my stomach clench.

"Draw a circle with the chalk and then outline it with

the salt," he instructed me. "Make it large enough you can lay inside it."

"Why do I need to be inside it?"

He made work of rolling up his sleeves and keeping his gaze diverted. "A safety measure."

I began drawing, the chalk dry on the skin of my fingers. "Afraid I'll call up a zombie horde by accident and they'll overrun the church?"

Finished with his sleeves, he glanced at me. "It's not out of the realm of possibility, but should things go wrong..." He looked away again. "We need to keep you contained."

"Wait." I sat back on my haunches, my task unfinished. In movies, they made drawing an even circle look easy. It's not. Mine was quite lopsided. "You're afraid of me? On second thought, I don't think I want to do this."

"Whatever happens, I will be here."

I gripped the chalk tighter. "Is that supposed to reassure me?"

He knelt and pried the stubby stick from my hand. The scent of his caramel and old libraries smell enveloped me. "I hoped it would."

Violet eyes stared into mine. My breath stuck in my chest. His strong fingers closed on top of my hand, and for a second, I lost track of my thoughts. I felt warm all over and my skin buzzed with his magic. "Does it come easy?" I drew a deep breath and blinked, breaking the spell. "Manipulating humans?"

The corner of his mouth twitched. "I've told you before, I will not exploit control or influence on you in any manner. What you sense and feel is all yours."

My pulse beat too loud in my ears. "I've never felt quite like—"

Katarina stormed in, hands full of glass jars and other items. "This is what I could find."

We broke apart. "Good," he told her. "Place them there."

I watched with a sense of dread as he went to work finishing my unbalanced circle. If we couldn't break this hex, what was I going to do? "How can you be sure this place is safe?" Memories of the previous attack played havoc in my mind, the flashbacks making me scan the enormous space, expecting a shadow to jump out.

Katarina sniffed, annoyed. "I've increased security. You're safe. Unfortunately," she added. She turned to Killion. "Anything else, master?"

He sent her off with a shake of his head.

She didn't understand what I'd been asking. I didn't fear the kind of attack we'd experienced with Jacqueline. I worried that Killion's careful planning might actually be necessary. "Are you sure about this?" I asked him.

Neither he nor Saint Anne moved, but I felt the irritation and damnation in both of their stoic gazes. "You still don't trust me?"

It was easy to forget at times that he was a dangerous supernatural who could snap my neck before I could blink. He'd also been a staunch ally and had assured me many times he would never lie to me. "I do."

Something passed between us again, and I hoped he knew I was telling the truth.

Ghost sniffed at the items Katarina had left. Killion took my hand and led me to the center of the circle. "This will require your focus and concentration."

"Don't we need to draw a pentagram or some ancient sigils or something?" The simple unadorned chalk outline seemed rather plain and boring for the seriousness of our work.

"Would that make you feel better?"

Actually, yes. "I thought we were performing magic. Doesn't that require a proper..." What was the term I was looking for? "Container?"

"You read the books I gave you on the subject?"

I'd been busy with school finals, but again, movies were my best friend when it came to research. "Of course. Loved them." I tried not to oversell the lie, but my bluff didn't fool him. He stared at me, unmoving, and I had to lockdown my need to fidget. "Okay, I scanned them. I'm taking one or two with me this weekend to read at work."

He moved away. "If you survive that long, it will be a miracle."

Although he said it under his breath, I bristled. "You're not exactly instilling confidence."

Ghost nudged a paper bag. Opening it, Killion removed several canisters and began sprinkling their contents around the inside of the chalk line. Some were a mixture of dried herbs and flowers. One held an orangey powder. "The longer the hex has to work on you, the more rooted it will be in your system. It's similar to an invasive vine and extracting the tendrils is of upmost importance before they alter your DNA. We must not leave any traces of it behind, or it will regrow."

"Awesome. What if the spell doesn't break it?"

He next grabbed an antique copper bottle, uncorked it, and moved toward me. A sickly sweet aroma clogged the air. "Hold still," he commanded, and dipped a finger in. It came out shiny with oil. Gently, he touched my forehead and drew something in the center, mumbling under his breath in Latin.

Heat snaked up from my pelvis, coiling up my spine and flooding my cheeks. His finger was warm, his violet eyes pools of desire I wanted to jump into. The words he spoke echoed in my ears, and for a heartbeat, we locked eyes as he fell silent.

I knew without a doubt that whatever was about to happen, I would not be the same afterwards. I wished that he and I could stay inside the circle, safe and quiet, away from the rest of the world forever.

Unfortunately, while it seemed I could administer life and death, I could not stop fate from doing what happened next.

TWELVE

Ghost jumped into the circle, breaking our concentration and messing up the herbs and powder. Killion let loose a curse in his native Romanian and moved to fix it. I released the breath I was holding, slightly disappointed, yet also relieved.

As I commanded Ghost to stay clear of the barrier line, he finished and nodded his head, as though satisfied. "Ready?"

What choice did I have? Another bluff fell from my lips. "Sure thing. Time's a-wasting. Let's get this over with so I can harvest Andy's soul and interrogate Simone."

Lying in the center, I swallowed hard. Killion waved a hand and a hundred candles around the space came to life. Saint Anne looked on, as did Ghost. He closed his eyes and said something in that other language.

When they opened, they homed in on me and I tried not to gasp. The violet pupils had turned red and his fangs were on full display. "Let us begin."

Ghost whined, and I had to bite my bottom lip not to do the same. Killion spoke the words of the spell, palms turned up to the ceiling. An orange energy sparked from his finger-tips and ran around the border of the circle.

The mark on my forehead heated, a frigid flame of magic, as though someone were driving an icicle into the spot between my brows. I gasped and put my hand on it, but then my gaze grayed out.

A fog surrounded me, blurring my vision and invading my nostrils, my ears, and filling my throat. I could hear Killion's deep voice, but could no longer see him, except for those glowing red eyes.

My teeth chattered, my limbs trembled, and my breath expelled in white plumes. The scent of grave dirt and old blood teased my nose. Then, his eyes disappeared in the ghostly fog.

But it wasn't fog. Layers upon layers of spirits floated above me, thick with vacant eyes. Frost particles covered their features and hung in the air.

Killion became a background hum. Time seemed suspended, death engulfing me. While I felt panic rising, I could no longer move. I attempted to call out, but my voice was locked inside my throat, my lips frozen.

Please stop, I mentally shouted at Kilian. *Something's wrong.*

The ghosts swirled around me, picking up speed. My stomach pitched, my jaw going tight. Although I was frozen to the spot, I felt as though I were moving with them. Like Dorothy swept up in a tornado, the world churned around me. A scream finally broke free from my mouth, but the sound was muted under the hammering pulse in my ears. Wind whipped and tore at my hair and clothes, sucking the oxygen from my lungs.

With no warning, everything stopped. I was unceremoniously dumped onto a rocky outcropping, banging my knees and skinning my palms. I stayed crouched, gasping for air, grateful that I could breathe again. Grit scratched my eyeballs. A nasty smell, like dead things left in the sun to rot, filled my nose.

Once my lungs had enough oxygen, I raised my head and scanned the environment. No chalk circle or herbs here. No Ghost, or master vampire, either.

A bleak landscape rolled out in front of me, the apparitions receding slowly like mist on a lake. As though a veil were being pulled back, I watched as concentric circles of headstones became visible in all directions. They leaned this way and that, covered in a glowing substance I couldn't name.

Legs shaking, I pushed to my feet. The world dipped and swayed, and I staggered on the circular precipice, trying to find my balance. Peering over the edge, I saw it was only a few feet to the ground, but I instinctively drew back. I did not want to go down there.

The graves were orderly, but bare, their markers lacking names and dates. Instead, each appeared to have a symbol carved on it. A glyph like the Jackal's.

"It is you." A female voice came from behind me.

I spun. My feet slid dangerously close to the edge, sending gravel scattering to the ground below. Sound lodged in my throat at the sight of the figure in red robes standing on the outcropping with me. The body under the material rippled as the fabric feathered out around her in a not-there breeze. She wore a cat mask over her features, giving her anonymity.

Or perhaps, like the jackal, she was half animal.

"Who are you?" My voice cracked. "What is this place?"

She cocked her head. As her gaze raked me from head to toe, I had the sensation of nails scrapping my brain.

A severe pressure invaded my skull and I clutched my head, squeezing my eyes shut. "Stop it!"

Jacqueline Vermouth had been a psychic in her pregrim life. She'd tried reading my mind the first time I met her, the sensation like a mosquito buzzing around in my skull. This was not dissimilar, only the cat-woman's intrusion was more like a million wasps. "You are the one the prophecy speaks of. So be it."

"Get...out...of...my head." I gritted my teeth and pushed back. The temperature inside me dropped to a level equal to the frigid environment. The pressure eased enough for me to crack open my eyes. A trio of half-human, half-animals appeared behind her—a falcon, a lion, and a monkey. Their flat eyes looked on as she continued to assess me. "I don't know what you're talking about." My breath was coming fast, my legs quivering from adrenaline. Surely, this wasn't Death's *friend*. "Your spell was supposed to break a hex."

Laughter, ragged in my ears, made me cover them. My stomach quivered and my brain screamed for me to run. But where?

One of her arms swept out from under the robes, motioning at the graves. "This is your fate. Your destiny. You cannot escape it."

Movement off to the side caught my attention and my heart battered against my ribs. The heaped-up ground in front of each headstone began to shift. A rotted hand shot up, another. The sand erupted. A skull emerged.

My stomach bottomed out and I pivoted to watch. Horror rising in my throat.

One by one, the corpses in the graves came to life. Most were little more than skeletons, rotted clothes and flesh hanging from their bones. Soulless eyes locked on me and they began to walk, drag, and pull themselves toward us.

I hated zombie movies with a passion. Living my own terrifying version of one was a hundred times worse. A thousand. "Why?" was all I could squeak out. "Why is this happening?"

She cackled, like a witch in a cartoon, raising both arms. Her nails were sharp daggers, the robe fabric forming wings. "The Undead master favors you. You *are* the one."

As the zombies closed in, reaching for me, she lifted off and flew away. A drone, like hundreds of wasps, rose with the skeletal figures. Mouths open, they emitted horrible moans, while her hybrids closed in, chittering and reaching for me.

Cold fingers latched onto my ankle. I glanced down into the empty eye socket of what had once been a man. Half his skull was on display, his mouth working. Was he trying to speak? Or, was he warming up his skeletal jaws to bite me?

I screamed.

THIRTEEN

Arctic air crushed me as my scream echoed over the misty land. I tore my gaze from the zombie latched onto my leg and kicked at it, shutting my eyes against the hundreds more closing in.

The monkey grabbed my arm and held it out. The lion bared his teeth and made to bite me.

The zombie climbed higher, his grip on my ankle and my attempts to kick him off causing me to fall. The lion's teeth raked my skin.

Another cry ripped from my lips, raw and agonizing, but I didn't hit the ground—at least not the rocky outcropping. Behind my closed lids, my vision whited out and a crackling noise exploded inside my head. As I tumbled through space, I grabbed my skull, my body spasming. I landed with a *harrumph* back in the circle.

Pain like a hundred fire balls erupted under my skin. A searing pain cut through my head and raced down my neck. My heart stopped for several seconds, my breath caught in a vise. When the spear of agony hit the base of my spine, the restriction around my lungs loosened and I gulped in air.

Curling into a fetal position and rolling onto my side, teeth chattering so hard I thought I'd shear off enamel, I rocked like a child. Small cries fell from my lips, sounding like the tiny mews of a kitten. Blinking at my surroundings, the moaning and chittering of the voices of the dead filled my ears.

"Chloe!" Killion's shout cut through them. Strong hands lifted me from the stone floor and I was cradled in his arms.

Candle smoke coated the air and Ghost jumped into the circle, pawing and whining at me. The raven was back, his wild eye spinning, as he flew down from the statue's shoulder and joined us.

"What happened?" Killion's gaze blazed with worry, but I couldn't speak, my body trembling and my skin itching. In spots it felt as though it were burning up. Did I have frostbite? Was the next stage numbness? "You're cold as ice."

He carried me out of the circle to one of the remaining pews in the shadows. We sat, him keeping me in his lap, and the bird landing on the arm rest. I was relieved to be back inside the church. The familiar sights and smells were welcomed.

The door opened, hinges squeaking. "Master?" Katarina rushed toward us. "What just happened? The entire place shook."

Killion barked an order over his shoulder. "Bring blankets and a hot drink. Hurry!"

Her reply was apprehensive. "We don't have blankets."

He growled something in Romanian, which made my neck hairs rise.

She backed away meekly. "This is a training and torture center, master. We interrogate sources. We don't coddle them."

His body tensed. I thought he was going to come up off the seat. "Then find a tapestry or shed your clothes," he snarled.

Disgust at the idea of sharing her apparel with me did the trick. "I'll find something." The door banged shut behind her.

I felt the slide of his jacket over my skin. Gently, he guided my arms into the sleeves. There was an immediate hush that came over me, a lingering warmth in the cloth that soothed my nerves.

I'd always believed vampires were cold, mythical creatures, but they were neither cool-skinned nor myth.

We stayed that way for a long time, and I appreciated him not pressing for information. The experience was already becoming dream-like, fading like the haze I'd found myself in. The gruesomeness of it, however, seemed etched into my bones. I wasn't sure I would ever forget the feel of the skeletal hand around my ankle, nor the chittering and moaning echoing in my ears.

Katarina returned with hot tea and a scratchy wool tapestry. I didn't particularly like either, but appreciated both. After leaving Killion's lap, I sat on the hard bench and gulped the liquid to alleviate the icy feeling in my stomach. It burned on the way down, and I welcomed it. Hopefully, Katarina hadn't poisoned me.

Together, the two studied me, him with concern, her with annoyance. He sat next to me, close enough that our legs touched. She crossed her arms and tapped a booted foot.

The last of the voices in my head were silenced. Finally, I was able to drag in a deep breath. Another. I rubbed my temples and finished off the beverage, handing the cup back to Katarina. She accepted it and Killion ordered her to find food, preferably high in sugar content. She dipped her head and left, no arguments or excuses this time. As she moved away, she did shoot me a disquieted look from the corner of her eye.

Ghost pawed at my leg and I lifted her, placing her in my lap and stroking her fur. She licked my face and I smiled at her. For once, I didn't mind her puppy breath. I snuggled her closer. "Are we sure that spell was to break a hex?" My teeth no longer chattered, but my voice was raw and it trembled as I spoke. "I don't think it worked."

"From the way you look, I'd say not." He leaned forward, scanning my face. "What happened?"

I closed my eyes to concentrate. Retracing the remnants of memory, I had to start at the end and work backward before I could wrap my mind around it. As I explained it to Killion, as best as I could, it felt like something was missing —not of the story, but of me. As if I'd left a piece of *me* behind.

"Cat woman said something about a prophecy," I told him. Her voice was still there, in my memory, but it seemed fuzzy. "She claimed I'm the one the vampire master favors." I opened my eyes in time to see his violet orbs darken.

"I am unaware of any prophecies, involving myself and a grim." He rose, pacing away. The raven followed, mimicking him. "This makes no sense. The prophecy, the experience...what is Death playing at?"

"You think he wanted this to happen?"

Killion stopped. "It certainly wasn't the correct spell to break a necromancy curse."

Ghost licked my hand and rolled over, displaying her belly. I rubbed it absentmindedly. "I wonder who he got it from, this friend of his? Could he or she have duped him?"

Killion stared up at Saint Anne's face. The raven did

the same. She appeared to return their gazes, as serene and divine as always. "No one dupes Death. There is more going on here than we are aware of."

My voice no longer trembled, but it came out quiet and surprisingly as serene as Anne's countenance. I knew the truth. "But you're the master vampire she referred to, whether you're aware of this prophecy or not. And the one you favor is Simone, not me. This whole thing is about her."

His head dipped, gaze dropping to the floor. "I'm afraid that may not be true."

"Why not?"

He glanced over his shoulder, but he didn't look me in the eye. Instead, he stared at Ghost, still wiggling in my lap.

When he didn't speak, I stood, the tapestry falling from my shoulders. I set her on the seat and she jumped down. "Why not?" I demanded. "Are you saying that you do? Favor me?" What did that even mean?

His lovely eyes were dark as the night, now, and a ripple of longing raced over me. I wanted to fall into them, fall into him. "This is unprecedented."

I didn't know if he was holding back the truth to shield me or taunt me, my need to know growing with every breath. "Please, Killion. Why me?"

A flash of sadness came and went quickly over his face. "I have not felt like this, since..." He shook his head. "You're right, it must refer to Simone. She is my second-in-command. I favor her, but I admit, I do not know what the prophecy means."

"How can you *not know*?" My stomach twisted. I wanted it to be about Simone, and yet, I also wanted to be important to him.

He took several steps toward me, as though he were about to put his hands on my shoulders. He didn't, but I felt the weight of his stare. "You are incredibly important to me. If, by chance, the prophecy is referring to you, however, then I'm not the vampire it speaks of."

Because he didn't favor me. I placed a hand on my stomach, a raw ache making it cramp. The voices in my head started up again, and I had to sit, gripping the pew. One came through loud and clear—the woman's. *He's lying.*

Finding my voice, I glared at him. "You said you'd never lie to me."

He looked taken aback. "I'm not."

"Then who is it?" I gritted my teeth, trying to banish the voice. "What other master vampire is there, and what would he want with me?"

He did touch me now, a careless brush of his fingers on my cheek. "I don't know, but I promise, I'll keep you safe."

He's lying, Cat Woman insisted again. *No one can. Not from me.*

Wild, unhinged laughter followed and my stomach dropped. Katarina burst in and Ghost came to full attention, her scruff rising. "Master!"

Killion was instantly on guard. "What is it?"

"We've got trouble." She shifted out of the way and Killion froze.

"Hey, mates." Death strode through the door, brushing past a wide-eyed Katarina. "We need to talk."

FOURTEEN

My stomach heaved, Death's energy causing my poor head to spin. The cacophony of voices became a high-pitched keening that sent flashbacks of what had happened with Jacqueline through my brain.

I made it as far as one of the torture chairs that had a bucket on the floor next to it. The tea and my earlier meal came up, seeming to tear out of me. Heat burned under my skin—part sickness, but mostly embarrassment.

A large spiderweb with a dead owner decorated the arm, the arachnid's legs curled inward. Hanging onto the chair, sticky from things I didn't want to think about, I shut my eyes against the spinning room. The keening gave way to what sounded like a wind tunnel and I remained bent at the waist, praying for the world to right itself and the spinning to stop.

A moment later, a cool, damp cloth pressed into my free hand and I blinked up at Katarina. For all her bluster, she'd come to my aid, and I nodded my thanks, grateful for the washcloth and the fact I only saw one of her.

My balance somewhat restored, and no further heaving

in sight, I washed my face with it. Ghost watched from her perch at my feet and the raven hid behind my legs. The vamp took the bucket and disappeared.

As I petted the dog to reassure her, the males spoke in low voices behind me. I slumped against the gross chair, willing my legs to stop trembling.

Three breaths in, a tiny movement of shadow on the floor snagged my attention. The web fluttered and a curled leg flicked open. Then another.

My heart dropped—the spider was coming back to life.

Katarina returned, glancing at Death and Killion as she joined me. "Something's wrong," she whispered.

"You think?" Besides the fact Death's presence made my body go haywire? Besides the fact the spell hadn't worked?

I chanced a sideways look at the two males. Killion's forehead was creased, that muscle jumping in his jaw. His arms were crossed and he appeared as though he might kill Death if given the tiniest provocation.

He also looked too pale again. Too...something.

Perhaps I wasn't the only one the hex bag had affected.

Death faced him, hands on hips, smiling as he spoke. It was a dead smile, no pun intended, and didn't reach his eyes. His posture thrummed with forced casualness.

The spider, fully functional once more, began climbing my leg. I gently shook it off. Forcing myself to my feet, I took an unsteady step toward the males, but stopped when my guts twinged. "You..." I raised my voice, drawing Death's attention. "You tricked me. That was no hex breaking spell. You sent me to zombieland. And now there's a vampire and a prophecy and..."

The expression he turned on me was part perplexed and part pure challenge. "I didn't send you anywhere, and the spell I provided should have done the trick." He shot an accusatory eye at Killion. "Think, Chloe. Your watcher, here, is the culprit behind all of this—you should ask him what he did to embellish that spell. He's using you for his own purposes. This last little stunt sent up several red flags to Smudgy."

My relationship with both of them had been taxed multiple times. I wanted to argue Killion's innocence, but I was on shaky ground. What my mentor had asked me to do with Jackal had started all of this, and it wasn't SMG business. It had been—and still was—personal.

I decided to save my breath on that point, but I did turn to Killion. "Did you modify it?"

He stilled, his stoic expression firmly in place, yet his energy licked at my nerves like salty flames. He pinned Death with a murderous glare. "I read it exactly as it is written. Perhaps you should examine what your witch wrote."

Death gave a dismissive grunt. Before he could launch into another accusation, I cut him off. "Why would any of this send up red flags at SMG?"

He puffed his lips and rocked back on his heels. "The place you ended up? It's not exactly where they want you."

"This may come as a surprise to everyone, but I didn't want to be there, either. Obviously, I never intended to visit whatever that place was, and you couldn't force me to do it again."

Killion walked to my side. "What *is* that place? Why doesn't SMG want her there?"

A mask fell over Death's face. "Above my pay grade. The point is, SMG is putting you on probation, Killion."

"Probation?" he and I chorused.

Death straightened, his previous casualness returning. "Using grim resources for your own means violates Code

16-11, Section B. Your hearing will be next week, and honestly? You'll be lucky to keep your appointment as an investigator." He motioned for me to follow him. "Come with me, Grave Girl. We have work to do."

I stayed planted, Killion's shoulder touching mine in solidarity. We exchanged a glance. "You can't do that," I said to Death. "He's my watcher."

Death strolled down the aisle and called over his shoulder, "Not anymore."

Killion's hand brushed mine. "Go with him." His voice was quiet, gentle. "I will see this is worked out, and I'll call you later." His pinkie hooked around mine. "I promise."

A pinkie swear? My mother used to make them to me when I was a kid. They were sacred pacts and we never broke them. Not one.

Death stopped at the double doors. "Now, Chloe."

The power in his voice made my limbs tremble. Being a grim meant he could compel me, as my boss, to do what he willed. He rarely used it, but I resented it—and him—all the same. "I'm not leaving without my watcher."

A grin, dark and threatening, spread across his face. "That's why I will be accompanying you to harvest Andy." He held open the door. "I'm your new watcher."

FIFTEEN

My voice sounded slightly hysterical as it echoed in the high ceilinged room. "You've got to be kidding."

The intense eyes continued to compel me. "We have a shapeshifter to harvest. Stay away from Killion until he's cleared of wrongdoing."

The tug was undeniable. I gritted my teeth and resisted anyway. "I can't be around you right now. You make me sick."

His left eye twitched. "You don't have to like me to do your job, Grim 281, and it *is* your job to do what I say."

"That's not what I meant. Your presence makes me literally sick to my stomach after that spell did...whatever it did." I huffed and pointed toward the bucket. "I may be a grim, but it appears I'm also a necromancer and being near the personification of Death apparently now turns my insides upside down."

Finally, the fact seemed to register, and he paused, a deep frown creasing his forehead. How could he force me to work with him when it would result in making me vomit?

Maybe that would save me from a watcher I didn't want. My hopes rose.

Only to be immediately dashed. "I'll keep my distance. Let's go."

My teeth ground together and I gathered Ghost and my bag. "You got me in to this, vamp master," I growled at Killion. "You better get me out."

He gave a slight bow, acknowledging he would.

Death waited for me in the parking lot. Across the street, the small, rundown bar was closing up. Several patrons stumbled out complaining.

Katarina's dogs whined and huffed at Ghost as we passed them, but stayed on the edges of the cemetery. The raven flew out with us and headed into the sky.

I adjusted my bag's strap and stopped a generous distance from my boss. A low level anxiety thrummed under my skin and fueled the burning in my stomach. Seemed like every time I thought I could trust either Killion or Death, something pulled the rug out from under me. Before I proceeded with the rest of the night's fun, I needed to set a few things straight. "Killion asked for my help as a friend and I gave it to him willingly. It had nothing to do with my grim duties, and although it has complicated things, I'm perfectly capable of taking care of Andy on my own."

Death watched the drunks stagger down the buckled sidewalk. A round of "Here Comes Santa Claus" started up, all three off-key. The older guy caught his foot on a piece of broken concrete and they tumbled as one to the ground. They lay there, laughing and swearing, their breath white in the chilly air.

Death smiled, watching them. "I don't make the rules, I just enforce them."

Right, and I was a big jolly elf. "I don't need a watcher anymore."

His gaze met mine across the expanse. "You've been going on luck and serendipity, and those have now run out. You need proper training and a firm hand. Besides, love,"—he winked—"why would you turn down working with me?"

He was always trying to lighten the moment and sway me in to believing it was all good fun. That we were buddies.

He continued on, assuming I would follow. I wanted to quit, there and then, but being a grim wasn't a normal job. I couldn't simply turn in my resignation. I was hip deep in something I didn't understand and couldn't control. I needed to figure out what was wrong with me, and I needed to save Professor O'Leary.

Biting my retort over the "firm hand" comment, I ran to catch up. Ghost loved running and jetted past me in a flash. Passing the drunks, my stomach twinged when I got close to Death. I pulled up, keeping several feet between us. Ghost sniffed at a bush. "Let's get this over with so I can go home and sleep. Where do we start, Oh Mighty Death? Do you have a location on the shifter?"

He glanced at me. "I do,"—he raised a finger as he marched on—"and because I have faith in you and know you can handle him, I'll leave you to it."

"What?" I mean, count me happy he wasn't going to helicopter-boss me, but now he was ditching me? "After that speech, you're bailing?"

"I'll be watching, like always." As he walked, his body began to fade. "Best behavior, Chloe, or I'll be looking over your shoulder twenty-four seven from here on out."

He'd done this on purpose to get me away from Killion, not because he actually wanted to be my watcher. "I can't tell you how motivating that is, but you haven't told me how to find Andy. Where is he?"

"Check your messages." He disappeared, leaving me a block from the church and in a lousy neighborhood.

"What the…?" one of the drunks mumbled. "Did you see that?"

"Go home," I called to him, fuming.

Taking out my phone, I saw a text from an unknown number with an address. The map showed it was four blocks from my location, but I was tired and chilled, my belly empty and my whole system on overload.

"Mind your own business," his friend yelled back.

The other two called me a few choice names and I was *this* close to pulling out my scythe and ending them.

Lucky for them, I didn't need their deaths on my hands. *Best behavior.*

Controlling my ill mood, I stood for a long moment, hearing them pick up their chorus and move on. I considered calling a ride service, but by the time they sent a driver, I could be at the house. I didn't want to chance Andy getting away again.

I started walking, struggling to think of anything to keep my mind off the necromancy stuff. Ghost stayed quiet but alert, and I hoped I didn't pass anything dead on the way. Before we crossed the street, a long, black limo slid to the curb.

Moss emerged and opened the door to the backseat. "Don't worry, he's not in there."

I almost wished he was. "Am I allowed to accept a ride? Isn't that off limits?"

His giant shoulders shrugged in his snappy, black driver's uniform. "Master said to give you a ride. Also a message—and I quote—'Watch your back, he's up to something.'"

Death was always up to something. "I'm done playing games tonight." I eyed the dark interior. "Got any hot chocolate?"

Moss gave me a lopsided grin. "Marshmallows, too."

"I'm in." Ghost jumped onto the seat and I slid inside, the warmth, combined with Killion's warm caramel and old libraries scent, made my tense, frigid muscles relax. I reeled off the address to Moss and checked the drink station.

A silver carafe of cocoa awaited me, along with a red bag of marshmallows. I popped one into my mouth as the limo glided forward and let the sugary goodness melt on my tongue. These weren't your store-bought variety; these were high-end, small batch treasures.

I poured a cup of chocolate and added a layer of marsh-mallows on top. Ghost whined, stomping her front paws on the seat Killion usually occupied, and I tossed one of the confections to her. She swallowed it whole and begged for another.

Psychopomp or not, too much sugar wasn't good for her, but I caved and gave her one more. Then I sank in the cushy seat, drank the cocoa, and sighed.

I ENDED up cooling my heels and drinking another cup after we arrived at the address. The tall, narrow house had seen better days, the concrete steps missing chunks. The front porch was cluttered with worn outdoor furniture, a collection of empty whiskey bottles on the railing, and a lone plastic Christmas tree doing its best to spread holiday cheer.

Most of the colored lights on the tree were burned out

and the star topper listed to one side. "What could these folks have that's worth stealing?" I asked nobody in particular. Scythe in hand, I leaned on the side of the limo.

Moss' window was down, Christmas tunes playing quietly in the background. "Magic," he said.

Ghost sat at my feet and I propped the scythe against a leg. "Seriously?" I glanced over the two-story, noticing the flicker of Andy's flashlight on the interior of the left downstairs window. I couldn't see a strange aura or feel odd energy around the place. "I don't sense any."

A beefy finger pointed toward the double-doored entrance. "See the wolf head?"

Squinting, I pushed off the car to lean forward. A metal plaque hung over the doors. "What about it?"

"That's the insignia of the local shifter clan. They probably use this as a safehouse. Their wards are invisible to vampires and humans, but they're present. My guess? He's looking for the power nexus. Something he can bring with him to make the ward mobile."

What a douche bag. "So I can't reap him."

"He could be trying to protect himself from more than you."

He was a thief. I had no doubt he had a few enemies. "The pack must realize he's in there. They've warded the place. They can smell him, at the very least, and the wards should be alerting them, right?"

"Maybe no one's home. Plus, it's a safehouse. They wouldn't assume he's stealing from them, only seeking refuge."

That made sense. I scanned the rundown neighborhood, ready to get this over with, but also curious. I didn't know any were-creatures, and learning more about them could help me down the road. "So they plunk a safehouse in a less-than-stellar location and ward it so it's basically invisible to humans and other supernaturals. Quite strategic." The beam disappeared. Andy had found what he wanted or was giving up. Either way, I was ready. "Is the nexus easy to carry? What does it look like?"

Moss shrugged. "Could be anything."

Helpful—*not*. I twirled the death blade in my hand. The sad tree on the porch drew my eye. "Like a Christmas decoration?"

He rubbed a knuckle across his chin. "I s'pose."

Was that what Andy had been doing all along—searching for the nexus object to protect himself from me? "Are there more of these safehouses in town?"

"Are there vampires in Louisiana?" He punctuated that with a toothy grin.

Taking the scythe, I strolled to the porch. Ghost trailed after me, sniffing everything. As I placed my foot on the bottom stair, I felt a charge of electricity zap me and lift the hair on my arms.

Ahh, there you are. While I could see the magic around the church, this type was different. This I could *feel*.

I paused, waiting to see if it would do anything further. When it didn't, I took the second step, the wood groaning under my weight. Again, nothing else happened.

Were the wards working? If Andy believed the nexus would protect him from me, I expected it and them to resist me entering this space.

Ghost bounded past and up to the top to look back at me, tail wagging. The magic didn't bother her at all. How close did I have to get before it would kick in?

Carefully, I took another step. The scythe vibrated in my hand. The tiny tree's lights flickered.

Getting warmer.

As my foot hit the top tread, the lights glowed brighter, all of them illuminated now.

Probably should have asked Moss what exactly the wards would do if I breached the boundary, but when I glanced over my shoulder at him, he gave me a thumbs-up. I took that to mean I could handle whatever was here.

Gripping the scythe tighter, I watched Ghost nose around at the porch debris. Nothing happened to her. I went all in and finished the climb.

Another shot of magic fired off, this time making my chest tight. If the ward had a silent alarm, I'd triggered it, and my pulse hammered, anticipating what type of harm might befall me if the house went on the attack.

Wards were the magic of witches. Shifters' extrasensory skills were off the charts and they had insane strength, but they didn't use magic in and of itself.

As I debated whether to check out the plastic tree, I heard rustling under the porch. "Please don't be a skunk," I muttered, peering over the rusty railing. It was the wrong time of year for them to be active, but stranger things had happened.

It was a skunk, all right, just not the black and white variety. Andy grunted softly as he tugged his legs out from the crawl space and reached back for something.

The scythe vibrated and Ghost sniffed the air. I, too, smelled the rangy scent of the man who was days past needing a shower and a shave. "Find what you were looking for?" I called as I skipped back down the steps.

Grunting, he yanked hard and a bag popped from the hole, causing him to lose his balance. He slipped on the frosty grass as he attempted to rise and run.

Ghost rushed forward, sinking her teeth into his leg as

she morphed. The shifter howled, literally, and dropped the bag. "Don't eat me!"

I finished my descent and stopped near him, holding out the scythe. "Sorry, Andy, but it's time."

He attempted to shake off the psychopomp. Ghost didn't let go. "Wait...I..." One hand dug in the bag. "We can make a deal. I've got some rare and valuable things in here. What do you like? Jewelry, food? I've got caviar. Rubies. Good stuff."

I doubted that. Why would shifters keep valuables in this place? "Hands where I can see them." I shook the blade at him, and hoped none of the neighbors peered out their windows or called the cops at the disturbance. "The nexus wasn't in the house. It's there." I cocked my chin toward the tree, the lights once again dim.

Andy froze, frowning. He started laughing, softly at first, then growing more animated as the truth sank in. He flopped onto his back, staring up at the night sky. "How did you know?"

Ghost glanced at me, as if perplexed by the laughing man. "It wouldn't have helped protect you from me anyway."

He sighed and sat up. A hand scratched at his beard and trailed over his long hair. "You're relentless, and I'm tired."

Seemed like the truth, but he'd outfoxed me enough times, I wasn't falling for it. "Let's wrap this up, then. Touch the blade."

The pale light from the porch flickered in his dark eyes. "I need a few more days. Can't we make some kind of deal? Just until after Christmas?"

Ghost growled and shook his pant leg. He raised both hands and gave me a pleading look.

"What's so important about Christmas?"

He seemed surprised. "Everything. Don't you like the holidays?"

No. "I can't make deals to extend your life."

He patted his chest in earnest. "I'm a troubleshooter. A fixer and you need a giant dose of holiday spirit. What's your biggest problem right now?"

"Nothing you can remedy. Touch the blade."

"Try me." Seeing my irritation, he called to Moss. "Why is she so mean? She has a problem, doesn't she? What is it?"

Before I could stop him, Moss said, "She's been cursed with necromantic powers and can't control them."

I sent the driver a death glare. Killion had told him. Great.

Andy's eyes grew wide as he met mine. A slow grin spread across his face. "So if you kill me, I'll come back to life?"

Possibly. "It only affects animals." *I hope.*

He patted his chest again. "I'm part animal!" Peals of fresh laughter rang out and echoed around the yard. "A grim who's cursed to be a necromancer! The irony is too much."

While it was ironic, I didn't find it funny. Mentally kicking myself, I lowered the weapon, debating what to do. The best option was to harvest him and run from his corpse as fast as possible.

The laughter died and he sucked in gulps of air, catching his breath. His hands reached out in appeal. "Seriously, I can help. Witches love me. I know a special one who's a necro. She'll know what to do, I swear on my grandmother's grave."

His grandmother probably wasn't even dead. Shifters lived long lives. "Why do witches love you?"

An indignant look crossed his hairy features. "Everybody does. I bring them things they need. Troubleshooter, remember? Number one fixer around here."

"What kind of things do you bring witches?"

"Rare herbs, bones, stuff for intricate spells. Powders and skins. You know, that sort of thing."

Gross. Still, I hesitated harvesting him. I needed help and I needed someone who wasn't Killion or Death to provide it.

Not that I trusted Andy, but he was straightforward with his manipulations—he wanted to live another few days. There had to be a good reason that Christmas was his goal, and that meant it probably had to do with someone he loved. I thought of Professor O' Leary and his daughter. Everyone had somebody. "Look, my boss is breathing down my neck and if I don't harvest you tonight, I'm in big trouble."

"You're a cursed grim." He smirked. "You can't control this new skill, right? How much more trouble can you be in?"

He wasn't wrong, yet, Death could make things much worse. I had people I cared about, and he could snuff them out with a twist of his hand, whether their life contracts were up or not. *Best behavior.*

Regardless of his voice in my head and the risk in front of me, a plan fell into place. Not a good plan, but one I needed to try. "Here's what I'm willing to do."

The blade buzzed, as if in warning. Ghost released Andy's leg and looked at me questioningly.

"Anything." He jumped to his feet, feral eyes glittering. "I'll take whatever deal you're offering."

"Just trust me, okay?"

As he opened his mouth to reply, I swung the scythe.

SIXTEEN

I don't actually cut off heads. All I need to do is touch them with the blade, which is somewhat anticlimactic, and *voila*.

The flat side of the steel banged against his arm and a shocked expression froze his features. Instantly, his spirit began to leave his body, the scythe handle hot in my hand.

Ghost leaped into action, snatching hold of it and both disappeared in a flash. Andy's corpse flopped over, his still startled features boring into me.

Moss tapped the door with his giant hand. "Smart not to trust a shifter. Their personalities are too mercurial and polarizing."

I glanced back at him. "I've heard the same about your kind."

He drew himself up with an affronted expression. "A vampire's word is gold. We may be cleverer than most, but we don't skulk in the shadows and…" His brows knit at my incredulous cough. "Fine, Grave Girl, we do a bit of that, and we occasionally might mislead humans, but if we give our word on something, we follow through."

I thought of Killion and his declaration he wouldn't lie to me. Ghost reappeared in a flash of cold air, and I returned my attention to Andy's corporeal body. He didn't so much as twitch.

The dog nudged my hand and I patted her, running my fingers through her fur. If this didn't work, so be it. I'd done my job, and I'd figure another way out of my predicament.

If it did? Well, I'd still done my job and I couldn't be held accountable for *accidentally* resurrecting Andy, since I was only following orders. Maybe then, Death would take my new necromancy skills more seriously, and I'd be able to buy Andy time to recruit one of his witches to help me.

A minute passed, then another. I checked my watch.

"What are you waiting for?" Moss called. "He's not coming back, and trust me that's a good thing."

Frustrated, I kicked at the sole of Andy's dirty sneaker. Ghost returned to her normal size and pounced on him, believing we were playing a game called, let's attack the dead shifter.

"Hey, Reaper?"

I kept my attention pinned on Andy's corpse. "One more minute."

"Think we better leave now."

The urgency in his voice made me glance up. My breath stuck in my chest.

From between neighboring houses and under trees, dozens of yellow eyes glared at me. The breeze blew the scent of wet dog and wild forest creatures past my nose.

"Oh, eww."

Ghost's hair stood at attention, a soft growl issuing from her tiny throat. I grabbed her and deposited her inside my jacket. She struggled, wanting out, and I tugged the zipper higher. "Stay."

Moving at a snail's pace, I backed toward the limo, keeping the scythe dangling loosely in my hand. Moss started the engine. "I'm a grim," I called to the creatures, feeling their aggression riding the breeze along with their distinct odors. I pointed to the lifeless body. "He was on my list. His contract was up two weeks ago."

A giant wolf stepped from the shadows near the house, its midnight black fur glistening in the silvery moonlight. It stood tall and proud, those fluorescent yellow eyes sizing me up. He was twice the normal size and his muscles flexed as he stepped to the body and sniffed.

I sensed he understood, but I was on hyperalert, readying for an attack. "We'll be going now." I took another step toward my escape. "Happy Holidays."

The alpha raised his head and growled, showing teeth, and the others made various yips and snarls. One by one, they emerged from the shadows, muscles tensed and fur rippling.

There was a menagerie of other beasts—bears, a lynx, coyotes, and a deer. All of their irises shone with that preternatural glow. I had the distinct impression they were not wishing me a happy holiday in return.

"Like I said, we're leaving." I didn't take my eyes off the alpha. "This location is safe with me."

His gaze flicked to Moss and back. His nose twitched and the others continued to close ranks.

"Him, too," I added. "Right, driver?" While I doubted Moss was his real name, I knew better than to share it with the pack. Killion had told me about the power in names and the compulsions magical creatures could amp up if they knew another's true identity.

"Right, boss," he said, but I heard a leering grin in his voice. He was enjoying this.

Ghost and I were mere feet from the safety of the backseat. My palm was slick with sweat and the scythe hummed, ready to protect me. In my peripheral vision, I noticed two coyotes moving in to cut off our retreat.

Fear coiled in my belly, but so did annoyance. I was a grim, for heaven's sake. I worked for SMG. That should afford me a certain amount of untouchability, right?

The pack didn't care. The alpha's top lip curled and the charged atmosphere went electric, causing the hair on my neck to stand up.

Now or never. In one fluid motion, I pivoted, raising the weapon. In the same instant, the coyotes attacked.

Gnashing teeth and razor sharp claws ripped through the air, tearing my clothes and sinking into my skin. I swung the blade, felt it connect, and the cries of those injured blended with my own. Ghost whimpered against my chest and clamored to get out as I lunged for the door handle.

It swung open on its own accord, or maybe thanks to vampire magic. Either way, I dove for the backseat, but one coyote latched onto my arm.

Moss gunned the motor, as I attempted to dislodge it. The second bit into my free arm, and I couldn't swing the blade now. Ghost jumped from my jacket, landing on the leather seat with the grace of a gymnast. She morphed into her psychopomp, filling the space and biting the closest coyote.

The animal screamed and released me, blood flowing in a stream. I made a fist and swung it at the other. My punch caught it in the jaw. It's eyes rolled up in its head, and at the same time, a shrill howl rose above the other noises and sent slick icicles down my spine.

The second coyote slumped to the ground and all activity ceased, the last of the brutal howl drifting into the air and dropping the temperature by another ten degrees. Reeling from pain, I pivoted and glanced toward the origin of the sound, expecting to see the alpha. Instead, he'd moved aside, along with several others, as a wolf, larger than the leader, stepped forward.

Gasping, I met its eyes and felt an involuntary shudder rack my body. His hair was orange, but there was a silver streak running from his nose to his tail.

Ghost's growl rumbled viciously and I held up a hand to hush her. The wolf loped toward me, eyes as silver as his stripe. He was tall enough on all fours to look me in the eye.

As the pack watched, he stopped nose to nose with me, and I held my breath.

Wait, did he just *grin?*

The misty moonlight cast a weird aura over him, but the scent—that I recognized. "Andy?"

His tongue shot out, and before I could stop him, he licked me.

SEVENTEEN

"Gross!" I stumbled back and thunked against the limo. Ghost barked and Andy looked crestfallen, as I wiped my cheek with a sleeve. Blood from the puncture wounds coated the fabric and I made a face, realizing I was probably now smeared with it. The bites burned and itched. "It is *you*, right?"

He lifted his head and howled, making my bones rattle. All righty then. "Okay, okay. My plan worked. Call off the beast squad and let's go somewhere we can talk."

The howl still echoing up and down the block, he looked over his massive shoulder at the others. Both coyotes slunk off to rejoin those at the edge of the perimeter. Andy angled his body sideways, blocking me like a shield. A series of throaty growls and snaps were directed at the alpha and the black wolf glared at both of us.

The intensity of that look made me ease toward the seat, but after a long stare down that seemed to involve telepathy, the alpha bobbed his head.

I wasn't sure if Andy had asked permission to leave or

demanded it, but either way, it was granted. As one, the animals faded back into the shadows.

A sigh of jittery relief left me. "Shift so we can go."

Andy faced me with doleful eyes.

"What? I'm sorry, okay? I had to reap you or Death would have, and he wouldn't have brought you back. We need to get out of here, so..." I motioned at him, my fingers bloody. "Do your thing. I won't peek, if you need privacy."

Taking the scythe and my bloody arm with me, I climbed into the backseat. Ghost jumped into my lap.

Moss caught my eye in the rearview. I saw his nostrils flare at the scent of my blood. "His kind don't ride in the master's vehicle."

I struggled to hide my eye roll. I was two coyote bites past carrying about Killion's rules. "Do you think I need a tetanus booster?"

He didn't answer, giving me a stare that would scorch metal. Scooting Ghost aside and checking the various hidden compartments under the seat and in the doors for a towel, I ignored him. My wounds would heal soon, but I hated dripping blood everywhere.

"I don't drive shifters."

I met his eyes in the mirror. "This is an emergency, Moss. What would Jesus do?"

He reared back, then swiveled to glance at me over the divider, brows drawn down. "Did you hit your head or something?"

"I noticed your necklace. I've seen you cross yourself. If you're a Christian vampire, more power to you, but I'm calling you out. Forget Andy. *I need your help.* Are you seriously going to abandon me in my moment of need?"

"I never claimed to be a Good Samaritan."

Touché. I found a stack of bar towels and staunched the

flow, stuffing them inside my torn jacket sleeves. "I could whack you with my scythe and send you to the great beyond to meet Jesus."

His eyes lit up. "You've seen him?"

Death save me. "Not in person."

He set his full lips, pressing them into a thin line as he audibly sighed. "The master will be very unhappy."

"He can take it up with me."

Hot, stinky breath hit my cheek. I whipped around to find Andy—still in wolf form—staring me in the face. "Dude, come on. This is no joke. I'm tired and you need to get in touch with your witch friend so I can break this hex."

The sad eyes stayed locked on mine. He whined softly and shook out his fur.

Understanding hit like a lightning bolt. "Oh, no. You can't be serious."

His muzzle twitched. "Rawry."

Sorry? I put my head in my hands. "It only works on animals." I felt like throwing the scythe or pounding my feet on the floor. "Since I brought you back in your wolf form, you can't shift?"

He panted, drool dripping from his tongue.

Scooting to the other side of the seat, I moved Ghost with me, creating as much room as possible. "Get in."

With huge paws and gangly legs, it took him several tries to compact his frame enough to fit. Moss kept up his grumblings and I held my nose against the smell. Finally, we were all in and the door closed.

The limo glided off into the night.

EIGHTEEN

M oss grumbled all the way back to my place, a real Scrooge. I instructed him to drop us off a block away so Vera, always on the lookout, wouldn't see the wolf at my side.

We slipped into a neighbor's yard, along the fence line to the rear of the duplex and I stopped Andy at the outside stairs that led to my apartment. "Can you contact your friend and communicate with her?"

He lowered his gaze to the ground. Did that mean no? Yes? Maybe?

The night air was sharp, the clouds thin and jagged, playing hide and seek with the moon again. I smelled like the two canines and longed for a hot shower and twelve hours of sleep.

"I don't speak wolf," I said, trying to be patient. This had been my idea, and it had backfired, but I needed that witch's help. "Can you paw the ground or something? Once for yes, two for no?"

The golden eyes rose and he used a massive foot to tap the frost tipped grass once. *Yes.*

Progress. I didn't know why he couldn't just shake or bob his head, but I'd take what I could get. "Awesome. So, it would be best if I don't reveal my, er, skills. Can you communicate with her and get her to write a spell, or whatever, to break the necro hex?"

His gaze fell again, and my stomach did as well.

"Not. Probably," a familiar, scratchy voice said from above my head.

I glanced up to find the raven dancing on the railing at the top of the landing. His claws dug in to the grayed wood, but couldn't seem to find stability. Tail feathers fluttered as though he were about to take flight, yet he didn't. "I don't know how you got out," I whispered, loudly, "but how do you know?"

"Mind. Read," he replied. At least that's what it sounded like. "No understand. Wolf."

I squinted at the bird attempting to decipher that. "I don't understand the wolf, or the witch won't understand him?" I glanced at Andy. He gave a one paw response, which didn't answer me. I waved a hand at him and ignored the raven. "Let's start again, one question at a time. We know I can't understand you; can't she do a spell to talk to you? That's what they do with their familiars, don't they?"

Ghost wiggled in my arms, wanting down. I set her near my feet and she promptly walked over to a pot of Vera's holly and peed on it.

"No. Doesn't," the bird replied for him.

At first, I thought he meant no as in 'negative.' My brain was slow and sluggish like my body. The bites were almost healed, leaving only pink skin at the puncture wounds, but the ordeal had taken more than blood out of me. "You don't *know?*" I clarified with Andy.

One paw. *Yes.*

"How about this—I'll write a note you can deliver to her. Will that work?"

His head lifted, expression brightening. Another yes, if that meant anything.

The raven confirmed it. "Work, work, work."

The wolf's ears twitched and his head swiveled toward the house. "Come upstairs and I'll write the note. Quietly," I added, giving him a stern look. "I don't need my landlady—"

"Chloe?"

The rear porch light nearly blinded me and the sound of Vera's voice coming from around the corner of the house froze me in place. I waved frantically for Andy to hide. He ducked behind the potted plant, as if that tiny bush could cloak his giant frame.

"Not there, you moron." I shooed him toward the fenced backyard. "Go!"

For such a large animal, he tiptoed off with quiet stealth. I spun as Vera shuffled into view, holding the lapels of her fuzzy bathrobe tight to her chest. "There you are. I thought I heard voices." She glanced over my shoulder and I stepped in front of her, hoping to block her view until the shifter was out of sight. She sniffed and made a face. "Who are you talking to?"

"Jelly bean," the raven croaked. "Jingle bells. Jolly old elf."

Saved by the bird. "Him." I motioned at the raven, and was glad when Ghost rushed to meet Vera, distracting her. "Do you know how he got free?"

Patting the dog, she clucked her tongue and shook a finger at the raven. "Naughty raven!" To me, she said, "It's my fault. I heard him calling your name and I felt bad for him, so I brought him downstairs to watch Christmas shows with me and Miss Pickles. Next thing I know, poof!" She splayed her fingers like fireworks going off. "He just disappeared."

"He called me by name?"

She nodded, her wrinkled jowls jiggling. A car drove past on the street around front, the motor fading away again in the chilly air. I wondered if Moss was checking up on me. "He's a smart one. You could train him so easily."

I wondered if when I broke the hex, the things I'd accidentally resurrected would go back to being dead. "Well, sounds like he's ready to go home." I raised my voice. "You can fly now. Go back to your owner."

He flapped his wings, stretching them out to the tips, as though he would lift off. For a second, his body did rise from the railing, and Vera sucked in an audible breath. He hung there, suspended, trying hard. I admit I felt relieved.

The beating wings sped up, and...he tilted sideways and squawked.

The wings beat the air in a panic. I dropped my bag and was moving before I could think. Regardless of the fact he had flown earlier, the raven somersaulted over the landing and kamikazed straight for the frozen ground.

I threw out my hands to catch him. Ghost was underfoot and I attempted not to step on or kick her. I bellyflopped, the impact knocking the air from my lungs. The bird plopped into my hands like a football, his claws scrabbling for purchase and managing to slice open both palms and dig into multiple fingers.

"Ouch." I was bleeding again. He rolled out of my hands and righted himself. Then he danced over to Ghost, squawking. "Jelly bean!"

Ghost barked and sniffed him in greeting. Vera chuckled. She waddled over to help me up. "Are you okay?"

"I will be." I brushed frost and dead grass from my thighs, my pants already dark with blood stains. I snagged my bag and Ghost. "Sorry we disturbed you. I'm going to hit the sack."

She sniffed the air again. "Were you working at the morgue? I thought you were off."

Yes, I smelled, but not of chemicals and embalming fluid. I went with it anyway. "Extra cleaning since it's been quiet."

Suspicions confirmed, she nodded. "Guess that's a good thing, right? How awful to lose a loved one at Chris—" she caught herself. Would everyone do this for the rest of my life—stop themselves from talking about death at the holidays? "If you need help bandaging your hands, or you change your mind, I have eggnog and cookies. We can watch *It's a Wonderful Life*."

The ache of missing my parents rose like a wave in my chest. I swallowed the lump that pushed into my throat. "Maybe I will," I told her.

She rubbed my shoulder and smiled. "Excellent." Ghost panted and reached her nose toward her. Vera scratched between her ears. "See you both in a bit, sweetie."

I waited until she'd disappeared and I heard her close the front door. Andy peeked his head over the top of the gate. "Come on," I whispered. "Everybody, please, be quiet."

The peace of my apartment was welcomed after the long, freaky day. I was shivering, partially from my chilled body, but more from exhaustion. I made a cup of strong coffee, fed the animals, and took a quick shower under very hot water. The combo kickstarted my brain and I sat at my desk to type the message. "What's her name?" I asked Andy.

He made a series of vocal noises and the raven trans-lated. "Airorah."

"Aorta?"

We tried the sequence again two more times, until I finally had Aurora written down. I confirmed it with the wolf, who tapped his paw once, and the raven hopped on my bed, singing, "La la la."

"Dear Aurora," I spoke aloud as I typed, so he could hear. "I am in desperate need of your professional services. I have been cursed and can now raise the dead without trying. I wish to break it." I knew she wouldn't do it for free, and didn't expect her to, but I had no idea what the going rate for hex-breaking services was. "Andy assures me you are a witch of great skill and knowledge. I'm happy to pay you for your time and services."

My bank account might take a hit, but I could use my bonus money. I gritted my teeth at the thought of putting my plans to purchase the vet clinic on hold, but I couldn't walk around resurrecting animals and insects like a necromantic Pied Piper.

"Please advise," I continued. "If possible, send word with Andy as to your terms and the cost. Thank you. Sincerely," – I hesitated. Should I give my name? An avatar seemed like a better idea. The raven hopped onto the back of the chair. The memory of Jacqueline's bumper sticker flashed through my mind: *Killin' it.*

I used it as my signature.

As if the raven read and understood, he squawked, "Kill! Kill!"

"Not that again." I shooed him away and printed the note. Eyeing the wolf, I frowned. How could he carry it? He had no collar, and while I had a few shirts for Ghost, they wouldn't fit over one of Andy's paws, let alone his body. If he used his teeth, it would be covered with slobber. "Well that's a pickle," I said, wondering if I needed more caffeine.

I searched my closet for a belt. I had none. I spent a while trying to concoct a fanny pack-like contraption, but nothing worked. Finally, I hit on an idea. I snuck downstairs to raid Vera's cat supplies. While her movie of choice played out on the TV, she snored loudly, head thrown back and Miss Pickles in her lap. At least, she wasn't waiting on me. Her other cats were settled on both sides of her, several dressed in red and green outfits.

In her guest room, which doubled for extra pet supplies, I found the stash and dug through a bag of collars and harnesses. Holding up different collars to check their size, I flinched when I pulled out one that had a bell. It jingled, but seemed to blend in with the Christmas movie, thank you, Clarence, so even though I froze, I heard nothing but more snores.

I peeked around the hall corner, where all I could see was Vera's feet on the ottoman. They didn't move and the snores continued. Taking the whole bag, I snuck past her, noting that Master Henry and Miss Pickles were now awake and watching me. I put a finger to my lips, as if they could understand, and tiptoed back upstairs two at a time.

Inside my apartment, I dumped the collection on the bed and began weeding out everything but the extra-large variety. There were no dog collars, since Velma needed all of those for the rescue.

For once, I was grateful for Vera's propensity to dish out treats and create fat cats. Nearly all of her felines had thick necks and required big collars.

I had to connect four to create one large enough to fit Andy's neck. I clipped a harness that had a weatherproof pouch made to display a therapy cat designation card to the handmade collar. Vera once had a seventeen-year-old feline who had qualified, and she'd taken her around to the hospitals and nursing homes, until Miss Mocha had passed on her twentieth birthday.

As I worked on attaching the homemade system to the werewolf's neck, he screwed up his nose and kept turning his face away.

"Cat like no," the raven told me. He clicked his beak. "Smell. Bad."

"Tough." I secured the contraption and tugged on it to make sure it held. "This is what we have to work with, and by the way, you don't exactly smell like roses, Andy."

A few minutes later, I watched him lope down the outside stairs and trot off into the shadows. I sprayed air freshener, and crawled into bed.

NINETEEN

Squawking and growling woke me before sunrise. I threw a pillow at the bird and dog, roughhousing with each other. Then groaned, and rolled over.

It was wasted effort, the pair deciding I wanted to play, too, and jumping onto my back. Rocking my weight side to side in an attempt to roll them only egged them on. I jerked the covers over my head to fend off the pecking and sloppy dog kisses that ensued.

"Pee. Dog," the raven announced, jumping up and down on me.

Ghost barked, seeming to agree.

Mumbling, I slowly made my way out of bed, pulled on my sweats, and stumbled to the backyard with them.

Shadows clung to the skeletal trees and dormant bushes. Vera's Santa smiled and waved at me from the patio, forever frozen in his good-natured tableau, as I watched Ghost sniff the frosted grass. The raven wobbled around, half-walking, half-flying here and there, his black body blending in with the landscape's edges and the gray and purple streaks of dawn.

Ghost did her duty and continued to investigate odors, wandering past the sleeping garden and into the jasmine and gardenia plants along the back fence. Several trees added cover there, their branches unmoving this morning. Birds twittered in the neighbor's yard, but none were awake yet in ours. The distant sounds of traffic drifted in and out as I yawned. "Come on you two," I called quietly. "Let's go."

My blood iced and my skin prickled a second before I heard Ghost growl. The raven flapped its wings and ran toward me, screeching, "Kill!"

My feet were moving before I could breathe. "Killion?" I hoped it was him, but Ghost's growl told me no.

I scanned in the direction the noise had come from. "Ghost," I called, no longer trying to be quiet. My slippers made crunching noises as I hustled along the garden path, stepping on dead pumpkin vines Vera hadn't cleaned up after Halloween. I stumbled on a rotting one, the not-yet-frozen vegetable mushy and soft. Could it be Andy?

I dismissed that as well. He didn't stir my blood or send gooseflesh over my body.

Vampire. I knew it from the twinge in my veins, the odor I caught on the chilly air. It was one of Killion's, but her normal lilies and graveyard dirt scent was bitter, like vinegar. "What do you want?" I hissed. "Just don't hurt the dog."

Laughable, since Ghost could take her out in her psychopomp form, and here I was with nothing to defend myself.

If anything, the air went even more still and flat; the neighboring birds hushed. I searched the fence line, looking for the shadow that didn't fit.

There. On my left, the outline of a head, the fuzzy glint

of magic—an extra layer over the natural shadows that hung heavily.

"Hello, grim." Simone stepped from her hiding place, Ghost giving her a slight berth. The black gloom clung to her, like thick, unyielding spider webs. "Your powers are growing."

"What are you doing here?"

"Few day lighters can sense a vampire."

I wasn't about to give her anything, so I kept the fact I could smell her to myself. Ghost curled her lip and growled. "Come," I said to the dog. "Porch."

She gave me a crestfallen look, but slowly joined the bird at the steps. For once, it was good she'd obeyed.

I stood my ground. "Did Killion send you?"

She ambled toward a grouping of rose bushes. "He asked me to guard you."

I nearly choked. "You're more likely to kill me."

Long, thin fingers trailed over the branches of the tallest bush, and snagged on the dead thorns. As they raked her skin, she breathed in a blissful sigh and then sucked the blood from her wounds. "We all have our cross to bear."

Total freak. "I'm actually glad you're here." It wasn't a total lie. "I need to ask you a few questions about the witch who sent the, uh, jackal-dude to take you out."

"The master told me. As I've already stated, I don't know any witches and I have no idea why one would want to kill me."

I wanted to kill her, so it wasn't a stretch for me. I kept that to myself, as well. The air between us crackled with electricity, and I had the distinct impression she was imagining all the ways she could hurt me, slowly and painfully.

I knew she was holding out. Problem was, vampires didn't play by human—or grim—rules. They thought differently and acted as such, too. If I was going to get to the bottom of this, for Killion's sake, I needed her cooperation.

"I know you believe the attack was random, but if you want to get me off your back, I have to figure out why the witch came after you. It shook Killion up—you're…" I forced out the word, "favored by him. I'm only digging deeper because he asked me to. Now I'm cursed with necromancy, and he's on probation from SMG. Don't you want to help me clear his name and make sure you're safe?"

She moved so fast, I didn't have time to blink. She hissed into my face. "I'm not at fault for this, and no, I don't want him to be reinstated with SMG or have his name cleared. He is a *master vampire.*" Her fangs flashed in the growing light. "He has more important business than investigating issues with *your* kind."

The smart thing would have been to step back, keep my cool, and not let her provoke me. All of my instincts were on high alert, and my survival one was taking the lead, encouraging me to get in the house. But I'd had enough of her and her ego. I shoved her away and was slightly surprised it worked. "Get out of my face."

Vampires possess enormous strength and stability and aren't easily caught off guard. My shove, however, set her back several feet, and I could only assume my grim abilities had kicked in due to the threat she'd presented.

She hissed again, and reached for me. I dodged her hand, but stayed planted. I considered the possibility she'd just offered. "Did you intentionally set this up so Killion would get kicked out of SMG?"

Ghost materialized next to me in her psychopomp form. She didn't growl or bare her teeth, but blocked the woman. Simone drew back. Smart. "I would never defy my master."

"Yet, you're threatening me when he sent you to protect me. Sorry, not buying that one."

"Humans." She spat on the ground. Eyes as black as night, her gaze went to the rooftop, the fuzzy rays of sunrise lifting the last layers of gray. "I'll let him know you refused my services."

She was gone in a flash and Ghost glanced at me. I patted her head, and we started for the porch. I was proud of myself for not backing down, and glad that my limbs weren't shaking.

Not much anyway.

The raven hopped back and forth on his claws. "Rawr! Kill!"

"Really?" I picked him up and Ghost shrank to puppy size. "Rawr?"

One beady eye studied me. "Santa?"

I laughed and opened the gate to access the stairs. At least that was better than *kill*. "I need coffee, and I'm definitely not Santa."

"Ho, ho, ho," he squawked.

I shut the gate behind us, hoping we hadn't woken Vera. The side of the house was still in shadow, and through the slats of the stairs, I noticed a person sitting on the bottom step of the stairs. My blood buzzed and my breath caught. I'd hoped Andy might be back by now, but once again, it wasn't him.

Simone. Gritting my teeth, I stopped a distance away. "Change of heart?"

But it wasn't lilies and grave dirt I smelled as the breeze blew by me. As I came around to the stair landing, Killion met my gaze, a single pale bar of light teasing across his features. "Simone is keeping something from us."

"You think?" Ghost jumped into his lap. "You're not

supposed to be here," I reminded him, and then I began climbing the steps. My leg brushed his arm, and lightning fast, he caught hold of my calf and stopped me.

Heat and cold raced up my skin in equal proportions. My fingers itched to reach out and touch his hair. "Chloe," he said, low and strained. "I am concerned for your safety."

I was more concerned with the way my pulse was jumping around like a caged bird. "I'm fine, but keep her away from me."

"I believe her loyalty to me is suspect. This is a difficult thing for me to understand—vampires have a code. She's taken my blood. She is bonded to me, yet..."

I controlled my breathing, hoping he wouldn't notice my response to his touch. Which was dumb, since he sensed everything. "Must be tough being in charge. Maybe bestowing your *favor* on her has caused her to desire more power—yours—and made you vulnerable."

He came to his feet, dragging his hand up my leg, my hip, to my waist. It rested there, and we were now face to face. Ghost nestled in the crook of his arm and his luscious scent flooded my nose. "You misunderstand the term. All those in my nest are favored by me, otherwise they wouldn't be part of my family. They've sworn an unbreakable oath. They've partaken of my blood. They cannot be disloyal."

"I've had your blood, yet, I'm *not* favored?"

He closed his eyes as if wrestling with his patience. He looked tired. "Partaking of a few drops of my blood created a bond between you and I, but not like that of a master to his family. That initiation is much more involved, more intense. It creates a pact among us. No member of the nest would dare to break it."

"I'm sticking with my assessment. You better watch your back. She doesn't like that you're working with SMG and she certainly doesn't like you working with me. She doesn't care if your name is cleared of wrongdoing. She wants you all to herself."

This gave him pause. He stood there, scrutinizing me. "You're sure?"

His lips were close enough to kiss. "Positive. She's definitely up to something." Like Death. "You shouldn't trust her."

"If I cannot..." His gaze dropped to my lips.

My legs trembled. The blood in my veins—the trace of his blood—warmed like melting butter. I swallowed hard, reminding my eager female parts urging me to kiss him that he had very sharp teeth.

I'd like to believe it was logic and common sense that led me to do what I did next, but my escape was more a result of the fact I hadn't had so much as a date, much less a kiss, in over a year, maybe two. I'd lost count.

I wanted to believe there was something between us, not just our partnership, not just the blood bond, but...

Such a bad idea to pursue that.

"Coffee?" I offered, and raced up the stairs to my apartment.

TWENTY

Killion and the raven followed me inside. I closed the door softly, wondering why I'd just invited the master vampire up for coffee when I'd been ordered to stay clear of him. "I subconsciously have a death wish," I muttered, leaning against the door and closing my eyes.

He put his hands on my arms, making me jump. I flicked my eyes open to see him staring at me with a frown. He'd set Ghost on the floor. "Why do you still fear me? I would never hurt you, and I certainly will not be the cause of your death."

His eyes were purple pools, mesmerizing. His concern was palpable. He was close again, so...enticing. The world was in those eyes. His heart was as well.

I fought against my desire. "We have to be quiet so Vera doesn't overhear."

He waved a hand. "She cannot hear us now."

The Undead master favors you. The woman's words clawed at my brain, my pulse skyrocketing. She'd talked about destiny, a prophecy...that I was the one.

But the one for what? To bring the dead back to life?

"You're shaking." Killion rubbed my upper arms through my sweatshirt. "What can I do?"

Suddenly, I no longer saw him. Instead, the graves of that other place clouded my vision. The sensation of being drawn back there wrapped around me. Then and now became layered, fragmented. I could see both my home and the precipice.

The graves burst open, row upon row of zombies rising from them. Chittering and moaning echoed in my ears. The cold touch of death made my breath frost on the air, even though it was a cozy seventy-four in my apartment.

"What is happening?" Killion snapped me back into focus. "Chloe, are you doing this?"

"That woman. The one who said I was part of the prophecy... She's pulling me there."

He stared at the sparkling fog between us. "She's trying to control you. You have to fight this."

I did. Yet, the floor felt like rocks under my feet. I could hear her whispering in my ears. "*Kill him,*" she instructed. "*His power will be yours.*"

"You need to...leave." My teeth chattered as I spoke. I blinked and cleared my vision of the other place. "Killion, you have to get out of here."

The crease on his forehead deepened. "I will not." He tugged me from the door and wrenched the blanket from my bed. "This is my fault. I should have studied that spell in detail before I performed the ritual."

We sat and he wrapped the material around me. I focused on his pretty eyes instead of the woman's voice still whispering in my head. "She's telling me to kill you."

"Kill!" the raven cackled and jumped around.

Killion continued to rub my arms, my back, my legs. "You're stronger than she is. Push her out."

"How?"

He dragged me into an embrace and warmth flashed through my veins. "Focus on me, now, not what happened with her. Wall her off."

In my mind, she laughed, the sound making my brain scream in pain. I ground my teeth. "With what?" Flashes of the scene flickered into being again, but weaker with Killion's arms around me.

"The rocks, the dirt from the graves, the zombies. Whatever is there. They're only props, Chloe. She's using all of that to mess with your mind and create a connection to it. Turn them against her."

I gritted my teeth, my body racked with spasms, daggers of ice attacking me. Waning and waxing like the day and night, my apartment and the precipice warred for my attention. I imagined the rocky cliff rising like a castle's walls around me, knocking her and the zombies away. She laughed again, but the sound was less painful, less sharp. Muted.

"That's right, grim." Her distant voice floated on the air. "You are powerful, but now you belong to—"

"No," my voice boomed out of me, a geyser of heat shot from my belly and into my chest. "I don't belong to anyone!" Killion's hold on me snapped like a rubber band. I rocketed to my feet. Ghost whined and hid under the bed. The raven cocked his head. "Kill?"

The blanket was now stifling, sweat dripping down my neck. I staggered, throwing it off and breaking free.

Killion caught me when my legs gave out and scooped me up like a bride. Gently, he set me on the bed, and then stared deeply in to my eyes, as if assuring himself I was a hundred percent back with him.

The room swam around me and I clung to his arm to

keep from pitching over. After a moment, I could steady myself. "I'm okay."

He lowered himself next to me. "I went back over the spell, dissected the words and meanings. I thought I understood it, but there are specific words in the old, regional witch tongue. One in particular—*yovumi*—is a take-off from ovum, egg, or origin. The way the text was written, I believed it meant the hex would be returned to the sender. After what has happened, it seems it returned you to the originator of the hex."

"That's a lot to understand. Try starting with: what is the old witch tongue?"

"They have their own alphabet and sacred language. Like the glyph in the Jackal's bag. The local one consists of a mixture of Latin, Creole, and more ancient tongues. Certain words are considered so sacred, many religions and cultures have tried to wipe them out of existence. Many witches use glyphs to replace the actual words."

"She said it was my destiny. My fate. What did she mean? *What* is?"

He said nothing and simply stared at me, as if willing me to put two and two together. I couldn't. None of this made sense. Or maybe my brain was stuttering because he was so close. My pulse was going crazy again, and I wasn't sure why.

"This all started with Simone and her attacker, who we assumed was sent to curse *her*. Yet, Simone claims to have had no interaction with any witch or know why one would. Either she's lying or she's oblivious to what she did to garner the witch's attention." I really wanted to believe the witch was after Simone and this was all about her destiny with those chittering zombies. Yet... "Is it possible Simone instigated this whole thing and had been playing the victim, and getting Cat Woman to come after both of us."

I saw how it unsettled him. If possible, he looked even more worn out. "I would normally stick to the fact she is part of my nest and would never commit treason, but, I will concede it is possible, if not probable."

"Has Simone done anything that might make you question her loyalties?"

He stood and paced to my desk. "She has made it clear that she disagrees with my handling of recent events concerning a peace treaty initiated with the shifter clans. She believes our nest should rule the city and subjugate other supernaturals. At one time, she rose to my lieutenant believing she would be my equal. The queen of the Undead here in Louisiana."

"Oh." Another overachiever. And possibly in more ways than one. I attempted to keep a straight face at the meaning I assumed was behind her becoming his queen. "You mean, you two..." I couldn't say it and hoped he understood.

"We were never lovers, if that's what you're asking. Although she would have liked to have pursued an intimate relationship. She is strategic and an asset to me as an advisor, but her philosophies about the role of vampires has significantly altered over time. She harkens back to the old ways and sees humans as food, other supernaturals as lesser than us."

Lovely.

He returned to the spot next to me, securing the blanket around my shoulders once more when I visibly shivered. If only he knew it wasn't from cold but because of him. "This territory is mine, but there are always those seeking to take it from me. Every vampire desires more power, and my nest is strong."

"But if someone on the inside, who knows everything about your businesses, as well as your personal life, were to attack you from within..."

He cradled my hand, the previous evening's wounds now healed. Still, he stroked over where the injuries had been as if he could see them. I melted at his gentleness. "Please let me worry about Simone. I didn't realize the necromancer had this kind of hold on you. How many times has she communicated with you?"

Exhaustion weighed on me as heavy as the blanket. I shook my head. "Just this once, but she's powerful. I mean, I think it was her voice I heard in the church, too, but she wasn't trying to get me to do anything, she just told me you were...lying about not being the master in the prophecy."

"I truly did not believe it was me. I am sorry."

Cat Woman had been right. "I have to break this connection with her and the sooner the better. I still don't see how she could curse me to begin with, at least not intentionally. And unless she's the one Death went to for the spell, how could she control the results? Dragging me to that precipice?"

"Let's assume she sent the creature after Simone, perhaps as you say, mistaking her for you and believing she is the one in the prophecy. But Jackal tried to kill Simone, not hex her."

I absentmindedly watched Ghost twirl in her bed three times before she laid down. "Which seems to suggest that the person of the prophecy was going to keep Cat Woman from doing something she planned, right? That's why she wanted to kill them."

He nodded and got up to pace the room once more. "What could she have planned?"

I could almost hear the chittering again and blocked it. "I'm going to go out on a limb and suggest raising the dead."

He stopped. "An army of the dead to do her bidding?"

A fresh chill pebbled my skin. No blanket could take away that coldness. "But she didn't stop Simone—or me—and now, I'm bound to her because of that stupid bag. If she thought I could stop her, why didn't she kill me when she had me on the rocks?"

"Her plans are not clear, and we are making assumptions. We should begin with why she created the jackal creature to begin with."

Silence fell as we considered possibilities. Faint peachy rays of sunlight danced with the curtain at the window over my desk. "Assuming Simone isn't behind this, maybe the witch sent Jackal because she isn't strong enough to take out a vampire?" I offered. "Or her magic is wonky?"

"That would definitely make it difficult to raise an army," he agreed. "Unless..."

I waited and when he didn't finish I prompted him. "Unless what?"

His phone dinged. "Speak of the vampire," he said, reading a message. "Simone reports that something has happened with the shifters."

I dropped the blanket and rose. "Is everything okay?"

He started toward the exit. "I'm sorry, I have to go. Several of my members are injured." Before he reached the door, he stopped short. "I can't leave you, though. You're too vulnerable."

I was, but no way would I admit it. "Go take care of your people. I'll be all right."

He stepped to me and took my chin between his finger

and thumb. "The Cat Woman has a hold on you. It's not safe for you to be alone."

I gently removed his grip. "It's also not safe for me to be with you, remember? If Death finds out, we could both be in serious trouble."

"You can't—"

"Trust him? I know. You two are a broken record when it comes to each other. I will handle him—and hopefully, I'll be clear of Cat Woman today. I'm going to learn who Death got that spell from and suss out what's going on with him." I gently guided Killion to the exit. "I'll let you know what I discover. Meantime, take care of your vampires."

"I'll leave Moss to keep an eye on you."

"While I like the guy, and I appreciate your concern, I don't need a babysitter."

"Do not think of him as such."

"Go," I relented, half-shoving him out the door.

His body was a brick wall and he planted his feet on the landing, reaching back and touching my arm. "Be careful."

The air felt charged between us. "You, too. I hope the others are okay."

For a heartbeat, I thought he might kiss me, but then he was gone. He disappeared around the corner, and the limo, a few yards down the block, purred to life. It sped off, and I was both relieved and disappointed he'd taken Moss. "I either need more sleep or a giant dose of coffee."

A tickling sensation danced over my skin and up the back of my neck. I had the feeling I was being watched.

As I stood on the landing, trying to act natural, I analyzed the energy. It wasn't Andy or Simone's, but it prickled my arms and made my chest tight.

I scanned the area, keeping my face neutral, even as I took a step toward the inside. The breeze danced with tree limbs, one of Vera's bushes scratching along the fence line. I almost called out, "Hello? Who's there?" but stopped myself. No sense sounding like a too-stupid-to-live horror movie heroine.

Coaching myself to look confident and hoping I appeared unconcerned, I stood my ground for another moment. Nothing changed, but I felt the heavy weight of someone's gaze. Survival instincts screaming again, I turned slowly and went in.

It was time to send Death a message.

TWENTY-ONE

After I fired off the email to SMG requesting Death's presence, I fed the dog and bird, checked the account Nita had set up for the lost and found sites—empty, to my disappointment—and jumped in the shower.

Hot water has a wonderful way of clearing my mind as well as cleaning my body. I found a bit of clarity, and when I stepped out, the raven was in the bathroom, perched on the vanity. Wrapping the towel around me, I shooed him off. "Haven't you heard of personal space? How did you get in here?"

He fluttered to the floor and danced over to the open door. I froze, thinking Death had arrived. Hair dripping, I peeked around the edge.

It wasn't Death; it was Tinder, the British clerk from SMG I'd met the morning after the robes chose me. Tall and lanky, he wore a newspaper boy hat cocked sideways over straight hair down to his ears. His skin was pale and he had acne scars that he tried to hide with shabby facial hair. He lounged at my desk, flicking a cigarette lighter open and closed. The chair squeaked with every movement. "About time, Grave Girl. What's ailin' ya?"

The bird hopped past, brushing my legs with a wing, and flew up to land in his lap. He fumbled the lighter and appeared amused.

I stayed behind the door. "What are you doing here? And how did you get in?"

"Your 911?" His gaze flicked over me as he stroked the bird's neck. "What's the emergency?"

"The message was for Death."

"He's busy."

"SMG sent you in his place?"

"I can leave." He stood, lifting the bird from his lap.

"Wait." I shut the door, tugged on my clothes, and pinned up my wet hair. The circles under my eyes stood out like dark bruises against my waxy skin.

Returning to the main room, I found him once again at my desk, enamored with the raven. "What's his name?"

"I have no idea."

"Kill," the bird said.

Tinder chuckled. "A grim with a bird named Kill? Hilarious."

"That's not his name, and...never mind. Here's why I sent the request." I told him the story, leaving out the prophecy and my suspicions about Simone's possible involvement. A furrow between his thin brows deepened with every addition. "I need help breaking this curse, and I have the feeling the necromancer is up to no good."

"Of course, she's up to no good. Are you dense? Necros are evil." He set the raven on the floor and paced. My already threadbare carpet was going to be worn to the floorboards by Christmas. "So your new ability only works on animals?"

"Yes."

"But you didn't raise Jackal?"

"No. I think the bag was keeping him alive, but it back-fired and caused his death."

"His internal organs, including his heart, were mummified?"

I nodded. "The fresh pieces came from someone—or some*thing*—else."

Dropping into the chair again, he looked stumped. There was a lot of that going around. "I've not heard of a hex bag that works like that, but mummification and man-beast hybrids point to ancient Egypt. Gods and demi-gods? Used to be plenty of them around. If Killion suspects yours was sent by a witch and she was controlling it—well, that sounds like a golem."

"A what?"

He gave me that *are you dense* expression again. "A monster made from clay, usually animated by a holy person. They're mentioned in the Old Testament and the Jews like to claim they're original to them, but plenty of cultures have brought inanimate beings to life with magic pre-Biblical times. They don't have free will and must obey their maker. Usually there's a word or a symbol that activates and deacti-vates their animation."

"This one had odd skin, but it wasn't clay."

"Some look as human as you and I."

I *was* human. Him? Jury was out. "Do you think Cat Woman gave Death the spell to supposedly break the curse?"

"Nah, why would Death go to her?" He scratched at a pimple on his cheek. "You've really stumbled into trouble. A grim who can raise the dead." He chuckled and shook his head.

"Tell me something I don't know."

He lifted his chin, as though accepting the challenge. "The Egyptian gods are long gone, but they left behind offspring, the demi-gods and other freaks of natures. Your hybrids may be related to them."

Perhaps Simone wasn't far off the mark. "Or Cat Woman created them."

"There used to be a secret sect who searched for a prophesied one they believed could give them power over life and death, make them immortal. Your Cat Woman may belong to that group."

"Prophecy?" Cold cramped my gut at his nod. "You know what it says?"

He shook his head. "Not my area, but I know the being they searched for is mythical. It has magic way beyond that of a vamp. She may have believed it was this Simone gal; now she thinks it's you, since the spell brought you to her instead."

"Power over life and death…" I couldn't make the pieces fit. "I'm a grim, yes, but only because I was in the wrong place at the wrong time, not because of any inherent magic."

"And now you can resurrect animals." He grinned.

"Because of her spell," I countered. "She did this to me. I can't be the one the prophecy refers to."

"Sure about that, Grave Girl?"

This was getting me nowhere. "Look, all I need to know is how do I break the curse?"

He snorted. "Do I look like a witch? How would I know?"

Irritation burned under my skin. "Can you suggest who might? I've reached out to someone, but I haven't heard back from her. I'm getting desperate."

"Witches and spell casters are bad news. Best stay away from them."

Still not helpful. "Are all the members of this sect part animal?" The memory of Jackal's smell, the sharp canines, those glassy eyes—all unwelcome. And then there were the ones on the precipice. "They can't be walking around like that without drawing attention."

He held up a finger. "Ah, well, the originals could change their appearance to look human, or create a glamour. They were demi-gods, after all. But their progeny?" He shrugged. "Diluted magic, at best. They'd need a powerful spell caster to help them hide their true form."

"They can die, right?"

"All things do eventually," he assured me. "Have you read the Book of the Dead?"

"You mean the grim manual?"

His chuckle told me I was providing him with oodles of entertainment. "The ancient Egyptian funerary text." At my blank look, he continued. "It's a collection of spells that assist the dead through the Underworld and into the afterlife. Humans and supernaturals alike have theorized that they could be tweaked to grant immortality—to turn someone into a god."

"Can they?" I prayed the answer was no.

He came to his feet and stretched, pocketing the lighter and checking his watch. "Let's hope not. Gotta run."

"What am I supposed to do?"

"Get rid of your Dr. Frankenstein." He sauntered to the door. "Or be prepared to take on a bunch of godlike creatures."

TWENTY-TWO

Frozen in place and baffled at both his nonchalance and my predicament, I stared at the open door for a few seconds. The bird cawed, bringing me out of my stupor. I ran out to chase Tinder down, but he'd disappeared.

I growled in frustration and kicked the railing, then froze when the snap of a twig off to the left sent my overly sensitive system a Code Red. The same feeling of being watched that I experienced earlier returned.

Scanning the perimeter of the side yard, the fence, and the overgrown space between our house and the neighbor's, I felt my patience with all creatures, living, dead, supernatural, and mundane, slipping away.

"Whoever you are, whatever you want," I said in a weary voice. "I don't have the time or the patience for games. Show yourself and tell me what you want."

The birds stopped singing, and nothing lightened the dread racing around in my chest. I had that eerie sensation of déja vu. Like my encounter with Simone, the sounds of car engines, folks out and about, and dogs barking, echoed through the air, yet seemed distant. As I scanned the mostly bare bushes and trees, my attention snagged on a pair of ice blue eyes. They peeked from a dark corner of the neighbor's yard.

Not Andy or Simone. Definitely not Killion. My arms offered up phantom pain as I wondered if the coyotes had tracked me down.

I sniffed but only caught the light fragrance of lavender and patchouli. Probably from someone who'd walked past on the sidewalk in front. I eased down the steps, hoping my visitor was neither a hybrid, nor an actual animal I'd resurrected.

At the bottom, I paused. The placement of the eyes suggested its head came to my stomach. "If you want to talk, talk. If I accidentally resurrected you, I'm sorry, but I'm not taking in any more pets. I can offer food and water, but you'll have to return to...wherever you came from." Keeping my voice calm and stepping off the last tread, I moved forward with calm deliberation. "Outside of that, if you're here to do me harm, I'd advise against it. I've had all the threats I can handle today, and shall we say, my unusual abilities, can cause you a lot of trouble."

I didn't exactly sound as confident as I wanted to, but I hoped the warning would be heeded. Clearing the edge of the dead grass, I stopped when the thing hissed and the whites of dagger shape fangs appeared. My bravado turned to a puddle of *yikes* in my belly.

I acknowledged the warning by taking a nice, big step in reverse, but I wasn't about to turn my back on it. "What's it going to be?" I crossed my arms and tried to affect an air of casual confidence like Killion and Death so often did. I wasn't going to hide inside my apartment or not be able to venture out into my own yard. "You want to talk or you want to fight?"

My bluff was exposed when something cold and wet poked me through my shirt from behind and I nearly jumped straight up in the air with a loud cry of fear.

Whirling, I found Andy at my side, a bag dangling by satin strings from his mouth. His neck scruff stood up and his eyes looked pleading. He made a whining noise.

"There you are," I said, relieved to see he'd returned and hopeful he'd brought help. He danced on his paws and sent his gaze to the apartment. "Are you okay?"

He head butted me, herding me toward the stairs. Strange sounds came from his throat, and the bag swung under his chin. I reached to take it, but stopped before I touched it. What if it was a trick? Another hexed item might make things worse.

A growl issued from the shadows, followed by a high-pitched squeal.

Raw fear raced up my spine. My eyes met Andy's and I saw the same in his. This time, he nearly knocked me down when he hit me with this massive head. He wasn't herding me; he was bolting for the steps to escape.

TWENTY-THREE

Done faking, I ran after him. There was a roar behind us as we took the wooden steps two at a time. I felt the staircase shudder from the impact of the beast when it hit, its massive paws clamoring after us.

As I threw myself at the entrance, nearly tumbling over Andy in the process of opening it, I caught sight of a sleek black panther. The thing raced up the steps, hitting the landing on the wood just as I slammed the door shut and threw the deadbolt.

Gasping, I looked at the shifter. "What was that?"

He dropped the bag and attempted to crawl under my bed. Ghost jumped around on top of the covers, barking at him. The raven was on my dresser, knocking various items to the floor. "Witch. Kill!"

I scrambled for my phone and texted Killion, then raised my voice to the heavens, or anyone listening. "True emergency here, Death. Nine-one-one times a hundred!"

The only response was a screeching noise from the door as the giant cat ran sizable nails down the wood. Then I remembered Killion was dealing with his own issues and felt guilty for bugging him.

At the panther's hiss and growl, the guilt evaporated.

I grabbed my scythe and stood armed and ready. My pulse did a tap dance and the handle warmed in anticipation. "I'm warning you," I yelled. "Leave me alone or I'll take you out."

"Chloe?" Vera called at the other door that she could access from inside our building.

Great. Just what I needed. "Yes, Miss Vera?"

"Do you have company, dear?"

Andy's backend stuck out from under the bed. At my feet, Ghost sniffed at the outside egress, and the bird danced on top of the dresser. "No, ma'am. Listening to a... podcast. Sorry, was it too loud?"

"Huh," she said, and I could almost envision her leaning her ear against the door. "I could have sworn I heard a man's voice earlier. You know how I feel about Killion being in there. I think he's a fine young man, but there are certain things I don't want going on under my roof."

There were so many issues with that statement, I was stumped for how to reply, but it was one of her rules —no men in the apartment.

My mentor certainly wasn't young, and although she believed we were involved romantically, I had to keep reminding myself he was my *pretend* boyfriend. A flashback of our morning exchange made a warm flush seep over my chest and neck. If my old-fashioned-values landlady knew what sometimes went on in here, I suspected she'd be far more upset than discovering I was having sex out of wedlock. "You did hear his voice," I told her. She was too smart to believe anything else. "He called and I had him on speakerphone."

"Oh." This seemed to appease her, and her voice brightened. "Well, I've made muffins. Come down and we'll have breakfast."

A knock sounded on the exterior door, making me jump. "Chloe, open up."

That's when I realized the scratching and yelling of the panther had stopped. But I wasn't excited about who had taken its place.

However, Death and I needed to talk. "I have to take a shower," I called to Vera. "I'll be down in a few minutes."

"Didn't you already take one? I heard the water running."

I bit my lip. "Your hearing is exceptional today," I muttered.

"Chloe?" Death spoke more quietly now, as though he sensed I was in trouble, but wasn't sure what was going on. I was surprised he'd even knocked. Like Killion and Tinder, he normally waltzed right in.

I undid the lock as quietly as possible and opened the door, putting a finger to my lips, before I called across the expanse to Vera, "I gave Ghost a bath. She rolled in something disgusting this morning."

"That silly girl." She chuckled. "All righty then. I'll see you in a few minutes."

Her heavy footsteps caused the stairs to squeak and I breathed a sigh of relief.

Death, in a holiday suit of dark green tweed, looked bemused. Ghost jumped up and down and barked at him to pet her. "Just think, she's around for ten more years, thanks to you."

Still half-hidden under the bed, Andy groaned and I realized my *faux pas*. If Death figured out I'd resurrected him, the shifter and I were both in a world of hurt.

Death whirled a finger, dropping his version of sound protection around us. "Where's the emergency?" He eyed Andy's flanks, which trembled at his voice. I'd mostly gotten over the slightly bone-chilling sound of it myself, but it could still affect me at times. Death scratched Ghost's ears. "And why is there a wolf trying to hide under your bed? Did he attack you?"

He reached down to grab Andy, but I managed to jump between them. "No, not him. We were attacked outside by a giant black panther. Didn't you see it?"

The corners of his eyes crinkled when he narrowed them. "That's why you called me? Over a panther? Reapers creepers, Chloe. I have important things to do, you know."

My grip on the scythe tightened. "A panther the size of Texas tried to take me out. Did you not see the gouge marks in the door from its claws? It's obviously a supernatural. Who exactly should I call?"

He grinned and ran a knuckle across my cheek. "I guess you don't call Ghostbusters for that." His longish hair was styled and I could smell product in it, subtle under the scent of his cologne. "Why didn't you call the vamp?"

I had, of course, but I didn't tell him that. Jerking away from his touch, I held his gaze. "There was an attack on some of his people."

He seemed genuinely surprised. "By whom?"

"Shifters."

Death turned away, ready to leave again. "Age old war. You'd best stay out of it."

"Hey, I don't feel sick when you're around me anymore. Did you do something to cause that? Wait, where are you going?"

"I told you, I have things to do. You don't get sick because your body is adjusting to the necromancy."

Abandoning me again? "My life is in mortal danger."

"The panther is gone, drama queen."

There was the pot calling the kettle black. "It could come back."

He faced me, one hand on the knob. "What are you scared of, Chloe? You're a grim."

As if that solved all my problems. "I'm also a necromancer, at the moment, who's got some crazy Cat Woman trying to do who knows what to me. She nearly pulled me back in to her world."

"*Her* world?"

"The one with the zombies rising from their graves and the animal hybrids trying to..." I shuddered. "Tinder said—"

"Tinder? Were you interrogating him about the professor's life contract?"

If only that were my biggest concern. "I need help. Otherwise you're going to have a dead grim on your hands."

Screwing up his face, he dropped his gaze to the floor, then brought it back to mine. "You got yourself into this jam because of your feelings for the vampire. Now you want me to fix everything for you."

Sticky anger bloomed in my chest. "Killion is my friend. I already explained that I had no idea helping him would go against the rules or end up with me in this situation." I clenched my teeth so I didn't say anything I'd regret later, but got the next words out. "I'm...sorry."

Disbelief colored his smile. "Good, lesson learned." He drew out a necklace from under his shirt collar, walked over, and dropped it over my head. "An amulet. It will protect you until we get this straightened out. Lay low for now. I gotta run."

It smelled like his cologne—a combination of musk and whiskey. I held up the red stone, feeling power radiating from it. Electricity buzzed along my fingers. "Why do you need a protection amulet?"

"I don't." He winked. "By the way, I know you're planning to bargain for Jamison O'Leary's life, but I can't make that deal. He has to die."

"Why?" The closeness of him unnerved me like always, but the reason he'd made a point to bring this up a second time did so even more. "When? Is it today? Tell me it's not. Please."

"Do not try to stop it. His contract is up." At my upset face, he grabbed my shoulder. "I'm serious. There are things you don't know about him. His demise will be a good thing."

I saw where this was going. "Is this some *greater good* thing? To balance the scales of the universe that you're so set on? Is he some kind of serial killer? Secret YouTube dissident? That's where you're going with this, isn't it? That my professor has a skeleton in his closet."

"Don't interfere. That's an order."

A shiver raced through my system, his command over me reinstating itself and reminding me of his control. "Can I at least say goodbye to him?"

"No. I promise he won't suffer, and your presence isn't needed. He'll go quietly, as his contract requires."

"But his daughter—"

"Will go on and make a life that he'll be proud of." He brushed my cheek again, and I fought the urge to slap his hand away. "You're a good person, Chloe, but you can't save everyone." Turning away once more, he patted Ghost's head. "We'll talk tomorrow. Like I said, lay low for now."

He seemed happy, almost excited. I studied the suit, coughed at the cologne filling my nose. "Are you going on a date?"

His laugh was deep and filled with irony. "Who would be reckless enough to date Death?"

He vanished.

Who indeed? I fingered the amulet. It seemed to come alive in my hand, glowing softly from some inner light. "You can come out now," I told Andy.

He made an odd, gurgling whine. The raven squawked. "Stuck."

"Oh, for grim's sake." I grabbed the shifter's hips and gave a tug. He'd jammed himself in good. When I finally managed to wrench him free, we both went sprawling backward.

The bag flew from his mouth and spun across the floor.

The amulet instantly created a ruby-red bubble around me. "What the...?" My fingers passed through the red haze, the texture light as air and feathery against my skin.

Ghost, Andy, and the raven stared, the canines both sniffing madly. I surveyed the bag, wet with Andy's slobbers. "What is that?"

He made a noise in the back of his throat. "Relp."

"Help," translated the bird.

Did Andy need help or did he mean it was help for me? "If this is supposed to break the curse, why is the protection amulet throwing a bubble around me?"

The shifter looked like he didn't have a clue. Ghost continued to sniff at it. "Don't touch," I warned. "It might be hexed."

Andy scooted his paws forward and dropped to his belly, letting out a huff. He made a series of Scooby Doo noises.

"Hexed. No," the bird translated as it teetered on the dresser, one wing smacking the framed picture of my parents. I caught it before it crashed to the floor. "You. Help."

Setting it aside, I stepped closer and inspected the bag. The material was a rich satin blue. It reminded me of something...

I straightened. The panther's glowing eyes.

The ruby bubble grew darker and thicker, making Andy and the bag fuzzy. It also caused a previously invisible sigil to appear on the cloth. Not like the glyph on Jackal's paper, but did I really trust Andy and his witch enough to defy the bubble and open it?

Biting my bottom lip, I angled a step closer. The crystal heated against my collarbone. A warning? If it was a protection talisman, from the embodiment of Death, no less, it should protect me from, well, anything, right?

Hovering over the satin, I reached down slowly, fingers dangling above the ties. They were silk and braided. The bubble resisted, as though it were attempting to pull me back, but I kept going. Just as I was about to make contact, gritting against the force the amulet threw at me, my phone blared.

I jerked and spun. What timing. Letting out the breath I'd been holding, I grabbed the cell, figuring it was Killion responding to my SOS. "Sorry, I know you're busy. It's under control now. Are your vampires okay?"

"Umm...Chloe?" The male voice was familiar, but didn't belong to the master vampire.

"Randy?" My thrumming pulse slowed. "Why are you calling me?"

The tech from the hospital paused before answering. "Geez, I didn't mean to upset you."

Randy had been trying to get me on a date for months. "Sorry, I thought you were someone else."

"Did you say...vampires? Who did you think I was?"

I rolled my eyes. "What do you want, Randy?"

He paused, then cleared his throat awkwardly. "I was wondering about the hospital Christmas party?"

Ugg. One guess where this was going. "What about it?"

"I thought, you know, I could pick you up. Maybe we could hit Olive Garden beforehand, grab some dinner."

Be still my heart. A text from Killion beeped the phone. "I really wish I could, but I'm...sick. Have a good time!" I hung up and read the message.

Killion was worried and on his way. I immediately dialed his number.

"Are you all right?" he demanded upon answering.

"The emergency's over. I'm fine and I apologize for disturbing you. How are your friends?"

His voice was strained. "Two are dead. For good this time," he added. "Mason should pull through, and I hope to get answers when he does. What happened to you?"

"Mason? He was attacked?" My protective streak rose like a lion. "I'll kill whoever did this.

"Are you sure you're safe?"

I eyed the blue bag. *Relatively.* "Don't worry about me. You have enough to handle right now."

"You sounded quite upset. Did Simone do something?"

"Not unless she can morph into a giant panther with killer blue eyes."

There was a hesitant pause. "A panther?"

"I'm okay. Really. I have a protection amulet now, and I'm working on getting this blasted necro curse lifted."

"As usual, I feel I have missed critical information in this story from you. An amulet? From whom?"

"I'll bring you up to speed later. I have to go before my

landlady busts in here and force feeds me breakfast. Take care of Mason."

"Yes. Be careful."

Once we disconnected, I went to the bathroom and turned on the shower, just to be sure Vera didn't get suspicious again. While the water ran, I picked up the scythe and returned to the satin bag.

The protective bubble hummed as though it liked the weapon. I used the blade to lift it by the strings and carry it to my desk. "Let's see what secrets you hold."

TWENTY-FOUR

The drawstrings were tied in a knot. Maneuvering to the desk, I cleared a space and used scissors to cut them. Three items fell out—an old medal, a rabbit's foot, and a beige parchment with writing.

The paper was decorated with a picture of an angel, wings spread. Using the tip of the scythe, I squared it up so I could read the words. It wasn't in English. "*Santé Michael Archangel...*" I stared at the rest, nonsensical to me, in Latin. I picked out a few words I could translate—*defend, spirit, virtue*. There was also God, Satan, and Amen.

"Not exactly what I expected," I muttered, carefully pushing the medal over to view the other side. My uncle Morty had a similar one on a keychain. "This is Saint Christopher. Your witch is Catholic?" I asked Andy.

His shoulders twitched with a shrug. "Rout row."

"Don't know," the bird echoed.

Dropping into my chair, I typed the first line into a search engine. "Bingo." Thousands of hits came up, and as I suspected, the top ones referenced Catholicism along with Saint Michael's prayer. I clicked on a link and read through a long article on the war against sin and combating Satan with the archangel's help. Another took me to an online version of the prayer.

Even with my limited deciphering skills, I saw some of the words didn't match up. Perhaps more of the witch's language that Killion had mentioned? Was it safe to use this stuff?

I toyed with the amulet as I compared the two line by line. The website offered an English version and I searched the terms that didn't match. A few hits came back, but they were on gaming apps and Reddit. I followed a few of the threads and found one person—avatar: Witch Finger—who seemed more knowledgeable about actual magic and spells than the rest.

Steam floated in from the bathroom. I got up, shut off the shower, and considered the medal and rabbit's foot. Both were types of talismans, much like the amulet around my neck. "Why would Death carry a protection amulet? And why does it not like this bag?"

The raven cawed and landed in my lap. He pecked at the rabbit's foot. "Luck."

The item appeared real. The thought of anyone hurting an innocent bunny to use its feet as lucky charms angered me. I reached for it and the bubble shivered but didn't stop me as I carefully stroked the white fur. It was soft against my skin; no painful zap or change in the bubble. "Would it be too much to ask for her to have included instructions?"

The raven cackled, then snatched up the medal and flew to the bed.

"Hey, not yours."

"Keepers. Finders." He ran when I came after it, keeping it in his mouth as he dashed for the closet.

"It's finders keepers." I tried bribing him to relinquish it, but he was stubborn. Corvids loved shiny things and were known as hoarders.

I considered threatening him with the scythe, but he already knew I'd never hurt him. "Bird,"—I really needed to name him or set him free—"just don't choke on it, okay?"

The thought made me stop. Jackal had the hex bag in his mouth. What if he'd stuffed it in there for safekeeping or to hide it from someone? Why had the bird had a piece of leather cord in its beak?

Vera's voice floated up the stairs, calling me for breakfast. I had to put that on hold, along with my questions about the amulet and Death. I fed the animals, using a cereal bowl to put some of Ghost's kibble down for Andy. When I texted Nita on my way down to ask if she knew Professor O'Leary's address, I was surprised when she replied with it a moment later. She was my closest friend for many reasons, and didn't ask why I wanted it, probably assuming the best about me and figuring I was sending him a Christmas card. By the time I sat at Vera's kitchen table, I had a the rough outline of a plan.

Coffee and a muffin were shoved in front of me and I dove in, suddenly hungry as a bear. "Delicious," I declared, to my landlady's delight.

"Did you get a new necklace?" she asked, eyes on the pendant.

"This old thing?" I stuffed the amulet under my shirt collar. "I found it in one of the containers I boxed up after... you know."

"It's pretty. For a moment, I could have sworn it glowed." She sipped coffee, handing me a napkin, and assuming I meant after my parents' deaths. Not wanting to upset me, she let it go. "I'm hitting the big sale at McCormick's today. Want to come?"

Wiping crumbs from my fingers, I shook my head, guilt slapping me at her obvious disappointment. "I'm afraid I have some things to take care of."

"You're always so busy. Can't it wait? I'll buy lunch." The bribe hung in the air between us.

I faltered, wanting to make her happy. "I wish I could, but this is important. Rain check?"

She sighed dramatically. "Work, work, work. If you're not at the coffee shop or the morgue, you're studying. It's Christmas, Chloe. If you take a few hours off to have fun, the world won't stop."

"Not for me," I mumbled, "but it will for someone else."

She leaned in. "What was that?"

Taking my plate to the sink, I pasted on a cheery smile. "Thanks for breakfast. Your cranberry orange muffins are the best." I hustled for the stairs, glancing back. "Even better than my aunt's, but don't tell her I said that."

The compliment did it, bringing a smile to her face, and letting me off the hook. As she got up to refill her coffee, I raced to get my things.

Placing the scythe and robes into my duffel, I stuffed the prayer and rabbit's foot in as well. Not every soul is harvested by a reaper—most go peacefully on their own. But if anyone or anything tried to stop me from saving the professor, I was going to be prepared. As I clipped on Ghost's lead, Andy and the raven hustled to the door. "Where do you think you're going?"

"Riff roo," the shifter said.

Either he was getting clearer or I was getting better at deciphering his speech. "I'm protected by this amulet. You're not. The panther could be out there."

"Jelly bean!" the bird cried, the medal falling to the floor. He flapped wildly. "Kill! Kill!"

"No killing."

I tried to move him aside, but he scooped up the medal once more and hopped onto Andy's back.

The shifter blocked the door when I reached for the handle. "Riff roo," he demanded.

Time was growing short. I didn't know how long the professor had. "Fine." I dug out the rabbit's foot and hooked it on his makeshift collar. "But if we're attacked, it's every man, animal, or whatever, for himself, understand?"

All heads bobbed, including Ghost's. Knowing this was a very bad idea, I led them out.

TWENTY-FIVE

Professor O'Leary's home had a pall over it, even in the bright light of day. A sticky gray energy coated everything, from the peeling paint of the old Victorian, to the tired courtyard in front. No decorations were to be seen, not even a wreath on the front door.

The wrought iron gate squeaked as I opened it and walked up the winding sidewalk. I'd instructed the animals to stay in the limo with Moss, so we didn't scare the professor.

The driver had been waiting for me down the block from the apartment, and while he groused again about the shifter, I was grateful Killion had sent him. I didn't have to figure out how to convince a ride service driver to allow a dog, wolf, and bird in his or her car. I'd let him examine the witch's version of the prayer but he didn't understand it. He did have a bevy of facts about the archangel.

Seemed Michael was nearly a god in his own right. Certainly not one to mess with.

On the short drive, I'd prepped a story to give my teacher, but it was weak. I had no idea how or when

O'Leary was supposed to die, and I couldn't exactly tie him up and keep him housebound.

Or could I?

If Death had warned me off interfering, it meant the professor's death was something I could prevent. A stroke or heart attack would be difficult, if not impossible, but caught in time, perhaps not fatal. Most likely, it was less daunting—an accident—and that I *could* intercede on.

Iron fleur-de-lis posts were screwed into the concrete steps, the connected railings rusted and flaking. The whole façade was sad, worn out, and the gloom was thick on the porch. This had once been a grand house and grounds, if the trellis work and corner scrolls were an indication.

The elaborate wooden door had an iron knocker with a face of a lion. Not what I expected. I pushed the stained doorbell that was nearly covered with dead ivy climbing the side of the house. Inside, a deep, melodic chime peeled, and a minute later, the curtain of the transom window rustled.

A young woman about my height cracked open the door. "Yeah?"

"Megan?" I tried to peer over her head into the interior without being obvious. "Is your dad home?"

Her brown eyes scanned me and my bag. Though my view of her was limited to a sliver, her black hair and heavy eye makeup gave her a goth appearance. She would have seemed older than fifteen if not for the acne on her chin.

She lifted said chin in defiance, attempting to look down her pierced nose at me. "You one of his groupies?"

"Sorry." I hesitated. "His what?"

She did an exaggerated eye roll only a teenage girl could pull off. "He's not here, and by the way, he's not interested. As in, not on the market. Stay away from him."

The door began to close. "Wait, I'm not"—*eww*—"after

your dad. He's my professor. He loaned me a book and I wanted to..."

I should have stuck my foot in the crack, but too late, she slammed the door in my face. The knocker seemed to smile, mocking me.

Smirking back at it, I rang the bell again. I honestly didn't expect her to answer, so when she whipped open the door and gave me a full on glower, I was taken aback. "I told you he's not here."

Ankh earrings hung from her lobes and her blood red shirt sported a large eye across the chest. "Cool shirt." She hadn't embraced goth fashion, but something else that kept coming up on my radar. "That's Egyptian, right?"

She didn't so much as glance down. "Eye of Ra. Go away."

"Have you heard of the Book of the Dead?"

Another exaggerated eye roll. "Everyone's heard of it."

News to me. "Have you read it?"

"It's online."

Of course it was. "A friend recommended it. Seems kind of...morbid, you know?"

"Wanting to understand the afterlife isn't morbid. It's fascinating."

She'd lost her mom. Of course, she'd explore anything that might give her hope and a belief in a soul existing after the final curtain. Was it possible she was my necromancer? "I'd better check it out. It's a bunch of spells, isn't it? Like...witchcraft?"

"Not all magic is witchcraft." She crossed her arms. "Wanting to live isn't wrong."

And if I didn't get a move on, her dad wasn't going to.

"Megan," a woman called from inside. I heard the click of heels on hardwood. "Who is it?"

"No one," the girl replied, beginning to close the door again. To me she said, "Dad's at school, like always."

"Wait." I'd bet money she was casting spells, possibly using those in the Egyptian tome, and that's why the house's energy was off. Magic was no toy and I wondered if it could exacerbate her depression. It might have even prompted her suicide attempts. I was pretty sure, though, she wasn't a necro or an actual witch. "I'd like to hear more about the —ouch!"

The pendant dug into my skin, a sharp knife of searing heat spreading across my collarbone. At the same time, the woman we'd seen at the shopping plaza emerged behind Megan.

"You," she said, and every hair on my body stood up in recognition.

The ruby bubble burst to life around me. My feet were moving of their own accord before I could breathe. I tripped, backing toward the steps, and caught myself on the railing. She wasn't wearing her cat mask, or sporting inch-long nails, but I knew who she was. I would never, ever, get that voice out of my head. "Stay away from me."

She shoved Megan aside and stepped across the threshold, quick as a vampire. The girl complained and a shrieking started in my head that nearly drowned her out. Energy crackled from Cat Woman's fingertips as she raised a hand, and between my panic and the push of the bubble, I lost my grasp on the railing and tumbled down the stairs.

Landing on my back, my skull struck concrete. Sunshine blinded me and cold from the sidewalk seeped quickly through my clothes. It wasn't a normal chill—this was a piercing bite of dark magic.

I scrambled to right myself, head spinning. Moss was

suddenly at my side, carrying my scythe. Andy, Ghost, and the raven appeared, as well.

"Oh good." The woman sounded delighted. Her eyes flashed, cat-like. "It's a party."

A bolt of magic flew at us and I screamed, throwing up my hands instinctively to shield us. The bubble instantly expanded, encompassing my posse.

Then, from out of nowhere, the panther emerged, teeth bared as it ran straight for us.

TWENTY-SIX

I screamed a second time, this one without fear and full of power. I was done cowering.

Ghost, Andy, the raven—I needed to protect them.

The bubble rippled, warping and trembling around us. The bird screeched in panic and Andy howled, blending with the intensity of my voice.

The ground shook. The shrieking in my head disappeared. My weapon flew from Moss's hold and the handle slapped into my palm. My tattoo felt like a soaring flame of fire against my skin.

As the panther soared through the air, its claws extended and its blue eyes blazed. I raised the death blade, and the raven lifted off my lap.

The bubble broke. With an odd tearing sound, the panther's claws, and then the rest of the animal, rent through the glowing veil. Instantly, it morphed into a woman in a silky, long maroon gown. The raven landed on one of her outstretched arms, and she murmured to it, petting its head before she glanced at me.

Loose curls, the color of black cherries, fell over her shoulders. Emerald green eyes snapped as she looked me over, her heavy liner giving Megan a run for her money. Her voice held the slightest Irish accent. "I'm indebted to you for saving my bird."

"Aurora?" I asked.

Behind her, Cat Woman/Ms. Leon marched down the steps. She raised a hand, electricity crackling from her fingertips as she readied her magic. "Daughter of the Nile, how dare you—"

"I am no daughter of yours." She winked at me and waved a hand through the air, a triquetra tattoo, each of its three interlaced arcs a different color, glowing bright on her inner wrist. "Hush."

The gal froze in mid-step. Her mouth hung open but no sound came out.

Wow. I needed to know how to do that.

I scrambled to my feet. "You're the raven's owner?"

He danced happily up and down her arm. "You need to go. My spell won't hold her for long." Andy whined and she glanced at him, her sharp-eyed gaze landing on the rabbit's foot, then flicking to me. "You'd protect the shifter over yourself?"

Behind her, one of Leon's eyes twitched, then her brows jerked. "Umm, I have this." I pulled out the amulet, and patted the scythe. "And this."

Her eyes narrowed when they took in the death blade. "Even you can be killed by the likes of her, grim."

I didn't doubt that, but it was unlikely with Death's protection. "How do I break her curse? I need something besides a prayer to an archangel."

The corner of her mouth quirked. "There is much

layered in those words, and you can't break the hex because there isn't one."

Leon's chin dropped, her lips pursing. I gripped the scythe tighter. "Yes, there is. As I told you in my note, I now raise dead animals without intending to. I need help to stop it, get rid of it, whatever."

The air around us became charged. Her eyes flashed the blue of her animal. "There's no hex or curse. The bag simply broke the protection charm that was hiding you, allowing her to find you and bring about the prophecy. You've always been a necromancer—she simply woke up your inherent abilities."

"My what?" It came out an embarrassing screech. "You've got me confused with someone else. I don't have inherent necromancy anything."

The frozen woman's fingers spasmed.

"We must leave," Aurora said. "I'm sorry, I can't help you further."

"Wait." I reached for her as she turned. "We can take my limo. I'll drop you anywhere you want to go."

My hand was shoved aside, as if she had an invisible shield around her body. She walked away, ignoring me, and I glanced over to see the other woman gaining in her fight against the immobilizing spell. Her face was livid, red enough it appeared her head might explode. Her obsidian eyes were pools of hate.

Dark fur began to sprout on Aurora. She was about to shift and leave me standing there with a deranged psychopath on my hands.

"What can I offer you?" I called. I couldn't let her get away. "What should I do?"

As if the Universe had an answer, I heard a crack of

lightning and the bubble gave me a giant push. Myself, Moss, Andy, and Ghost were shoved toward the car. Just before Aurora morphed fully into her panther shape, she called over her shoulder. "Run!"

TWENTY-SEVEN

I didn't need to be told twice. The pack of us bolted for the limo, as if the hounds of hell were on our heels.

The vampire's fangs, as well as Andy's canines, were on display. The bubble trembled but held as Leon raced across the yard, throwing lightning at us.

The shifter and I launched ourselves into the backseat. Moss slid into the driver's and gunned the engine. The backend of the vehicle dipped and we jetted off.

Another hit of the woman's magic slammed into us , but it only propelled the limo faster. Tires squealed as Moss took the turn at the end of the block, the far side of the car becoming airborne.

Heart racing, I kept the scythe on my lap. I checked that my psychopomp was okay. She appeared so, barking viciously toward the direction of our attacker.

Andy panted, avoiding my eyes. His gaze was glued to the rear window, as well. I had the feeling his stare had more to do with Aurora than Ms. Leon.

I shook from head to toe. Witches, ancient magic, secret

sects...and a young girl caught up in it all. A girl whose mother was already dead and father was about to be.

"The master wishes me to bring you to The Beaumont," Moss informed me.

By his slight lisp, I knew his fangs were still out. Danger did that. Andy had covered his, but the alert ears and focused concentration told me he was still on guard.

"We've been ordered to stay away from each other while he's on probation." And we'd already broken that missive once. "I need to go to the university."

His eyes met mine in the rearview. They had a faint ring of red around the irises. "I can't defy his orders. Besides, you're his partner. Shouldn't you work on this case *with him?*"

Partners. The word gave me an idea. "You're brilliant, Moss." It would do no good to fight him, but maybe... "You can take me to the hotel after we make a pitstop on campus. Please. My professor's life is on the line, and if you help me, we may be able to save two lives tonight."

He glanced at the road, then back to my reflection. I gave him my pleading face. As a kid, I used to use it on Aunt Camille when I had sleepovers at her and Uncle Morty's. It worked for all kinds of things—getting an extra homemade cookie, a bonus hour before bed to sit up with them, another story about my parents.

It shouldn't have compelled a vampire, yet something about it did. He blew out an exasperated sigh and took the next left, heading north. "You'll vouch for me when the master disciplines me?"

"I'll make sure there's no discipline, I promise."

From his dismissive snort, he didn't put much faith in my persuasive skills with his boss. Shifting Ghost aside, I took out my phone. Killion had texted and called numerous times. I replied to the last message, insisting I was okay and telling him Moss had saved the day. I added that I would see him as soon as I had secured a grim contract. I figured he'd be less upset if he thought I was on a job. Which I was, in a way.

Next, I opened an SMG case form and filled it out with as many details as I thought prudent. I insisted there was something big going on that threatened the cosmic scale and humanity, and an investigation was called for. I needed to word it just right so SMG would not be able to say no.

The farther away we got from the professor's house, the smaller and thinner the bubble became. I breathed easier and emailed the form, stating I needed my partner's help with the investigation. "Cross your paws," I told Ghost.

Moss ignored the signs about Staff Only when we arrived at the campus and he drove into the lot reserved for teachers and administrative employees. Due to the holidays, only a small assortment of vehicles were there. The front row was reserved for the big wigs, but he ignored that, too.

I didn't spend any energy worrying about it, since he didn't have a parking sticker to begin with. Really, who would bother a limo? The dean and other officials were probably off in Mexico or on some Caribbean cruise, and campus security was light.

The professor's office was in the Graham Lithgow Building, named after one of the founders. Unfortunately, that was clear across campus from the lot, but I might as well confirm his vehicle was here before I went that direction.

Exiting the car with my bag, I peered at the half dozen cars around us. I had no idea what he drove, and I hoped he hadn't already left, or that I wasn't about to spend hours searching for him. Andy got out and stood next to me. He lifted his nose, sniffing the air. His muzzle pivoted toward the southeast.

"You can smell him, can't you? Is he here?"

Moss joined us. "That's his van." He pointed to an older blue Toyota in the direction Andy's nose had indicated.

"How do you know?"

"I ran his name through the DMV database."

"You can do that?"

He looked offended. "Of course. Can't you?"

Andy loped over to the van. A trim piece on the driver's side was missing, and there was a slight dent on the rear passenger door. He sniffed around the tires, raised his nose once more, and this time turned west. Ghost mimicked him and her nose lifted in the same direction. Andy took off like a bloodhound on the trail, and Ghost darted after him. Moss and I exchanged a look and followed.

We ended up outside the library, the central water fountain turned off for the break. Three stories of large, blue tinted windows reflected the late morning sun. Andy approached the wide concrete steps, but I called him back. "You can't go in there." He glanced at me and seemed forlorn, then trotted to my side. "You're sure he's here?"

One paw smacked the ground. "Rees rin rear."

Unfortunately, I no longer had the bird to translate. I kind of missed him. "Your witchy friend seemed surprised I would protect you."

One massive shoulder shrugged. He gave me sad eyes, glanced down.

"I appreciate what she did." Ghost sat at my feet and watched me, as if listening intently. "But she still didn't answer my questions. When we're done here, can you get her to talk to me? I'd also like to know why she attacked us earlier."

The paw stayed on the ground. His eyes did, too.

"What's wrong?"

He hung his head. I really needed that raven back.

"Did you tick her off or something?"

His haunches sagged and he sat wearily. "Ree runed re."

Perplexed, I simply stared. "I have no idea what that means."

"She dumped me,'" Moss volunteered.

Now, I was doubly perplexed. "You can understand him?"

The vamp looked slightly embarrassed. "Can we just get on with this before the master kills me—for good this time?"

I peered at the shifter. "You and Aurora had a thing, didn't you?"

A solemn nod. His paw thumped the ground once. He lifted his muzzle and howled. The mournful notes echoed off the building.

"Stop that. If anyone notices a wolf running around, they'll panic and call animal control. We'll get in big trouble. Go back to the car."

Head down, he lumbered off to the lot, and I felt guilty. What was I supposed to do? I wasn't here to play matchmaker, and I had my own relationship issues. I was hardly one to offer advice.

Although it was winter break, the library had limited hours for staff and students. I didn't understand why anyone would keep studying when they didn't have to, but there were always people who didn't have family to celebrate with and grad students trying to complete their theses.

It also gave professors like O'Leary a chance to work on articles and books, the world of publish or perish constantly breathing down their necks. For some, the quiet campus and sanctuary of the library was a great place to hide from the real world. I wondered if O'Leary was doing a bit of that, as well.

"I'll take the first floor," I told Moss, securing Ghost in my bag. "You scan the second. Text me if you see a fortyish man in tweed and glasses. If neither of us find him, we'll meet on the third level."

"What exactly do you plan to do with him?"

"We find him and get him to come with us to a safe place. I can't let him die today."

The big man stared down at me. "You're defying Death again?"

Apparently, my reputation was getting around. "No lectures, okay?"

He grinned. "You won't get any from me. You're beginning to grow on me, Grave Girl."

High praise from him. I smiled back, but speared him with a finger. "Drop the nickname. But thanks for helping me."

He dipped his head in acknowledgment. "Just following the master's orders."

Sure. I could see in his eyes that he enjoyed being rebellious, and like Killion, he seemed to root for anyone who could rub Death the wrong way.

The entrance was composed of one revolving glass door that led in, and a second that spit folks back out. We made it into the lobby and luck—no rabbit's foot needed—was on our side.

Professor O'Leary leaned on the raised front desk in the center of the brightly lit vestibule, smiling at the woman behind it. She was touching her hair and laughing at something he said. Apparently one of his *groupies*.

"That's him," I uttered. Maybe I should tell Nita to go for it. She certainly had it all over the librarian. "I'll handle this."

As I approached, the woman's smile fell and she hurriedly put on a pair of reading glasses. O'Leary turned to see why.

"Hey," I said in my best student voice. I raised a hand in an awkward wave. "Just the man I was looking for."

It came out sounding like I was a groupie, too, so I corrected it. "The *teacher* I was looking for."

Ms. Hazel Brady, according to her lanyard ID, scowled. "No dogs allowed."

Busted. I glanced down to see Ghost half out of the duffel and peeking around my waist. "I couldn't leave her outside. She's just a puppy and I only need a moment of the professor's time."

Her glare nearly singed my hair. "It's vacation for him, too, you know."

Protective are we? Territorial? "I am *really* sorry to bother you," I told him. "But this is important."

He gathered the stack of books at his elbow. "Have a lovely holiday," he said to Hazel.

She blushed. "You, too, Jamie."

Jamie? Definitely a groupie.

O'Leary seemed unnerved at Moss' appearance near the exit, but being the smooth guy he was, the vampire went out ahead of us. "My cousin," I said, in way of explanation.

Since Moss was as black as the night and had the girth of a bouncer, this made O'Leary do a double-take. He said nothing until we were on the sidewalk. "Okay, Chloe, what's this about?"

Movement to my left made me freeze. The blood in my veins warmed and the scent of caramel and old libraries hit me.

"Yes, Chloe," Killion said, joining us and looking like he wanted to stake me. "What *is* this about?"

TWENTY-EIGHT

"Killion," I choked out, "what are you doing here?" I cut my gaze to the driver and lowered my voice. "I thought we had a deal."

Moss, the traitor, shrugged. "He's the master."

"Master?" O'Leary frowned deeply. "I think we should wait and discuss this um, whatever this is, when classes resume, Ms. Frost."

He started to pivot and Killion's hand shot out. The professor's eyes widened as he froze mid-stride. Killion looked him over. "*This* is grim business?"

Busted. "I need to keep him alive. His daughter is involved in the—er—" I stopped, realizing O'Leary could hear me. "Situation with me." I winked, hoping Killion understood. "But everything is fine." I smiled and nodded at my teacher, who looked as though he were in the middle of a nightmare. "Can he hear me?" I whispered to my mentor.

Killion dipped his chin.

"Did you know Ms. Leon is at your house?" I asked O'Leary. "I believe she's leading Megan down a dangerous path."

O'Leary's lips moved, but no sound came out.

Killion rubbed his free hand over his face. Although he'd told me vampires didn't need to sleep, he sure looked like he needed some. The hand holding O'Leary immobile snapped its fingers and the man's eyes rolled up in his head.

Quicker than I could blink, Moss caught the professor as he slumped, then lifted him in a fireman's hold.

Ms. Brady ran out. "Oh my goodness. Jamison, are you all right?" She whirled on me. "What have you done? I'm calling the po—"

Killion stepped in front of me and smiled at her. "All is well. Nothing for you to worry about." Her fearful demeanor went slack, then morphed into a mirror of his, a hesitant smile raising the corner of her lips. She nodded, in thrall to him. "Good," he said. "Return inside and continue with your work. The professor is safe."

She didn't so much as glance at Moss or me, pivoting in her conservative brown shoes and gliding up the steps. As she reached the glass entrance, she snuck a glance back at Killion and made a motion with her thumb and pinky finger. "Call me."

Unbelievable. "You have a new admirer." I was annoyed he'd used his powers on her and O'Leary, but relieved at the same time. Things were getting way too problematic. "Please tell me she won't remember you assaulting my teacher."

He faced me, the smile gone. "Not if I so will it."

A simple yes or no would be too easy. "I need a place to stash O'Leary."

Ghost went crazy, wanting him to pet her. He did, ruffling her ears, even as he glowered at me. "This is your plan? Keep the educator alive? He is safe now and will remain so until..."

"Let me guess—*you so will it*?" I might have put a bit too much bite in it.

He leaned in and my skin tingled. "Yes. You are in serious danger, and yet you choose to help this human escape his death contract."

My body wanted to step back, get him out of my personal space. I held firm, lifting my chin. "His daughter is involved with Cat Woman. I didn't realize it until a little while ago, but I know if he dies, Megan will, too. I'm not sure how she's tied into this, but—"

He raised a hand to interrupt. "We'll figure it out." He grabbed me by the arm and propelled me forward. The amulet trembled at his touch. "At my place, where you'll both be safe."

I wanted to resist on principle. Feeling like I was out of options, I didn't.

TWENTY-NINE

In the parking lot, a bright red convertible sat next to the limo. Two creatures circled each other—Simone was squaring off with Andy.

Her fingers were claws, her fangs on full display. His scruff stood on end, teeth bared. He growled low and ominously, as Moss looked on, entertained.

The driver had stuck O'Leary in the front passenger seat of the limo, and he slumped unconscious against the window. A good thing, too, since a supernatural World War III was about to break out.

Exasperated, I marched forward. "Knock it off," I said to Simone. I had my own bone to pick with her, and I wondered if Killion still believed she was trying to usurp him. "The shifter is with me."

Her response? She flipped me off with a single claw and hissed, licking her fangs. She then lunged and took a swipe at Andy.

He was more graceful than I'd seen so far. He dodged it and bit her above her wrist.

She howled in rage and punched his muzzle. He

released his hold and they returned to their fighting corners, circling each other again.

"I said, knock it off. Both of you." Jumping between two supernatural creatures during a fight was stupid, but I felt semi-responsible for Andy.

Ghost gnashed her teeth, raring to jump in herself, and I glanced at Killion for backup.

His expression was less than sympathetic. "Some of our own were attacked by his kind." He didn't seem pleased, yet he showed no signs of commanding his lieutenant to halt. "Emotions are running high." He studied Andy with wary interest. "Is that the shifter you were supposed to harvest?"

I shoved Ghost into his arms, pulling out the scythe from my bag. The handle immediately warmed, sensing I was ready for battle, and the afternoon sun glinted off the blade. *Kill*, it whispered.

I strolled between the enemies, catching Simone's eyes. "I know you're upset, but Andy had nothing to do with what happened, and he is under my care. *Stand down.*"

"Or what?" She spit on the ground. "You think you can kill me? Go ahead and try."

"I've been waiting for a reason, so thank you for giving me one."

I reared back to swing and she swiped her claws at me.

In quick succession, the bubble sprang to life, Ghost morphed, and Andy bounded in front of me. Killion grabbed her and jerked her away, and Moss said, "You're telegraphing your slice."

It was my turn to hold up a single digit that spoke volumes.

"That will do, Simone," Killion growled. "None here are your enemy."

"I wouldn't go that far," I said.

She hissed again and it was only his clamp on her that kept her from coming after me.

"Enough," Killion's voice boomed out of him, echoing off the cars. She relented, and even I felt the command inside my bones.

"I won't kill you." *This time.* I lowered the weapon. "But if you harm Andy, I will make you taste the blade, and I assure you, you won't like it."

She turned in Killion's hold, facing him. "You don't know the beast wasn't part of the kill party."

"I trust Chloe," he countered.

I stroked Andy's head. "He wasn't." I hoped that was true. He'd been gone a long time, and I couldn't swear to his whereabouts. "You're endangering all of us with this display in public in broad daylight."

Killion murmured something I couldn't hear and her fangs retracted. He escorted her to her car, and with one last scornful glance at me, she peeled off and left.

The master vampire watched until she was out of sight. I calmed Ghost and Andy, herding them to the limo, but I scowled at Moss. "You couldn't have intervened before we got here?"

He grinned in a manner that reminded me he was a vampire and liked shifters about as much as I did Simone. "Where's the fun in that?"

Ghost returned to her normal size. She jumped in as if she owned the limo and the amulet vibrated as Killion took my elbow to guide me in. He sat and scrunched up his sensitive nose. "It smells like dog in here."

Andy whined. Ghost hopped into my lap and Andy watched as the vampire adjusted his jacket, closing the door on him. The wolf's dark eyes met mine and seemed to ask where he was going to sit.

"The penthouse," Killion ordered Moss.

"Yes, sir."

"Wait." I reached for the door handle on my side. "Andy comes or I stay."

Killion rubbed a hand over his face. "And what would you have me do with the professor?"

I cracked open the door, ready to make good on my claim. "Take him to the penthouse. Andy and I will figure out how to save Megan."

Killion grabbed my arm before I could bail. The amulet trembled. "Why is everything hard with you?"

I met his gaze straight on. Raw emotion coated his features. Simone wasn't the only one hurt and angry about what had happened with the nest.

I closed the door. "I'm sorry about your friends and I appreciate you defying SMG's mandate to help me. But Andy is also helping me. I need him."

Killion glanced out his window at the shifter and sighed. He opened the door. "Get in."

Andy looked pleased, and he climbed onto the empty seat facing us. Ghost thought it was great and crawled onto his back. She began grooming him as we drove off.

"Why do you wear Death's amulet?" Killion asked.

"Why were you defending Simone?" I countered.

He rubbed his eyes. "She has restored my faith in her."

I fingered the pendant, confused and annoyed, but what could I do about it? "He gave it to me for protection."

"He's keeping tabs on you. It acts as a tracking beacon."

"You would find something wrong with his act of kindness, no matter what. When I'm in danger, it creates a bubble around me and anyone I want. If it hadn't been for this, I would be dead right now. Cat Woman plays dirty."

"She doesn't want you dead. Under her control, yes."

He fished out his phone and showed me a message. "SMG has temporarily suspended my probation due to an *investigation* you need my assistance with. Do you know anything about this?"

"It worked?" I did a fist pump. "You can thank me by having your chef make me one of those shrimp bowls."

He pocketed the cell. "Tell me what happened with O'Leary's daughter."

By the time we reached the hotel, I'd given him the details. It felt good to be working together again, the early morning's intimacy seeming far off. Still, he appeared tired and distracted.

Upstairs in the penthouse, I made myself at home. Moss deposited the professor on one of the plush antique couches and Killion's butler/chef greeted me and stoked a fire in the hearth. Within minutes, Pennyworth set a full lunch buffet out for us, including my coveted étouffée with his home-made sauce. Once my belly was full, I felt more like myself.

"You and Simone are getting along now," I stated around a mouthful of cheesecake. I needed the carbs. "How exactly did she restore your faith so easily?"

Killion played with his wine, turning the cut crystal glass in circles by the stem. "She is my concern, not yours."

I had more to say, but it seemed now wasn't the time. I couldn't hold one fact back, though. "I don't trust her."

He nodded, but refused to discuss it further.

Once I was finished eating, the two of us examined the professor's reading material and I dug his laptop from his leather briefcase. On that I discovered an e-copy of the Book of the Dead, as well as interesting theories the man had been working on. He referenced a written work long thought destroyed in the ancient Alexandria library fire that held the formula for creating—"Holy reapers," I murmured, turning the screen so Killion could see it. "My professor believes human-animal hybrids are the next stage in evolution. Look at this."

He read the passage and tapped the table with his fingers. "This is most concerning."

"This must be the research he mentioned to Nita and I. He plans to publish an article about the viability of it. Looks like he's hoping to get private funding." I clicked on another file, this one containing a list of academic journals, and labs, O'Leary believed would be interested in his discovery. He already had letters from two R&D groups, wanting to contract with him. I now understood Death's warning about the man needing to die. I paraphrased as I scanned. "He claims to have a viable formula that will change everything. History, anthropology, archaeology, even theology will be rewritten."

"He previously worked for an R&D group, doing genetic manipulation on animals. I believe he and his team were close to a major breakthrough, but due to his wife's cancer, he left the field quite suddenly. Not far down the road, scientists—especially those privately funded—will add to their already extreme experiments." Killion stared unseeing at the hearth's flames. Light flickered across his strained features. "Who knows what monstrosities they'll create?"

I shut the laptop and sat back. "This could also out you and the other supernaturals. I didn't read the whole thing, but he claims the original shifters were ancient hybrids, and that they still exist today."

His gaze flicked to Andy, who rested in front of the fireplace. Ghost had curled up next to him. "He'll be a laughing stock among most of his peers, initially. But if he can prove he can create one... We can't allow that to happen."

"Do you believe him? That he has this formula?"

His troubled eyes met mine. "If he does, we need to get it and destroy it."

I replaced the laptop in the bag, my chest heavy. "Cat Woman. This Ms. Leon. She's behind it all, isn't she?"

"It appears so."

Together, Killion and I stood over the professor. I shivered at the thought of stopping him, one way or another.

"Okay, then." I rubbed my hands to warm them, but at this point, I could have held them in the fire and it wouldn't have made any difference. "Guess it's time to wake him up."

THIRTY

K illion touched the professor's shoulder and said, "Wake."

Just like that, O'Leary blinked open his eyes and made a soft, surprised noise.

"Hey," I said, kneeling in front of him. Killion assisted him to a sitting position. "How do you feel?"

His unfocused eyes darted between us. "Where am I?"

"You fainted," Killion volunteered. "We brought you here. You're safe. Your vitals are stable, but you probably succumbed to low blood sugar."

Or magic.

O'Leary made a groaning noise and rubbed his head. "I've never done that before." He glanced up at Killion. "Are you a doctor?"

The vampire motioned toward the dining room. "My chef has prepared food. Come eat."

O'Leary swayed when he stood, and together, we walked him to one of the soft, high-backed, velvet chairs. He gripped the arms while he stared at the lavish display. "This is generous but I'm not hungry."

Pennyworth appeared and slid a steaming bowl of gumbo in front of him. "Of course, you are. I prepared this especially for you. Eat up."

Now, he didn't even hesitate, and I wondered if the butler/chef was compelling him. Truth be told, I suspected the delicious scents were a natural attractor. I certainly had trouble resisting them.

While O'Leary ate, Pennyworth refilled Killion's wine glass and brought a cup of coffee for me. "Two sugars, one cream, just the way you like it." His tray also held a black coffee, which he sat in front of O'Leary.

I watched in amazement as my teacher slurped down the soup in record time, along with consuming a slice of fresh baked bread. The loaf was still warm, even though it had been sitting on the table since we'd arrived.

There were also chocolate chip cookies, and I helped myself to one. I passed the plate to Killion, but the vampire shook his head.

O'Leary wiped his mouth on the cloth napkin that cost more than my shirt, and smiled with pleasure. "I haven't had gumbo this good, since..." His face blanched and I knew he'd intended to mention his wife. The pain of losing her was still fresh.

I'd found there wasn't much that chocolate didn't help, so I passed him the plate. He took two, then glanced around, much more alert—and suspicious—now that his 'blood sugar' was back to normal. "Where did you say we are?"

"My place," Killion supplied smoothly. "The Beaumont Hotel."

O'Leary seemed mildly impressed. "You live here?"

"He owns the place," I said around a bite of delicious goodness. The cookies were absolutely to die for.

"You're a doctor *and* you own the hotel?" He sipped his coffee, then took a longer drink. "Wow, this is incredible."

I nodded. "He has fresh beans flown in from Paris daily."

"I remember that you said you needed to talk to me, and you were discussing Megan and my friend." He rubbed his temple. "The details are fuzzy. Can you refresh my memory?"

Killion and I exchanged a glance and I launched in. "I met Megan, and she seems like a really nice girl." That was the best I could come up with. It was better than accusing her of trying to raise her dead mother.

O'Leary's face turned apprehensive. "She is."

"It appears she has an"—*unhealthy*—"interest in ancient Egyptian mythology."

Killion sat forward and toyed with his drink, clearing his throat. He was obviously unimpressed with my interview technique. "I noticed your books, professor. When I realized who you were, the theories you've put forth in your published papers, I was incredulous. I'm a huge fan of your ideas."

The male ego is hard to override. O'Leary was surprised, but also delighted. "You've read my papers?"

"I have a great interest in animal-human hybrids."

Andy, now awake, peeked over the couch. O'Leary, who was facing Killion, didn't notice, but I feared seeing a giant wolf in the penthouse might cause the professor to faint for real. Carefully, I shook my head at the shifter and made a down motion with my hand. He grumbled a bit, then collapsed back to the floor.

Hearing the noise, O'Leary glanced his way, but saw nothing but the glowing fire.

"Is that why Megan has such an interest in Egyptian symbols?" I asked. "Because of your work?"

He smiled, looking like a proud parent. "She's drawn to science."

"Tell us more about your theory," Killion prompted.

"Hybrids are not simply a possibility, and I believe they never were myths. Yes, we can grow human organs inside animals, but focusing on that alone is limiting." Fervor about his beliefs made his eyes shine brighter. "The ancients embraced the idea that we could be faster, smarter, and stronger, if we combined superior attributes belonging to our animal brothers with our own. We could see in the dark, for instance, and move with silent speed. After all, we share much DNA with them already. Genetic manipulation is not a modern invention. Our ancient forbearers have recorded many instances of it. Humans, pigs, and apes have the most similarities, and I've been attempting to prove my theories that, at one time, these superior beings—gods—who embodied the most powerful traits of animals, existed. The best news is, I finally have the lost formula we need to create them."

The dread was back. I played dumb. "Lost formula?"

"Another academic has come forward. You saw her the other day."

"Ms. Leon from Cairo," I confirmed.

He nodded. "She has worked at several research companies and is now a curator at a museum. She found a set of hidden parchments, along with a text that is aiding us in deciphering the formula. She's a huge fan of my research, a true believer. She...borrowed the papers and brought them to me. They were written by the hybrids, and they detail the process of cross-manipulation to ensure healthy outcomes.

Superior beings are a reality—do you know what this could mean?"

The end of humans?

He took our collective silence—which was a combination of fascination and horror—as an opportunity to answer his own question. "We can extend the average human life by decades. Cure disease, explore the world in more depth —the oceans, space." He leaned in. "We can control our environment, rather than letting Mother Nature do so with earthquakes, hurricanes, wildfires."

"We could become gods," Killion said.

For all the positives O'Leary had rattled off, there were extreme negatives he'd failed to mention. I wanted to list those as argument, but right now, I needed to get my hands on that formula. I needed to destroy it, and also figure out how to stop Cat Woman.

I pulled out my phone. "What's Ms. Leon's full name?" I knew she hadn't 'borrowed' the formula from some museum. She was doing her own experiments. "I'd like to look her up."

O'Leary fiddled with his napkin. "I'm afraid she's asked to stay out of the limelight—she's quite an introvert— that's why she gave the documentation to me. I must respect her wishes and keep her identity a secret."

"She's staying with you?" Killion fixed his gaze on the man.

O'Leary blustered a bit and firmly placed his napkin on the table, as though preparing to leave. "It's not like that. We're not...involved. She's simply helping me with my project, and we're strategizing the best way to release the information to the public."

I wished I could extract what I needed without the use of force. Unfortunately, that would take too long, and the professor was definitely ready to bug out. I caught Killion's eye. "I need her name, and he must stay here."

Killion waved his hand at the man now making to stand. "Sit and tell Chloe the woman's name."

O'Leary's brain tried to resist, but the very thing he admired about hybrids won out. Killion was more powerful than he was. Gritting his teeth, his eyes darted around and he plopped into his seat. "Sekhmet Leon."

"Sekhmet?" Killion seemed to pale. "The Egyptian goddess?"

"Of course not, but she *was* named after her."

The master vampire shut his eyes, and I felt everything in me go very still. His hands balled into fists and I swear he paled. This couldn't be good.

I was afraid to ask, but there was no turning back now. "Who is she?"

"She protected the Pharaohs," he said, "in ancient Egypt."

"Cat Woman is a...goddess?"

His nod made my delicious meal threaten to come up. "We are talking about archaic dark magic and nearly immortal hybrids who've been around since gods and goddesses roamed the earth."

"But shouldn't being a goddess make her a good guy... girl...being?" I was unsure of the correct term.

He pointed a finger at my phone. "Look her up."

"Have you two lost your minds?" O'Leary flicked his gaze between us. "Sekh is not a goddess, she's a dedicated researcher and currently a museum curator."

Killion pinned him with a glare.

He fell silent.

I read the first entry, noting the images with it of a woman with a cat head, and nearly dropped the phone. The awful memories of the precipice rushed over me. I swallowed and read out loud, "Sekhmet, translates as: The One Who Is Mighty or Powerful, but she's also known as..." I took a breath. "Mistress of Dread? Lady of Slaughter? Oh, everyone's favorite—She Who Mauls."

O'Leary waved it away. "My friend and colleague is not the goddess, Chloe."

I swallowed my fear and pushed back my chair. "Unfortunately, I believe she is." It made sense after what I'd witnessed, whether I wanted to admit it or not. Better to be safe than sorry. "And she's got your daughter."

THIRTY-ONE

"Call Megan," I told him. "Ask her to meet us here."

His brows scrunched, causing two lines to form between them. "My daughter is perfectly safe with Ms. Leon. You're being ridiculous."

Killion snapped his fingers. "Call her."

While I was under no compulsion, my body still twitched from his tone. O'Leary fought it, but went to his bag and withdrew his phone. He now noticed the canines by the fireplace, pausing momentarily. "Is that a...?"

"Yes," I told him. "He won't harm you."

O'Leary retreated several steps, keeping a wary eye on the wolf, and typed out a message. "She hates it when I call." He returned to the table and peered at Killion. "What did you say your name was?"

"I didn't."

"Is there a reason you have a wolf as pet?"

Andy whined. Killion silenced him with a sharp cough. "My name is Killion Reveux, and he isn't a pet. If you'd like to use him for one of your experiments, I can certainly arrange it."

Andy jumped to his feet and howled. I smacked the vampire's arm. "Killion!"

The professor gave both of us a polite smile, one I'd seen in class plenty of times right before O'Leary dressed down a student. "I appreciate your help," he said, "but I believe it's time for me to go."

"I'm afraid you can't." I couldn't divulge the truth about my grim status, but I needed him to understand how serious this was. "Mr. Reveux and I are investigators for a special...organization, and we're working a dangerous case that involves this woman, Sekhmet." I tried to convey confidence, as well as urgency. "We need you and Megan to remain here, where it's safe, until we...eliminate the threat."

That got his attention, but disbelief colored his response. "So you're with the FBI? CIA?"

Killion came to my rescue. "A clandestine group you haven't heard of, hence its covert status. I assure you it's real, and so is the peril your new friend presents."

"You're a doctor, own this hotel, and now, you wish me to believe you're also an undercover agent?" O'Leary chuckled before studying me once more. "Is this a hoax, Ms. Frost?" He made a show of scanning the corners of the room as though looking for hidden cameras. "Am I being videoed for some social media prank?"

I shook my head. "This is no prank, professor." I checked his phone's screen, but Megan hadn't responded. "Call her."

"I'm sorry, but I really must leave."

Strong-willed. I admired that about him. Before he could move toward his laptop and books, however, Killion was in front of him. "Relax."

The man swayed and grabbed for the table, dropping

his cell and nearly knocking over Killion's wine glass. The vampire caught him. "You're weak. I must insist you rest."

Mesmerized once more, the fight went out of him. I grabbed his phone from the floor, and Killion maneuvered him to the sofa. I found Megan's number and hit call.

Voicemail. When Killion glanced at me, I shook my head. "I'll try from mine." Kids often ignored messages from parents, when possible, but an unknown number might get her to answer.

As the butler brought an afghan to wrap around the now sleeping O'Leary, I dialed. It still went to voicemail. As I listened to her try to be cool on the message, I thanked my lucky stars I wasn't a teenager anymore.

At the beep, I hesitated. Should I go hardcore and try to scare her in to responding? Or the opposite: snag the fly with honey? Neither would work if Ms. Lady of Slaughter, had already harmed her.

Killion watched expectantly as the silence dragged out. I cleared my throat. "Hey, M. We met earlier today, and I'm interested in what you were telling me." I went for casual, avoiding offering my name or insinuating I was freaked out that Sekhmet might be holding her against her will. "I'm hitting The Smoking Bean for a peppermint mocha latte. I love how they put a candy cane in them, don't you? Can you meet me there in thirty minutes? There's this woman who knows about that book you were studying. She's going to be there. She said she knows how to, you know"—I lowered my voice—"raise the D.E.A.D. Like, for real. I thought you'd want to talk to her. Anyway, see you at The Bean."

I disconnected, and Killion raised a brow. "You believe that will work?"

"Yes." *Probably not.* "If she's still in charge of her

freewill, hopefully, she'll be interested enough to come. If Sekhmet is controlling her, and gets the message, perhaps they'll both show up."

"What if the goddess does accompany her?"

"I'm the one she wants, right? I'll get her to trade Megan for me."

"I don't care for this plan." He glowered, the illumination from the fireplace outlining his face. "You can't stop her. Whatever she intends, you're playing right in to it."

"But I'll have you, Andy, and Ghost." At her name, the dog jumped up and shook herself. "Plus, I have the amulet and the scythe."

"I *am* powerful." The vampire moved toward me. "But I have not fed in days, and I cannot, even at my strongest, handle an ancient goddess."

To tell the truth, I was pretty surprised at that admission. I'd never heard him concede he wasn't the most powerful creature around. Moreover, I could tell he wasn't at his best, and hadn't been since our time at the morgue. I was worried. "Can you, umm, feed?"

His violet eyes darkened, and I didn't miss the way his gaze dropped to the side of my neck. It lingered there long enough to make my knees weak. "Only if you're—"

The door burst open and Simone rushed in, her appearance disheveled. "Master!"

Killion moved to her side instantly, the moment between us over. "What is it? What's happened?"

"It's Mason." Her voice trembled with an Oscar-worthy delivery. "He's awake."

Killion cast a glance back at me and my heart sank. "Go," I told him. "He needs you."

"Do not leave here," he commanded. "I'll return as soon as I can, and we'll regroup."

"But Megan's going to meet me—"

He pinned me with that gaze, and I felt as though I were silently reprimanded.

"You're right," I admitted. "It's too dangerous. I'll just..." I gave the buffet what I hoped was a yearning look. "Eat."

Doubt clouded his eyes, and I thought briefly he might put me in an unconscious state, too. But he thought better of it, coming to take my hands in his. "Please, Chloe. Promise me you'll remain here until I return."

That might be worse than having him put me under. Promises were serious matters and I didn't take them lightly. "Killion," I whined, attempting to draw my hands away. "Mason needs you and you need to feed. What you don't need is to worry about me."

His grip tightened. "Promise. Me."

"Master, please," Simone cried.

I wanted to tell her to shut it, but I stayed focused on Killion. I wrapped a pinky finger around his. "I won't go after Sekhmet until you return. I'll stay clear of the coffeeshop, Megan, all of it. I'll read O'Leary's notes in more depth, okay?"

The relief in his features surprised me with its intensity. He held up our entwined pinkies. "You promise?"

He was going to get me, no matter what. I blew out a huffy breath. "Yes, I promise! Geez, you act like you don't trust me."

He leaned in and brushed hair behind my ears. "I trust you with my life."

Then he kissed me.

THIRTY-TWO

My body flushed, my bones melting. It was a chaste kiss, soft and warm, his lips barely brushing the corner of my mouth before he turned and walked out.

Rendered immobile, I didn't miss the scowl Simone sent my way as she trailed after him. Whatever malice her look promised caused the amulet to flare, sending a bubble around me. Interestingly enough, it hadn't reacted to Killion's kiss.

Slowly, I raised my fingers to touch the spot where his lips had been. It wasn't uncommon for folks in our area, where there was a heavy French and Creole influence, to throw kisses around like confetti.

This meant more. Regardless of the fact he was my friend and mentor, he and I had crossed an invisible line. A threshold, and there was no turning back. My mind scrambled for the correct term for what I felt, but all I could come up with was *magnetism*.

Nita was right—I'd been out of the dating world so long, I was a disaster. I'd shut down that side of myself, focusing on my education and the goal of buying back the clinic. I'd completely suppressed my libido. Now, it seemed, a simple kiss could send me into a system-wide shock.

The bubble throbbed, an intense pressure hitting me on all sides. It was as if it had read my mind and decided to warn me that daydreams about a vampire were dangerous to my health.

The pounding didn't stop, and I staggered, grabbing my skull. "Ugg. Cool it, already." I made it to the dining table and fell into Killion's abandoned chair. My vision blurred and my fingers and toes went cold. The necklace eased up on the pressure with each pulse, but as it did so, the cold seeped through my legs and along my arms.

Pennyworth appeared. "You look a fright. May I bring you something? Warm tea, perhaps?"

I tried to say yes, but my teeth chattered and my voice lodged in my throat. I simply nodded and he vanished.

The frigidness crept into my belly and flooded my chest. My lungs iced over and I attempted to call out, alert him that I needed help, yet I couldn't draw breath. I planted my hands on the table, knocking over the crystal goblet. Scarlet wine soaked the white tablecloth, looking for the world like blood.

The amulet turned icy-hot. I would have gasped, if I could have sucked in air. Everything inside me felt barren, desolate, futile. Time seemed to stretch out in an endless frozen landscape. I saw people being born, then dying. Buildings rising and falling. Layers upon layers of ghosts roaming the stark city.

Each recalled a previous generation, as though they were stuck in time loops, replaying the lives they'd already lived. The future superimposed itself on top of them. The clothes and buildings continued to change, but the terrain became apocalyptic, the sky bleak and gray. The very hotel

I sat in was reduced to rubble, and still my body, my heart was cold, remote. I felt detached from it all, centuries, millennia, stretching out in wave after wave of sameness. No joy, no love, only survival.

Was this what it felt like to be a vampire? To live, but not truly be alive? To see the things and people that once brought you happiness be extinguished, only for some other form to take their place? To know their ghosts continued to be stuck in time, like your previous life as a human?

A piece of the broken goblet bit into the skin of my hand. Stars danced on the edge of my vision. I reached up and tore the amulet from my neck. The chain broke easily and I flung it aside. It landed at the butler's feet, as he returned with my tea.

The bubble burst, a thousand sparkles of light disintegrating in a show of fireworks. The hold it had on me vanished. Lungs burning, I sucked in oxygen and clung to the edges of the table, the frost in my ribs melting.

"Are you all right?" Pennyworth hustled past the necklace and set the drink in front of me. "May I get you a blanket?"

It took two tries for me to respond through numb lips. "That would be...awe...some."

With trembling fingers and shaking legs, I bundled myself in front of the fireplace and sipped the tea, warming my hands on the cup. Andy and Ghost cuddled next to me, the professor sleeping on the other sofa. My brain continued to feel foggy, my synapses sluggish. Once I was warm, however, I knew what I had to do.

First and foremost, not crush on a vampire, no matter how sexy he was. Even if our working relationship was too close for comfort these days, and getting a taste of what it was like to be Undead made me sympathize with Killion on a whole new level, it was suicide. If that was truly how he felt inside, it made my heart ache for him. Even if he experienced so much as an inkling of it, it was still too much for me.

Secondly, the number of ghosts I'd seen gave me pause. Most of the time, souls stuck on earth had somehow avoided their contract's expiration date. They could also be shades— their contracts hadn't expired, and even though their bodies were out of commission, their souls were still tethered here.

Death was big on balancing the scales and making sure souls weren't hovering between here and the spirit world. I'd been assigned several who'd needed help moving on. Not all grims went after ghosts, but I wasn't the only one on earth who could see and interact with them. Who had left all those souls lingering in their time loops, and why hadn't Death or SMG stepped in and cleaned them up? I'd have to ask him next time I saw him.

The butler left the necklace where it lay, and it twinkled across the room on the floor. The window shades were drawn, only the wall sconces and hearth flames lighting the room. I could feel the crystal beckoning to me, its energy glowing. Why had Death really given it to me?

It had protected me, but what was the demonstration at the table about? Had he engineered it to scare me off Killion? I tucked that thought away and finished my tea. I had more to worry about than myself. Megan was Sekhmet's prisoner, one way or another, and the professor seemed to be her tool to help her create monsters. She had to be stopped.

Shrugging off the blanket, I set the cup on the coffee table and stood. My legs were still a bit shaky, but strong enough. Ghost and Andy hopped down and looked at me expectantly.

"Can I get you something else?" Pennyworth asked, instantly available and anticipating my every whim.

"No, but thank you. I have to go out." I picked up the amulet. With the chain broken, I could no longer hang it around my neck, and I wasn't sure I wanted to. I stuffed it in a pocket. "I'll be back in a bit."

He smiled in a practiced manner, patient and calm. "The master said you shouldn't leave."

"Don't worry, I'm honoring my promise to avoid Sekhmet. I have a friend I need to visit." I slipped on my jacket and grabbed my bag. "Keep an eye on him for me, will you?" I motioned at O'Leary. "I know he's knocked out, but don't let anyone in unless it's me or Killion, okay?"

It might be a moot point, since Death could go where he pleased, and no vampire could keep him out. I considered leaving the amulet on O'Leary, but I had the distinct impression it wouldn't work on him. Right now, I needed it as much, if not more, than my professor.

"I really must insist you stay." The butler moved in close, and although he was still smiling, his intent was clear. "It's for your own good."

"Yeah, well." I flashed the scythe. "Unless you wish me to end your Undead life, I suggest you let me pass."

His hesitation lasted about as long as the irritation that dimmed his smile. He gave a mock bow. "As you wish."

"I'll explain to Killion that you had no choice," I assured him. "And my plan is to return before he even knows I'm gone."

"Be careful, Ms. Frost." He stood dutifully at the door as the canines and I walked out. "I rather like you, and I would hate for you to die."

Aww. That was sweet. "I feel the same about you."

The canines and I descended to the first floor. Tiny

rivulets of rain dotted the windows. Several guests gave double-takes as we crossed the lobby. I suspected Moss or another vamp might be watching the front, so I steered us toward the rear exit and into the courtyard.

December had done nothing to the plants and trees here, thanks to glamour. Bushes flowered as though it were the heart of summer. The trees' leaves were luscious and green, the grass healthy and inviting one to discard their shoes and walk through it. Ivy vined over the stone walls and jasmine scented the air.

Bees and butterflies roamed the private, enclosed grounds. A scantily clad nymph, cast in concrete, spilled water into a giant upturned shell, the fountain bubbling and attracting various birds. Coins that folks had made wishes on shone from the watery depths, although there was no sun to reflect off them.

We followed a brick path to the rear gate, and I flinched as it squeaked when I opened it. Scanning what I could see of the garden behind us and the street in front, I noticed no movement. My blood didn't react, so it appeared we were alone.

Once we were a block away, I said to Andy, "Take me to see Aurora."

He made a questioning noise. "Ruff?"

"I need to speak to her and you know where she lives." I motioned with my hand toward the road ahead. "Lead the way."

He pawed the ground twice.

No.

I tapped the bag. "Then I'll send you to the Great Beyond."

He hung his head.

"I get that you're reluctant to see her after what

happened, but I have to find out what she knows. She may have the key to help me stop an apocalypse."

Along with a dramatic sigh, he rolled his eyes. With a long-suffering glance to the south, he started walking.

Ghost and I followed. When we arrived at our destination twenty minutes later, I wished I'd stayed at the penthouse.

THIRTY-THREE

"A cemetery?" I glared at the shifter. "Are you kidding me?"

We stood at the gated entrance of Evil Eye Burials. No lie, that was its name. A half-wall of stones running around the property at the south end of town formed a fence with a towering black iron gate that kept it divided from the rest of the area.

I'd lived in Dante's Grove all my life and never noticed this place. Ancient oaks, mystical yews, and weeping willows sheltered rows of raised beds containing graves, along with plenty of crypts and impressive mausoleums. There were dozens of statues, but not the usual kind, like mournful angels standing watch over the various burials. Instead, there were giant ravens, skeleton grims, and yes, evil eyes, decorating the various entombments.

Although it was cloudy, I had to shield my eyes to see through a hazy mist that clung to the property. Adding to the fog was the presence of dozens of ghosts.

Magic hung in the air and stung the insides of my nose, as if I'd snorted pepper. I had the feeling the gloom and general depressiveness was part of a glamour to keep humans away.

It was effective. I wanted to turn tail and run.

"This is where your girlfriend lives?" I asked Andy.

His nose twitched as he stared through the metal bars. One paw lifted and smacked the ground. "Ri ruv rer."

I love her.

I felt bad for him, but this explained why he'd wanted one last Christmas here. I fumbled in my bag and brought out the scythe. It hummed to life. The ghost closest to us suddenly realized we were there. Previously, he and his friends had been floating aimlessly, but now their heads swiveled in unison toward us and his dead eyes locked on me.

Nothing better than a bunch of earthbound spirits focusing on you with murder in their eyes. I swung the blade and brought it down on the rusted padlock. That caused a spark, but the metal and the magic it was infused with, gave way.

As I shoved the dual gates open, they screeched in warning. Ghost morphed, becoming her psychopomp self as the ghosts were drawn to the blade like moths to a silver flame. I readied the weapon. They bared their teeth and lunged at me, but seemed to avoid the blade no matter how I swung it.

Magic.

When I finally made contact with one of them, there was a flash of light so bright I had to shield my eyes.

That was new. When the light faded, I saw that they'd all disappeared, but Ghost was still with me. I hadn't felt the normal bliss I did with soul transference, either. "Why didn't you take the spirit over?"

She gave no response and I noticed Andy was gone, as

well. I cursed, hoping I hadn't accidentally sent him to the great beyond again. I saw no wolf corpse, so that was a good sign. Had he run off, leaving me to confront Aurora myself?

"Andy," I hissed, searching around grave markers, crypts, and statues. "Get out here."

Head down, he slunk from behind an overgrown bush and eyed the scythe with unease. Seemingly convinced we were safe, Ghost returned to puppy size. Her long-haired ears twitched and she turned to face the largest of the mausoleums at the rear of the grounds. She sniffed the air.

The pointed roof towered over the others, and as I studied it, I heard a woman humming. "Proceed with caution," I warned my companions.

The sky above grew darker the farther in we ventured. The humming grew neither louder nor softer. I kept my weapon raised and ready in case anything supernatural attacked. No traffic sounds or birds cut through the heavy magical barrier. My breathing sounded too loud in my ears, and I swear I could feel the eyes of the statues watching us. We all three jumped at every snap of a twig or creak of a tree branch.

As we reached the mausoleum, I gripped the scythe tighter. A willow next to the towering building had to be at least a hundred years old. It hadn't dropped its leaves, and they created a long, rustling curtain that blanketed one side of the tomb. More pliable limbs slid over the concrete steps leading to the door. Pillars decorated the front and gargoyle statues with open mouths glared down at us from the roof.

I hesitated, considering my options. Should I knock? Barge in and hope I didn't get zapped by her wards? "You're sure she's here?" I asked Andy, even though I could still hear the humming. That, too, could be misleading.

He raised a paw and scratched at the door, the exterior of it bearing a bronze panther.

"Knock, knock," I called, using the iron knocker. I figured I'd hedge my bets. If she was as powerful as I suspected, she already knew we were here. "It's me, Chloe, Andy's friend. I'm coming in. I just want to talk."

Inch by slow inch, I pushed on the heavy door, the sound of grinding, stone on stone, making my teeth vibrate.

What met me when I finally peeked around the opening was not the witch, nor the panther.

Flapping wings and sharp talons came at my face. "Kill!" screamed the raven.

THIRTY-FOUR

The amulet immediately kicked in, although with less intensity than normal, forming a protective shield, rather than a bubble.

The obnoxious raven smacked into the rosy colored wall of energy and bounced off, hitting a concrete tomb to my left. Squawking again, this time in pain, or perhaps surprise, his wild eye rolled.

I lowered the blade and glared at him as he righted himself. "I fix your broken wing, never mind bringing you back from the dead, and this is how you repay me?"

The humming stopped. One beady eye regarded me and he toddled forward. "Jelly bean!"

The shield disappeared, and the bird, Ghost, and Andy had a reunion. I scanned the shadowy interior. "Hello?" My voice echoed off the stark walls, an assortment of concrete tombs resting helter-skelter as far as I could see. Here were the sorrowful angel statues, along with fairies, goddesses, and female saints in robes. "I know you're here, Aurora. Please come out and talk to me."

Silence. I started forward, keeping the weapon raised. A

razorblade sensation cut along my spine, and I assumed it was some type of ward, but the scythe only vibrated at a low hum, making my fingers tingle, and the amulet stayed quiet.

The bird skipped ahead, the shifter and dog taking up positions at my sides. The gloom deepened as we moved into the dark depths, a heavy humidity pressing down on me. It *was* damp, yet the scent of dry paper hung in the air. Along with it, the odor of burning herbs and fragrances—sage and essential oils. I recognized them from the metaphysical shop Nita dragged me to more often than I cared for. I liked frankincense, rose, and jasmine, which were lighter than my friend's preferred sandalwood and patchouli. My nose caught both of those riding the otherwise stale air.

"All I need is advice," I called. "It's not just about me anymore. The young girl at the house earlier—she's in mortal danger from that necromancer."

Sapphire blue eyes blinked at me from a corner and I stopped short. A tall, weeping angel was on my right and Ghost sniffed at the base.

"Do not pee on that," I warned her. Then I spoke to the panther with more force. "I mean you no harm and I *did* save your familiar." I hoped she saw that as a good thing. The raven wasn't the brightest bird in the unkindness—a term used to describe a flock of ravens. "You owe me. He was deader than my boots."

The eyes vanished. Ghost sniffed toward the place they had been, and I snatched her up to keep her morbid curiosity from getting her into trouble.

A ball of light the size of a marble came to life, revealing Aurora in human form. Her hair was piled high on her head, a long robe of the same color hung to her feet. "His name is Corvus," she said. The raven hopped and flapped his wings, his body disappearing into the gloom. She turned and began walking on silent feet. "Follow me."

The marble grew and floated about a foot higher than my head in front of us, lighting the way. Regaining my composure, I lowered the scythe and prayed I wasn't walking in to a worse situation than I was already in. "Corvus, huh?" My voice echoed off the stone walls of some sort of hallway as we continued. I couldn't tell if we were going up or down, or even which direction. The name was cliché, but I wasn't about to mention that. "I see what you did there." I chuckled, the sound scratchy, revealing my nerves.

The humming began again, but I realized there was a differently quality to it. Not her voice, it seemed to be coming from the walls. Or perhaps the statues.

"Yes, well," she said, "as long as he's fed, the bird cares not what he's called."

"Sounds like my dog."

The end of the hall brightened, spotlighting her in a subtle luminescence from a pair of elaborate metal sconces on either side of a wide wooden door. The entrance appeared to have been carved straight from the trunk of a tree. She glanced back, sending a glare at Andy. "Animals are that way."

He whined and ducked behind me.

There was an indentation in the upper center of the wood and she placed her hand on it, bowed her head, and uttered words I couldn't make out. The door groaned, shifting to allow us in. I chuckled nervously again—what was up with that?—and then cleared my throat. I was about to enter a witch's lair. Was that the right term? I might be no smarter than the raven. "Open sesame doesn't work?"

My joke fell flat. She glanced my way as the door inched its way back. "You may enter, the shifter may not."

"But he—"

A hand cut through the air. "No arguments."

Once again, I found myself coming to his defense. This was getting to be a bad habit. "I don't know why you're angry at him, but he's obviously in love with you, and he's had a rough few days. Cut him some slack, okay?"

Her body blocked my view of the interior chamber. "The blame for our breakup is solely on him, and if he is not man enough to shift and speak to me as he should—"

Ah, so *that* was it. "He can't," I interrupted. "He was a noncompliant soul and I had to harvest him. Then I resurrected him, but this weird necromancy I've been cursed with only works on animals." I reached back and hauled him forward by the makeshift collar, the rabbit's foot swinging. "Hence, he came back in wolf form. He's stuck this way."

The starchiness in her face evaporated. She dropped her gaze to his. "Is this true?"

The door finished sliding open and warm light flooded over us. The shifter sank down, rolled over, and showed her his belly.

I saw the faintest quiver of her lips. "Yes, indeed, I guess I have amends to make. Get up," she commanded, and he jumped to his feet like he'd been poked with a cattle prod. His eyes were wide and he panted, a goofy smile on his muzzle now. "You may enter."

As I stepped across the threshold, another entire world opened up before me. "Whoa," was all I could say.

THIRTY-FIVE

Aurora's home was part atrium, part laboratory, and part library. Rows of shelved books rose two stories around us. Skylights and a single wall of glass windows allowed significant daylight to penetrate the space. Plants of all sizes and varieties dotted every open surface, along with more statues.

A fire crackled cheerfully in a large brick hearth, complete with a huge purple cauldron, bubbling over the flames. Water trickled down a stone section near the glass panels, forming a pool. A work station was set up in the middle, made from more dark planks like the door. It was covered with blue bottles, droppers, and copper bowls. There was also an expensive microscope, along with other tools.

She glided toward it. A black cat, stretched across several open books, glared at us as we followed.

Corvus cawed and flew to a swing connected to a tree branch growing from a live specimen near the waterfall. Andy went straight to the hearth and lay down, watching Aurora warily.

I needed to make this visit quick, but I also needed to get on her good side. "My mom always loved plants," I volunteered. Ghost sniffed the air and eyed the cat, her tiny tail trying to wag against my ribs as I held her close. "You have an amazing collection."

Aurora gently lifted the feline off the books and set her on a velvet pillow under the tree before returning. "They are necessary for my work, but also, they make me happy."

Happy was good. "You have a lovely...home?"

She met my eyes, hers twinkling. "And you have lots of questions."

You ain't kidding. "Why did you attack us earlier? At my place?"

She closed the open volumes and moved a stack of books out of the way. Under them was a yellowed map of what appeared to be Dante's Grove. There were circles and markings on various buildings. "I apologize for scaring you. The area reeked of the Undead. I've had several unfortunate encounters with them, and I feared your request for help was a trap. They don't care for witches, and we have no use for them."

Did *anyone* like vampires? Killion needed to get his PR people to work on their image. "Why was the raven at Simone's?"

"Ah, Simone." Her slender fingers glided over the map, tapping on a spot that I realized was the location of the vamp's house. "I'm tracking an evil enchantress who recently showed up in town."

"Cat Woman?"

Her thin brows dipped. "Sorry?"

"The gal from Cairo who was at my professor's house. You were watching her?"

"Yes, that's her. Corvus alerted me when she sent the

shiftling to the vampire's."

So he was good for something. "Shiftling? You mean the jackal?"

"She's gifted at creating disgusting creatures, isn't she?"

"I thought he was some type of hybrid-golem thingie."

Her lips twitched from holding back a smile. "You're not far off. She's one of the last of a sect that has been playing with various animal-human designs for millennia. A type of gene splicing, you might say, with magic."

"Genetic engineering? That's highly complex stuff."

"Hence the magic. She's clever, dangerous, and powerful. You should steer clear of her."

"Too late for that." I explained in detail what had happened to me from the moment I'd dissected her creature. "That's why I reached out to you."

Aurora leaned her elbows on the high table, engrossed in my story. "His organs were mummified?"

I nodded and continued until the whole of it was out, including my experience on the precipice and Tinder's theory. "What do you think? Could she responsible for it?"

She took up a leather journal and pen and began writing furiously. "Fascinating. Yes, she's capable of all of that, and more. We used to believe her sect was attempting to replicate the old gods, but this confirms my belief that her goal is quite different. I think Cosima wants to be a god herself. But to clarify, I wrote the spell to break the curse."

"You? You're friends with Death?"

"I wouldn't say we're friends, exactly."

That I understood. "Well, it backfired and that's why I ended up confronting this Cosima in her cat form."

"Cat form?"

I nodded. "That's why I named her Cat Woman."

She tapped the pen against her chin. "Again, to clarify,

you weren't hexed." Setting the journal down, she shifted through a set of parchments and singled one out. "Your master vampire is correct. My spell was designed to return the curse to its originator. But I don't believe Cosima's bag was designed for cursing. It's part *anime vita*, which is designed to keep her creature alive, and that relied on the glyph. When the glyph became smudged, that part of the enchantment backfired, causing the thing's demise. However, what I've discovered about her creatures suggests they don't live long anyway. Not yet. She's still searching for a certain ingredient for this genetic manipulation to work the way she wants." Unrolling the parchment, she scanned several symbols and made another note. "The other part of her enchantment bag was meant to trigger inherent magic in her target. Magic that was dormant."

"Such as a gene that wasn't turned on in the DNA?"

She nodded.

"What kind would that be?"

"Your kind." Again, she gave me a knowing smile. "You are very unique."

Not the first time I'd heard that. "Killion calls me an enigma, but I'm just a grim, and the only *magic* I have comes from the scythe and the robes."

"Surely you know that's not true." A skeptical brow arched. "The bubble you summoned at the house today? Grims don't have that sort of power."

"You know lots of grims, do you?"

"One or two."

Interesting. "The bubble was caused by a protection amulet Death gave me. Tell me about Cosima and her necromancy. How do I turn it off?"

She hesitated, then cocked her head. "I'm the necromancer—along with you, of course."

Not for long. "You are?"

A nod. "There's no real use for it, unless you deal in black magic, so I keep it suppressed, but yes, it's a natural ability I have."

Suppressing it seemed like a good idea. "Cosima calls herself Sekhmet and Killion believes she might actually be the Egyptian goddess."

Her tinkling laughter filled the space, and Andy raised his head, ears twitching, as if soaking it up. "Heavens, no." She reached for a pair of shears and began cutting flower buds from a lavender plant next to the book stack. "Cosima is old, but not that ancient."

The scent of the herb drew me in. My mother had always grown large pots of it at our front door. She often treated my headaches by putting flower buds in warm compresses for my neck and shoulders. She also steamed the leaves, along with eucalyptus, to open my sinuses when I had a cold. "What exactly does she want with me?"

She took a copper bowl from a tiny pedestal formed in the shape of animal paws and placed a handful of buds in it. Next, she drew out a glass honey jar and added a dip of the golden stuff to the pot. "Sounds like she wants the original grim to grant life to her shiftlings."

Each time she answered me, I ended up with more questions. "The original grim?"

She nodded but didn't elaborate, adding water from a pitcher to the pot. "Have a seat." Ghost squirmed in my arms. "You may put her down. Nothing here will harm her."

I was more worried about her *doing* the harm. Giving in, I released the dog and kept an eye on her as she sniffed at all the possible things she could knock over, dig up, or pee on.

Aurora held both hands over the pot and her lips moved

soundlessly. The water began to bubble. Steam rose, and I dropped my bag and scythe to the floor and sat on a stool, watching it warily. She peeked at the concoction and must have deemed it satisfactory, because she lowered her hands and bent to pull a cup and strainer from a shelf under the table. "Grim Zero is her missing ingredient."

"But I'm Grim 281."

"Sure, in this incarnation."

"What are you talking about?"

The light in her eyes dimmed and her amusement faded. "They didn't tell you. Goddess be." She made tsking noises as she strained the liquid. "Protecting you, I suppose."

"Who is 'they?'" The steaming drink appeared in front of me, and once again I thought of my mom. The scent had a calming effect, even though my brain didn't like what she was suggesting. "SMG?"

"Drink," she said, retrieving a second cup and pouring herself some. She smiled ruefully when I didn't touch mine. "I assure you, it's quite safe. I have no reason to poison you." She eyed me over the edge as she took a sip, and winked. "Yet, anyway."

"Very reassuring," I grumbled.

Returning her drink to the counter, she sighed. "Yes, I assume Soul Management Group has its reasons, but this is a dangerous state for you to be in, not remembering who you truly are. You are the original grim, Chloe. The one who worked among the gods at the beginning of humanity. You alone held power over life *and* death. You've been reincarnated, but you're who Cosima seeks." Her sleeve dragged across the parchment as she patted my hand. "That must be why she enchanted the bag—to turn on your necromancy."

"That's crazy." My suddenly shaking fingers reached for the cup, wishing there was something stronger than tea in it. "You've confused me with someone else. I'm Chloe Frost, a twenty-four-year-old college student struggling to get her degree and make a life for herself. I accidentally killed a grim a few months ago and ended up having to take his robes and this job for one year."

"Accidentally? That was no accident. Being a grim is in your blood. The magic may have been suppressed, but it rose to defend you when Avi Gustafson attacked you."

A click echoed in my brain, a rightness, yet I couldn't wrap my head around it. I eyed the concoction and wondered if she'd been drinking too much of her own potions. "You might want to try coffee instead of whatever hallucinogens are in this."

She crossed her arms. "How do you explain your inability to die?"

What? My cup hit the tabletop, liquid splashing over the side. "I *did* die. The night I accidentally killed Avi. Killion brought me back to life."

A bark of disbelief echoed in the room. "No vampire resurrected you. You did that yourself."

"*I died.* My ghost was floating above my body and Killion put drops of his blood in my mouth. Which, yes, was as disgusting as it sounds, but that's what saved me." That and my mother's ghost telling me it wasn't my time yet.

"And the night of the accident? Who brought you back when you perished alongside your parents?"

I shot up off the stool. "How do you know what happened to them?"

"I know a great many things about you, Grim Zero. I've spent my life training to help you. Apparently, at the moment, I know more about your true history than *you* do."

My fingers balled into fists. "I didn't die that night. I walked away with nothing more than a few scratches and a concussion."

She uncrossed her arms and placed both hands on the countertop, leaning toward me. "You resurrected yourself, Chloe. You are a necromancer."

It was all too much. Head shaking in a wordless "no," I hastily stepped back, colliding with the stool. It toppled over and clanged to the ground. Andy and Ghost were instantly up and on alert. Ghost came to my side and whined. "That's not..."

"Possible?" She tapped the counter with a scarlet nail. "It certainly is, because you are Grim Zero."

My head shook so hard, strands of hair fell from my ponytail. "I'm not a necromancer. I've been cursed."

"Corvus died. I arrived at Simone's in time to see him be smashed under Cosima's shiftling. You resurrected him."

"I've brought back a few animals, because of her curse." My voice kept faltering. "I'm not...just... No."

Her lips pursed. She studied the work table, nails tapping. "You don't know about your birth either, do you?"

I sucked in a gulp of air; my breath stuck in my chest. Had she somehow seen my original birth certificate? Another impossibility. I hadn't even seen it until I'd been going through my parents' things after their funerals. "You're some kind of freaky stalker, aren't you? I'm out of here."

"Wait." She swept around the table and held up her hands to stop me. "I'm not a stalker. I'm a watcher—not like the master vampire who's been assigned to be your partner. I watch for evil. For magic gone awry. Generations of my family have been assigned to track sorcerers and enchantresses such as Cosima. To keep SMG informed about their activities."

An NSA for the Soul Management Group? My stomach churned.

Aurora lowered her hands. "She's been under the radar for decades and then turned up a few weeks ago. I suspect because of you stepping once more into your grim powers."

I didn't much care about Cosima at that moment. "But how do you know about...?"

She took a deep breath and spoke in a reassuring tone. "What happened to you twenty-four years ago?"

I nodded, swallowing my fear. She appeared to be barely older than me. Looks could be deceiving when it came to age and magic, though. Killion was three hundred but didn't appear a day over thirty. "How do you know about my birth certificate? It was an error. My uncle explained it to me."

"Did he?" Her eyes snapped with challenge once more. "He explained how you were stillborn? How the doctor attempted to resuscitate you, but declared you dead? How you miraculously took your first breath *five minutes* later, while your mother held your lifeless body in her arms and grieved?"

My lungs shut down, my throat burning with words I couldn't say. Tears welled in my eyes as I shuffled away from her. "You can't know that," I forced out.

She reached for me, slowly, entreating me. "I do know it, and you do, too. Deep down, you know who you are. Once you accept that you are Grim Zero, then we can fight Cosima. Together."

My vision blurred and a sudden burst of adrenaline surged through my trembling body. Turning on my heels, I ran for the still open door.

THIRTY-SIX

The light from her room only illuminated the hall so far, and I ended up in the shadowy gloom once again. No glowing ball appeared, but I sensed Ghost on my heels. She could see fine in the murkiness of the crypt. Me? Not so much.

I stumbled into a weeping angel, tripping over my own feet. Staggering, I fell and whacked my head on the corner of a crypt. Sharp pain knifed through my temple and I ended up sprawled on the chilly floor.

Sobbing, I sat up and rocked, holding my head. Warm blood oozed through my fingers.

What Aurora had told me was totally whacked. Yet other things made more sense now. How I'd been able to kill Gustafson. Why the robes had chosen me.

Ghost squeezed her wet nose between my hands and licked me. For once, her stinky breath was welcomed. I gripped her in a tight hug and rested my hot face in her fur, and we sat that way for several minutes. My sobs stopped and I could once more breathe.

Shoving my emotions in that deep hole where I

normally kept them, I pushed hair out of my face. Regardless of what Aurora had told me, or how she knew it, I had to stop Cosima and save Megan.

Or did I?

I didn't owe SMG or Death anything. If Aurora was telling the truth, they'd deceived me.

But to leave that girl in the hands of Cosima?

I couldn't do it.

Soft light appeared above my head. "Chloe, I'm sorry. That was insensitive of me." Aurora sat across from us. "I truly didn't realize the extent SMG had blocked your memories, and I'm very familiar with the pain of losing those you love."

My cheeks were damp and I brushed the wetness away with my sleeve. My poor brain went numb—similar to what I'd felt after my parents' deaths.

I could curl in a ball and check out. Stop talking like I had then. Sleep for endless days.

Or I could pick one thing to focus on and move forward, like Dr. Maxwell, my grief counselor, always advised.

Lives hung in the balance.

But I was so utterly exhausted.

Aurora stayed silent as I let the pendulum swing back and forth between taking up my scythe to help Megan or checking out. Andy arrived, and Ghost continued to lick my face, whining now.

I thought of my mom. My dad. How proud they'd always been of me. How much they wanted me to be happy.

Megan's face swam in my vision. Professor O'Leary's.

I drew a deep breath and patted Ghost to reassure her. "I'll sort these revelations later. Right now, I need your help to stop Cosima and whatever she's planning."

Aurora held out a hand. Begrudgingly, I accepted it, allowing her to help me to my feet. I swayed slightly and she peered at the side of my head, examining the injury. "Let's care for that wound. We can brainstorm while we do."

"I heal pretty fast." The world dipped when I started to walk, so I allowed her and Andy to guide me back inside. "It's part of my grim...magic."

She led me inside to a chair near the fireplace, her cat side-eyeing me while Corvus danced on his perch. She shoved the cup—still warm—into my hands and commanded me to drink. "I'll get something to clean the cut."

The liquid now had an earthier aroma, but also a dash of cinnamon. That and the honey made drinking it slightly less horrible. I still only managed to get down a couple of sips before I dumped the rest in the water pool.

When she returned, she took the empty cup, seeming pleased I'd caved. She used a washcloth to clean the blood from my cheek and temple. I gritted my teeth when she rubbed salve into the wound, and focused on the story she told about how Cosima's ancestors had been searching for the elusive magic of the prophecy to create hybrids to do their bidding. How Aurora's family had selflessly taken on the responsibility thousands of years ago to stop them.

"What exactly do they want the creatures to do?" I asked. I was imagining the Jackal fetching Cosima's slippers or bringing her a glass of wine.

"Subjugate humans. Turn them into slaves."

"Oh, good. Nothing major, then." My head throbbed—both from the injury and the implications.

"Those who lust for power are never satisfied."

I thought of Simone. "She could do that with these shiftlings? I'm not sure I understand how."

She checked me over, as if searching for other wounds. "They have hands and feet like we do, but they also have the eyesight, hearing, and other faculties of animals. With her magic, she could use them to be her eyes and ears anywhere in the world, day or night. They could carry weapons and easily overpower even the strongest humans."

I eased back in the soft chair and watched the flames crackle in the hearth. The wood didn't seem to burn—more magic, I assumed. Handy. "Why hasn't SMG done something to stop this sect?"

She repacked her first aid kit. "Cosima's ancestors initially protected demi-gods and they went after Death. SMG tasked you—Grim Zero—with protecting him and harvesting the demi-gods. You did your job well, eliminating most of them, but the sect had collected their nearly pure blood. With that, they began creating golems and hybrids. Those creatures are soulless, however, so it was difficult for SMG to track them. When the sect again tried to eliminate Death, believing if they did, the shiftlings would be safe, you sacrificed yourself for him, knowing you would resurrect. However, things didn't work as planned."

"Lovely," I grumbled, filing that away for the talk Death and I were going to have soon. "How exactly did they kill me?"

She drew a finger across her neck. "After they cut off your head, they drained your blood. There are few entities, even magical ones, who can come back from such extremes."

My stomach flip-flopped.

She squeezed my arm. "You did significant damage to the sect, though. Those left disappeared, and eventually, it was assumed they had all died. The demi-god magic was gone for good. What no one realized was that Cosima's sect was regrouping. They were testing all types of magic and hybrid combinations to design new gods. They searched for the original formula, even though it was believed to have been destroyed by you. And while they didn't find it, that didn't stop them. One of their experiments created the first human-animal shifters."

O'Leary was correct after all. "You're descended from those mad scientists?"

A gruff noise burst from her mouth. "I may be a necromancer, but I'm no shifter."

Andy whined as though offended. I narrowed my eyes at her. "You're a panther."

She snapped the antique box shut. "That's transfiguration. Any witch worth her magic can do that. That's what Cosima does—how she appeared to you as this cat woman."

"You must both be powerful."

"As are you."

I didn't feel like it. "I still think it's a stretch for her to believe she can take over the world."

Aurora shrugged. "She'll have support for manipulating humans from many of those in the magical community."

Like Simone. "If Grim Zero hunted them" —I was uncomfortable calling myself that—"and Cosima believes I'm this reaper of legend, why would she come after me? Why not disappear again?"

"Her ultimate goal is to figure out how to create an immortal and you hold the key."

I definitely had a concussion. I couldn't quite track what seemed obvious to her. "How?"

"Your blood. It allows you to have power over life *and* death, remember. You can resurrect yourself because of it, and she's hoping it will do the same for her new batch of shiftlings. She just needs the right formula."

"She has the original."

Her eyes widened. "You've seen it?"

"My professor has it." I fiddled with the end of my braid, a nervous habit. "Why would SMG allow me to reincarnate if they knew someone could use me like this?"

"I don't pretend to know how that organization thinks, but as I mentioned, we did believe the sect had died out." She tapped a finger to her chin. "Which is why Cosima needs help from your teacher. He must have the skills to assist her in fashioning her new breed of shiftlings. Her current ones die too easily. She needs a better host to start with, and his daughter would make the perfect specimen to experiment on." She pondered this a moment and nodded. "That must be her ultimate goal. Use the girl, have her father do the transplants, and, if she can collect your blood, she'll have everything she needs to bring her shiftlings to life and keep them that way."

I sat up too fast and a kaleidoscope of light and colors flashed in front of me. I gripped the arm rest and swallowed down nausea. "Professor O'Leary would never perform such an experiment, especially on his own daughter. That's nuts, not to mention illegal and amoral."

"You said he's very excited about the prospect of proving hybrids are possible, and Cosima can convince anyone to do her bidding. Enchantress, remember? If she has him under her control, together they can create the creatures to enslave humans and do as she commands."

I thought of the thrall the Undead often used. "Is an enchantress similar to a vampire?"

She let loose another of those harsh laughs. "Close, but no. That's why the Undead and the shifters detest each other so much. The shifters, and their predecessors, believe they are superior and have conquered death, but it's the vampires who have succeeded in cheating it."

"Vampires still die."

"Yet, on the whole, they live far longer. In one of my volumes,"—she pointed to the shelves—"it mentions the first shiftlings using vampire blood to stay healthy. It took a cocktail of that, along with heavy doses of black magic and necromancy, to keep them functioning."

The attack on Killion's people. "Would Cosima use shifters to get vampire blood for her?"

"Certainly. There are few other supernaturals who can overpower one and drain it. But that must have been for the current creatures. Once she has yours, she won't need blood from the Undead."

I rubbed my eyes and realized my healing abilities were finally kicking in. I could move my head without the room swaying. "Simone hates humans and wants to subjugate them, too."

Aurora didn't seem surprised. "Perhaps the two of them have teamed up."

Wasn't that a happy thought? "Professor O'Leary won't experiment on Megan," I insisted.

"But Cosima will."

While the fire warmed the room, I felt chilled to the bone. "She must have a weakness," I stated. "She's...killable, correct?"

The witch sighed. "Yes, but you're not going to like what you have to do to accomplish it."

"Just tell me," I said, and prayed I could still save the professor and his daughter.

THIRTY-SEVEN

Ghost and I left her place half an hour later. I needed to return to the penthouse before Killion realized I was gone, and I had a lot to think about.

I texted the ride company I preferred as I trudged across a vacant lot, telling them to pick me up at the convenience store a block away. The sky was unnaturally dark for the winter afternoon, storm clouds so low I felt like I could reach up and touch them. When I glanced back toward Aurora's graveyard, it had disappeared. I stopped and stared, wishing I had that kind of magic. Then maybe I could sneak up on Cosima and destroy her and her plans.

Trudging on, my head barely registered any pain, but I felt off. Like the sky overhead, my perspective of the world around me seemed to be closing in. Grim Zero. The thought kept swirling around. As I walked, Ghost kept an eye on me in between sniffing and marking spots. She seemed aware of my unease, and potentially understood on some level, what we were about to go up against.

Once this was over—if I survived—I had a date to return and start reading the histories stored on Aurora's shelves.

She had assured me I would; she just didn't know how many times within one lifetime I could bring myself back from death.

My phone dinged, bringing me out of my revelry. I had nearly made it to the back of the convenience store. Wind blew dry leaves across my feet, and the noise of cars and people coming and going from the place was oddly comforting. The world had no idea what might happen soon.

Nita: *Megan O'Leary is here. Says she's meeting you. Where r u?*

I considered how to respond. I was actually surprised the girl had shown up, and while I longed to swoop in and attempt a rescue, it wouldn't work. Cosima had to be with her or at least nearby. I had to check my impulsive need to save everyone—Death would be proud—and stick to the strategy I was working on. That plan relied heavily on the support of Killion and his vampires.

With the exception of Simone.

Me: *Can't make it. Tell her I'm sorry. Fell and hit my head. Have to take it easy.*

Her response was all kinds of worried and asking if I was okay. Luckily, she had to work until five or she would've insisted on rushing to my bedside. At least this got me out of the hospital Christmas party.

I assured her I was fine and was in good care, hinting that Killion was taking care of me.

As I slowed to pocket my phone, I felt a tug under my breastbone. Ghost growled, and as I followed the direction of her gaze, I saw a tattered cat stumbling toward us. From its matted hair and somewhat deflated rear end, I knew it had been dead.

Sighing, I shushed the dog. "Leave it be. Let's go." I

figured if it followed us the rest of the way, I'd have to clean it up and let Vera find it a home.

Turning away, the cold slide of Death seeped into my bones. Of course, he'd turn up. I steeled myself for the lecture I was about to get for my interference with Professor O'Leary's scheduled death.

"There you are." He materialized out of nowhere and glanced at my collarbone, noting the missing necklace. "Where have you been?"

Killion was right. "The necklace is a tracker, isn't it?" I fished it from my pocket and tossed it at him. He caught it mid-air. Still in his suit, he was nevertheless mussed. The tie was loose, the top button of his dress shirt undone. His pants were wrinkled. "Why aren't you wearing it?"

"Answer the question. I want to hear you say it."

"I don't need this to track you, and you know it. You're one of mine."

My bones quivered at the statement, confirming it. *Yes, and I once gave my life for you.* I wondered if that was the real reason I had some form of immortality in each incarnation. Eventually, I would die again, and, like Aurora had mentioned during our talk, who knew how many times I could resurrect myself?

The cat meowed, a sound that was scratchy and grating. "I'm not *yours*," I clarified. Maybe, like this poor thing, I had nine lives. "And I don't want the amulet."

He toyed with the metal links and the broken ones were suddenly fixed. He sauntered to me and dropped the chain over my head. The crystal once more fell to the hollow of my throat. "Your independence is admirable, and I respect it, but this is a direct order." His eyes pinned me, glowing with preternatural intensity. *The ominous 'death' glare.*

"We're up against dangerous forces and I will not lose you to them. Wear the necklace."

A shiver of rebellion went through me, my binding grim contract at war with my stubbornness and the fact I knew his secrets—at least some of them—now.

He playfully tugged at the end of my braid, pulling it from under my jacket. I noticed a smear of black on his neck, and a red imprint on the edge of his shirt collar. "Who was she?"

The clouds rumbled. The cat slid its dirty body against my leg. Death chuckled, but there was something hollow in it. "Relationships aren't my thing."

He was too close, too overbearing, and lying to my face. He hadn't mentioned O'Leary, and that was good, although I sensed there was a reason. I needed to wrap this up, get away from him, and return to the penthouse.

I flicked a finger at the tell-tale lipstick. "Just meaning-less hookups then?" I kept my tone casual, even as I touched the black smear and my finger came away with kohl eyeliner. Plain old humans couldn't see him, but someone like Cosima, our enchantress? Oh yeah, I bet she could. "Let me guess: a grim? A witch? A vampire?"

Since he hated vampires, he screwed up his nose. "Fine, you caught me." He glanced around as though someone might be eavesdropping. "I'm doing a bit of undercover work. It seems your case has generated concern with Smudgy and I'm getting cozy with one of the individuals who could be disrupting the natural order of things."

Another suspicion confirmed. My mouth formed the word 'traitor,' but I clamped down on it.

The revulsion wouldn't be denied however, and I did move away, bending to pick up Ghost. Pain shot through my head. When I righted myself, I staggered and he grabbed my elbow.

"What happened to you?" He brushed at my temple, and even thought the wound was healed, seemed to be able to sense it had been there.

I broke his hold. "Did you find me for a reason?"

His concern cooled considerably and he pulled a slip of paper from his pocket. "Your next reaper assignment."

I accepted it without looking at the name. "Great. I'll get right on it."

He inhaled. "You smell of sage and sweetgrass." He moved closer again, and sniffed at my hair.

I took another step back, Ghost in my arms, the cat following at my feet. "Just trying to clear my aura or chakras, or whatever. Get rid of the cooties, you know. I'm full of negative energy right now."

In his eyes, I saw when he realized I was lying and then seemed to conclude where I had been. "You're going down a perilous rabbit hole, Chloe. You should let me handle this."

"You mean with the shiftlings? The demi-gods? Or are we talking about today's hook-up?"

His eyes hardened. "You can't take them alone."

I hate it when anyone tells me I can't do something. "But you can? How? By screwing Cosima? Not sure I understand how that plan is going to work out for the rest of us."

"You are far too smart for your own good." He winked, but again it was hollow. "If you want to be part of the solution, it will require more than going against my orders and keeping O'Leary at the hotel under Killion's influence."

He *did* know what I'd done. There was no satisfaction

in the proof, though. "I was expecting a lecture, a few threats."

"Why do you think I hammered home the order *not* to interfere with his death? Because I knew you'd disobey me. You delight in defying me."

Wait...he wanted me to *save* O'Leary? "What are you playing at?" I couldn't help myself, I had to know. "Are you on Cosima's side? Her sect tried to kill you, don't you remember?"

His brow shot up and he put a hand to his heart, as if horrified at the accusation. "You think that little of me? That I would work with them to tyrannize humans?"

I didn't know what to think. Ghost whined and I tried to reassure her with a pat. "All I want is the truth."

He stuck both hands in his pockets, casual and detached once more, rocking back on his heels. "The truth is complicated, and we don't have much time to foil her."

My phone buzzed with the ride service driver letting me know he was waiting. "Then talk fast," I said as I began walking. "And don't think I won't come after you myself if you lie to me, or put my friends in harm's way."

He fell into step, his tone amused. "I wouldn't expect any less."

"How do we stop her?" I already had a plan brewing, but I wanted to know what his 'undercover' work was going to provide.

He patted my back. "We use you, my brave grim, as bait."

THIRTY-EIGHT

The driver, Rafael, implicitly told me animals were not allowed in Veronica.

Yes, he'd named his car. Maybe someday when I had a vehicle, I would name mine, too. Something catchy, though, like Jelly Bean. Right now, I was in a hurry and struggled not to say anything offensive to him.

"Do something," I growled at Death. "We're on a deadline."

"While I agree, I'm afraid I can't interfere with a human's free will."

The free will card. He liked to throw that around when it was convenient for him. "You interfere with mine all the time."

Rafael frowned, not able to see Death and sure I had Fruit Loops for brains. I heard the car locks slam down and I raised an irritated eyebrow at my companion.

"Try using more charm," he suggested.

Under my breath, I told him where to stick that idea and said to the driver, "I'll double your rate. My destination is only a few blocks from here." To emphasize the point, I fished out a tattered pile of bills from my pocket. My tip money from my last shift at The Bean. I was relieved I hadn't washed the pants yet. I counted out thirty dollars and held it out to the man. "Seriously, it'll take you five minutes to drive us there."

He eyed the remaining crumpled bills in my other hand, then dropped his wary, but greedy gaze, to the dog and cat at my feet. "What is that smell?"

A previously dead cat who spread the scent of carrion with every move she made. I peeled off a five and added it to the bribe. "Buy some air fresheners."

Death waved a hand through the air above the cat and her fur went from dirty and mottled to fresh and clean, puffing out as if she'd just arrived from the groomer's. The scent of shampoo and rosewater floated around us. Rafael's face brightened and the corners of his dark eyes relaxed. He stared at the feline. "How did you do that?"

"Such a coincidence." I forced a smile and ignored the question. "Her name is Veronica, too."

The cat meowed and arched seductively. He smiled and batted his lashes at her. "Really?"

"Must be fate." I reached through his open window to tap the lock button. "Even better, she's available for adoption."

I clamored into the backseat before he could protest, and by the time we arrived at The Beaumont, Rafael had fallen head over whiskers for the cat, thanks to me singing her praises and making up a whole lot of baloney.

While schmoozing the driver, I had to listen to Death explain his plan to use me to draw out Cosima and how we could end her and her shiftlings once and for all. He insisted she had not been his date, and that he'd used the tryst to inquire about her supposed job where she'd discovered the coveted missing formula. The whole thing was intricate, involving an archaeological dig, the museum, and several covert exchanges between her and an unknown entity who'd assisted her.

It was challenging to act like he wasn't there and worst to not blurt out the doubts I had. The one thing that hit home was that Cosima was not working alone. However, Death was sure we could handle her and her creatures, using his strategy.

Me? Not sure at all.

We sidled up to the hotel and it pained me to hand over the money to Rafael but I did. To Death I whispered, "I believe the current shiftlings have been feeding on vampire blood. They may be stronger than you think."

He patted my leg. "Get some sleep and we'll regroup in the morning."

I gathered Ghost and my bag, while making a mental note to discuss his handsy-ness and the fact I didn't like it. On the sidewalk, I watched as Rafael drove off, Death still riding for free. My boss waved through the rear window and Killion's doorman rushed out to ask if he could carry my bag. "Wait," he said, looking down his nose as only a proper vampire could do. "You weren't supposed to leave the premises."

"And if your master finds out I did, you'll be in big trouble." I kept the bag and brushed past him, putting a finger to my lips. "Let's keep this between the two of us."

He bristled but held the door for me. I was tired and smelly, and although I wasn't normally a drinker, I needed something strong. I glanced at the threatening sky before sweeping into the swanky hotel and setting Ghost down. the traditional and exceptionally tasteful holiday decorations twinkled merrily away.

Part of me hoped Killion wasn't back yet, and the other needed to see him in the worst way. What had changed with me that the vampire had become the one I depended on for support in my wacko life?

The desk clerk called to me as I sped past her. "Ms. Frost? Can I offer your dog a complimentary grooming?" Ghost ran around behind the massive cherry desk and she lifted the dog, smiling at the kisses she received. "It's no problem at all."

"Very generous, but we'll have to take a raincheck."

"Of course." She put her down and we headed for the elevators.

"You sure have a lot of fans," I told Ghost.

She licked her distorted reflection in the mirrored panel as the glass box ascended. Dozens of thoughts, ideas, and my greatest fears pinged around in my mind, blotting out the view through the clear view of the immense columns, green plants, and cozy gathering places growing smaller below.

Arriving at the penthouse floor, I readied myself for the possible impending confrontation if Killion were already here, and considered the odds of my own plan—which seemed much saner, if that were possible, than Death's. I needed to bounce my ideas off Killion and his strategic mind.

The elevator dinged and the door slid open with a melodic sigh. Ghost and I walked to the massive double wooden doors of the suite and I paused, waiting for the rush of my blood and the skip of my pulse, signaling Killion was inside.

Neither happened. All I sensed was the butler.

Which made me hesitate, wondering if Killion was okay. Maybe I was paranoid, but it was unusual for him not to message me, not to show up unexpectedly when I least wanted him to. The attack on his nest had been serious and I prayed Mason had provided valuable intel. I was extremely suspicious of Simone, but lacked concrete evidence. For now, I had a good idea why the shifters had attacked, and I drew out my phone to let Killion know. My thumbs hovered over the keyboard before I started my message.

Me: *Don't retaliate on the shifters until we've talked. Also, watch out for Simone.*

I hit send. Planning to do a quick check of Professor O'Leary before I gorged myself on whatever Pennyworth could put in front of me, I pushed open the double doors and entered.

Only it wasn't the butler waiting for me.

"There you are." Simone rose from a chair positioned in front of the entrance, her movements feline and graceful as ever. "I've been waiting a long time for this."

I'd barely caught her scent when she zapped me with a stun stick. The chain around my neck broke once more, and the stone hit the ground right before I did. Frozen, I suddenly knew what Professor O'Leary must have felt like when Killion had immobilized him.

Ghost went into a frenzy, barking, and jumping at the vampire. Before the dog could shift into her psychopomp form, Simone zapped her, too, making anger roar through my motionless body. That emotion surged like a wave, pushing me to my feet, my grim strength overcoming the electrical charge, although I wobbled and staggered. My lips moved, but the sounds that came out were garbled. I sounded like Andy. "Ri rill hill yoo."

Looking amused, Simone punched me in the chest, lifting me off the ground and sending me through the air.

I hit a bookshelf, forcing the air from my lungs. I crumpled to the rug, a large, heavy volume falling on my head. Flickering white lights danced in my peripheral vision as she approached in her high-heeled boots. She jerked me up by my jacket lapels and brought her fist to my face this time. My head snapped back and I lost consciousness.

THIRTY-NINE

I woke sometime later in the dark. My body shivered with cold even though I was mashed against another body. I picked up a whiff of car exhaust that made me sneeze.

That action created a fresh wave of pain that knifed through the back of my skull over the rumbling of an engine. I groaned, lifting a hand to rub it and brushed metal.

A car trunk. Grappling around, I tried not to panic as the blurry details of what had happened skipped through my mind. Simone. The weapon, the amulet... *Ghost*!

Heart suddenly in my throat, I searched for a furry body. The dog wasn't there, but I wasn't sure if that was good or bad.

I was going to kill Simone.

My fingers touched tweed, and a light, male snore echoed in the space.

Professor O'Leary. She'd brought my teacher along for the ride.

Where was she taking us? And for what purpose?

My suspicions rushed back, making my already

pounding head pick up the tempo. I gritted my teeth and shifted as best as I could within the limited space, searching for my phone.

It was gone, and so was the necklace. I had no scythe, robes, psychopomp, phone, or magical GPS tracker. It was just me, Chloe Frost, and a man in a coma-like stasis.

Awesome.

The car hit a pothole. We slowed, then made a turn. I trailed my hands along the trunk, searching for the safety release latch. It should glow in the dark, but I saw nothing to indicate it existed. Cars made after 2002 were required to have one—then it hit me. *American* cars. Simone's convertible was an import, and even if it had arrived with the safety mechanism, she'd yanked it out.

Double on the awesomeness.

I attempted peeling up the thin carpet to get at the spare and jack, but with O'Leary and I packed in like fangirls at a Justin Bieber concert, that was impossible.

Another bump and O'Leary's elbow smacked into my very sore face. Had Simone broken my nose? Gingerly, I touched the area, and it came away wet. Blood. My diaphragm hurt, too.

We slowed, made another turn and came to a stop. O'Leary stirred but fell back to snoring. I closed my eyes and sent out a mental message to Death and Killion.

Help. I've been kidnapped by Simone. O'Leary is with us.

Problem was, I had no clue where we were, so even if those two picked up on the psychic emergency call, how would they find me?

Get Andy. He can pick up my trail from the hotel.

The engine shut off. I figured I could play the next minute in one of two ways—lie there and pretend I was still unconscious, which would cause the vamp to have to carry me to my grave, or, when she popped the trunk, yell my grim reaper head off and come out swinging.

The key inserted into the lock. The trunk began to peel open.

I balled up both fists and screamed.

FORTY

My attack made her laugh, due to the fact that when I sprung to take a swing at her, my jacket was trapped under the professor's dead weight and I snapped back like a rubber band, landing on top of him.

The jarring stirred him, and that gave me momentary hope that he might come to and help me.

That was snuffed out when he snored loudly in my ear.

"Nice try." Simone touched my forehead and I felt my body freeze.

A man with huge biceps and a bald head rolled a large cart, like the home improvement stores supplied to shoppers, to the car and lifted me. He dumped me unceremoniously on the cold unforgiving metal and I landed half on my side, legs sprawled.

I tried to roll over—an effort in futility. The surroundings looked familiar and I stopped struggling, but my mind had trouble processing where we were. "The university?" My throat was barely able to force any sound, and the words came out a whisper.

O'Leary landed on top of me, knocking the air from my

lungs. I grimaced when one of his hands landed on my breast. This was all kinds of wrong. My fingers twitched, but I couldn't move to shove it away.

The twitch empowered me, though. I started focusing on my fingers, my toes, drilling all of my willpower into moving them.

You're more powerful than you realize. Aurora's words rang in my head. How, though? Even with focused effort, I couldn't make any part of me do more. I needed my robes and scythe. At the moment, even my tattoo was silent as the grave.

The cart wheels squeaked, grating against my eardrums, as Simone's minion wheeled us to the biology building. Campus was deserted; not a single person emerged from any of the structures along the way.

She stroked the man's back and made flirty small talk, as he took us to the rear of the brick building. I tried to ignore them and focus on drawing up my power, but the scorching hot kiss he gave her before he pushed us up the ramp to the back entrance made me want to vomit. Smiling wickedly, she whispered something in his ear and waved a hand causing the locked doors to open.

I'd been here many times, completing labs and practicing techniques. In the lower level clinic, I'd sutured wounds, cleaned ears, set and bandaged broken bones. I knew before the minion took the next turn that we were headed for a suite, where a sophisticated operating theater for veterinary students was set up. We all were required to watch various procedures before we could participate in any of them.

After entering the spacious room filled with equipment, a surgical table, and an anesthesia cart, minion shoved the professor off me and unto the floor. A familiar voice said, "You found the grim. Very good."

"Told you I'd bring her to you." Simone leaned forward and jerked my head up by my hair. I saw Cosima and I shouted expletives, which made both of them laugh, because my suggestions regarding what they could do to themselves came out as whispers. They didn't pack much punch.

The adrenaline gave me another power surge, though, and my right leg moved an inch.

While I had none of my weapons, I saw possible ones all around the room. Strange symbols and glyphs had been painted on the ceiling above the surgical table in what appeared to be blood. On top of that, there was a body under a white sheet.

Come on, Chloe, think!

Simone dropped my head and easily tossed me off the cart, where I banged into O'Leary. Neither woman had noticed my leg, and as Cosima assured Simone she would help the vampire cement her position in the Undead Nation, I managed to turn my head and get close to his ear. "Wake up," I shout-whispered. "I know you can do it. Please, Professor, I need your help. So does Megan. Wake up!"

Minion swung the cart around, smacking it into my back. O'Leary blinked and made a low noise in his throat, but resumed his unnatural slumber.

Frustration roared through me and my entire body shook. My back met a wall cabinet near the wash sink, and my foot nailed one of the doors. Luckily, the sound was covered up by the squeaking cart, as the minion headed for the exit.

I can do this. Just...have...to find...my power.

Closing my eyes tight, I dug for it. Aurora had explained it was tied to my emotions, so I tried to ride them, especially the anger burning through me. Her logic seemed accurate, as I searched for all of the emotions, lining them up like soldiers, to test. Who would be the strongest? I had to break free from Simone's grip.

The anger was combined with a good deal of hate for what she had done. On the heels of that came fear she had harmed Killion in her quest to take his place. The heat of it raged and suffused my body. My fingers curled in to fists.

Yes!

Unfortunately, they slackened just as fast. The rage seemed to burn too fast. I opened my eyes, gasping from the exertion.

Cosima rattled on about the surgery and the best way to have O'Leary perform it, but I could see Simone didn't care. The vampire glanced at the door, as if longing to chase down her lover and resume their make out session.

Magnetism. Sexual desire. I brought up the memory of that morning with Killion and warmth poured into my anatomy. I imagined his hands on me, his lips. What it might feel like for his fangs to scrape my skin.

And whoa, boy, my body lit up like a Ferris wheel. I let the fantasy play out, start-to-finish, and nearly self-combusted. I was so caught off guard by the concentrated intensity of my response, I lost control of the energy almost immediately. It scared me to be so strongly attracted to him.

"Where's the bag?" Simone asked.

Cosima withdrew a burlap container like the one Jackal had choked on and tossed it at her. "This should do the trick."

Simone gave it a sniff. "You're sure? This will incapacitate him?"

My blood ran cold. *Killion.*

"Money-back guarantee." Cosima waved her away. "Now, I must get to work."

I screamed out another telepathic message, this one to the master vampire only, but felt helpless. She flipped back the sheet and I gasped. Megan, nearly as white as her covering and stripped of her makeup, appeared twelve rather than sixteen.

Bile rose in my throat. I latched onto the horror of what I anticipated was about to happen and my hands curled into fists once more. I dug in to that feeling, cold steel in my gut.

The pureness of it fed my limbs with a desire to...well, kill. I could hear the scythe whispering the word, even though it wasn't near. The tattoo came to life, as well. I could sense Megan ebbing away, one terrible, slow heartbeat at a time.

A wave of emotion that held all the wrongs done in the world, all the accidents and bad things that had happened to good people, crashed into me. People like my parents.

Their smiling faces flashed through my mind. Happy times, family dinners, vacations to the beach. Homemade cookies and Christmas presents. Them smiling proudly from the audience at my graduation. I shifted ever so slowly onto my hands and knees.

I was wobbly, but neither Simone, nor Cosima, paid me any attention. The vampire glided to the door, ready to escape.

"Wait," Cosima called. "One more thing. Use that strength of yours to get the grim on the table. I need a transfusion of her blood to make this work."

From my place on the floor, I calculated what it would take to reach the surgical tray and its collection of blades.

Simone snarled. "Can't you do anything yourself?"

My legs put up resistance when I attempted to stand and lunge for the tray.

The door opened and Simone jumped back. I would have, too, if I hadn't been under her stifling control. Three grotesque figures shuffled in, each a mix of animal and human.

"I really hate vampires," Cosima said. "You're all so entitled."

The shiftlings sniffed at Simone and she backpedaled, then fled once they turned to Cosima. The room filled with the disgusting odors of the shiftlings, who looked on in silence. A lion, a monkey, and a falcon.

The enchantress motioned them in. "You're late."

With her escape, Simone's magic seeped away. I wanted to stop her and whatever she was about to do, but I had to trust Killion could handle her. My priority had to be Megan. I continued to act incapacitated.

Cosima stepped around the table and headed for Professor O'Leary. The lion peered at me, his mane thin and missing chunks. The scrutiny made my skin crawl. Were he and the others like Jackal, more golem than demi-god? Was there a glyph hidden somewhere on them that I could damage?

"Put the grim on that table over there." Cosima pointed to a second exam table. "I'll get to her in a moment."

I played dead, closing my eyes and going limp. The feel of their hands made my stomach flip, but I couldn't fight all three at once. Better to save my strength for when it really mattered.

Cosima muttered words over O'Leary, and he opened his eyes. She cooed over him for a moment before assisting him to sit up. "There's been a terrible accident," she said, dragging him to his feet and over to see his daughter. "I'm afraid Megan is dying."

His addled brain couldn't make sense of it, and he peppered her with questions as he checked Megan's vitals. Cosima's explanations were vague, but all eyes were on her. I reached for that powerful force inside me again, and primed my rage this time by opening the door to my disheartenment, my grief. That dam had been closed for months, abandoned in the shadows of my heart. Yet, it was still vicious in its torrent, the heartache not having dissipated. If anything, my anguish felt fresh and explosive.

"Only you can save her." Cosima continued her manipulation of the professor with every word. "The deed must be done, and exactly as we discussed. This is your chance! You can put your theories to the test."

He leaned heavily on the table, trying to rouse Megan. "She needs a hospital. A doctor."

"You're a doctor," the enchantress countered. "You can save her. I know you can." She marched to a cage and drew off the covering. I'd paid no attention to it, nor the noise coming from it, and now my pulse raced anew. A panther sprang to its feet and snarled, and Cosima tugged the tray of scalpels close. "Megan would want you to do this for her."

Stunned, I asked, "Aurora?" but it came out too soft to be heard.

Cosima stroked O'Leary's hand. His expression softened. Every touch, every word, held magic.

She began dressing him in surgical garments, keeping him facing away from her guests. After leaving me on the second table, the lion continued to peer at me, and I feared he was aware of my subterfuge.

I dug deeper into the wellspring of magic, willing myself to bring forth power. What kind, I had no idea, but when I focused on the ceiling and saw the symbols inside the circle, a fissure of enlightenment popped in my brain. I was a grim and a necromancer. I could raise dead animals simply by being near them—no spell or symbol required.

One of the sigils was the same eye from Megan's shirt. It seemed to glow brighter than the others. Another was a glyph like the one on the paper that had been in Jackal's mouth. If I could mar it in some way, would the creatures die?

Cosima picked up a scalpel and handed it to O'Leary.

As she did, I poured all my will into resurrecting the dead in the room.

Granted, the shiftlings appeared to be alive, but they'd taken on the abilities of the innocent animals they'd been merged with. The souls of the lion, falcon, and monkey were no longer present. *They* weren't alive, in the strictest sense of the word.

"We'll begin with something simple," Cosima purred to my professor. "The liver. Then we'll replace your daughter's eyes with those of the panther's."

Organ transplant, *simple?*

Perhaps with magic it was. My suspicious nature told me she had no interest in making Megan a hybrid, however, but she needed the girl's organs. Most likely to replace those mummified versions in the shiflings.

"But we can't," O'Leary argued. "That is a specialized..."

Once more, Cosima laid a hand on him, and his words drifted off, the glazed look returning to his eyes. "You'll make history. Megan will live on in infamy and you'll be a worldwide success. Go ahead and start. I'll set up the blood transfusion."

In a zombie state, he accepted the scalpel.

Now or never. I rolled off and surged to my feet. Cosima's hand shot out, lightning bolts crackling. I dodged left and most of them missed me, but white hot pain raked my arm where one struck. The skin sizzled. I cried out, and swore maliciously.

"You can't fight me, and you can't run." She took a step in my direction. "And why would you want to? I can give you the world, Grim Zero, but you must work with me. Stop this pointless resistance and join us, or this will end like last time."

She continued her advance and I backed up, running into the wash station. "All I need are a few drops of your blood."

Over my dead... Maybe I shouldn't tempt fate. "Your contract is up." My voice was barely audible. I sounded as though I had been screaming all night at a rock concert. "You're noncompliant. I'm here to reap you and your...shiftlings."

She stopped, gave me an incredulous look, and laughed. "You couldn't reap a fly right now."

My palm seared with heat, as if the death blade rested in my palm, ready to work. *Kill*, it whispered again in my ear.

Another power-tripping surge rippled through me, this one as ancient as hers. It started at my toes and rocketed up my body, reminding me of who I really was. *I am Grim Zero.*

The acknowledgement gave me a burst of strength. Knowingness. I had done this before. I could do it again—and be smarter about it.

I smiled at her, a calm steeling over me. "Let's give it a try."

She lunged, her magic slamming into me like a freight

train. Her ringed fingers went around my neck and she lifted me off the floor. Fresh waves of agony shot through me as she worked at crushing my windpipe.

I slammed a hand against her chest. She grunted, and under my palm, I sensed her heartbeat. The *thudthudthud* echoed through my system. The rush of her blood sounded in my ears.

Next to her heart sat the seat of her soul.

Her spirit was strong and fought, but there was a subtle click when my grim power latched onto it. Her eyes widened—she felt it, too. The torrent inside me intensified, while her creatures shuffled toward us, ready to defend her.

My fingers splayed and I felt a heady rush. Her spirit lost some of its fight. *Come to me.*

She swayed. Her grip on my neck loosened. One of her hands attempted to knock mine from her chest. "Nooo!"

Thunder boomed—not outside.

In the room.

She dropped me, but I stayed standing, grabbing the back of her neck with my free hand so I could keep my other pressed against her beating heart. A heart that was slowing, skipping, coming to a halt.

My vision blurred and I felt it—the moment her soul released itself to my care.

She muttered in another language, words to thwart me, but her knees gave out, her physical body no longer able to resist. The shiftlings stopped their advance.

Gasping, I held on, staring into her eyes. Confusion and fear danced in them. I felt no guilt at all. "Cosima," I purred. "You've been reaped."

The light left her eyes. She crumpled to the ground.

I let her, eyeing the confused shiftlings.

Professor O'Leary blinked at me, waking from his

dream state and staring at her corpse. "What happened?" He glanced around, fear clear on his features as he took in the creatures, the cage with the pissed off panther, and Megan. All his attention zeroed in on her. He shook her, and checked for a pulse. His horrified gaze came up to meet mine. "What have you done?"

Before I could answer, the shiftlings attacked.

FORTY-ONE

L ion knocked me on my back, stronger than I anticipated seeing as his creator was dead.

"Get Megan out of here," I yelled at O'Leary.

Lion lunged for me and I rolled, then crawled to the panther, who was clawing at the bars. It possessed those crystal blue eyes that were so familiar. "Please be Aurora," I muttered under my breath. As I released the hatch, she bolted. At the same time, the falcon drove its beak into my shoulder.

Aurora took it down with a giant paw, her panther sleek and completely enraged. As the two fought, O'Leary lifted Megan from the surgical table and ran for the door.

Monkey waylaid him, and the lion once more pounced on me.

He pinned me under him, warm blood from my shoulder soaking my shirt. I peered up into his golden eyes. "Come to me," I said, shoving away my fear of the leering teeth that were as long as my hand. "Remember who you are, what you once were." My voice was jagged, shaky.

"Wake up from the nightmare. Come back to the land of the living."

The beast roared and I cringed. The sounds of bones cracking and popping filled my ears. The circle of images overhead quaked, a split creating a jagged break through one heavy coal line. The ground shook, items falling from the shelves. The falcon and monkey stopped to glance around.

Aurora took advantage of the distraction and sunk her teeth into the bird's throat. Above me, his companion fought the shift happening to his mixed-up body. The animal's screams of pain echoed through the room.

More plaster rained down from the ceiling. A large chunk crashed next to my head and I peeked over to see the eye of Ra staring back.

Spittle hit my cheek and when I dared glance at the lion, I saw he was more animal than human now. It seemed oddly weird to encourage the shift, since he was likely to maul me to death, but I did. "You didn't deserve what happened to you and I'm sorry," I croaked. My mouth felt like it was filled with plaster dust. My blood continued to run out of me and I felt lightheaded. "It's time to take back your life. To be whole and wild again."

I could feel Cosima's ghost hovering nearby and arguing with me. Even in death, she was trying to control what was happening. "You'll lose everything!" her voice rose over the cacophony as she shouted to her shiftlings. "Don't let her change you. We can still rule the world!"

I'd had enough of her. "Shut it, already." I fought the encroaching darkness. "Save...Megan..." I called to O'Leary and Aurora.

I could no longer see what had happened to the falcon, the monkey, or the panther. The animal morphing over me bellowed once more, blocking out the light. The energy of the room went electric, and I covered my head. Had I done something worse than the enchantress?

The ground stopped shaking and a weird, eerie silence fell. My various pains came rushing back in all their glory and I moaned, my arms going limp. But I felt a weak bliss filling my chest—the kind that came when a soul passed over. For a second, I wondered if it was mine.

A wet tongue licked my cheek. Hot breath wafted over my face. I cracked open one eye, then the other. The lion's face was only a few inches from mine, a look of gratitude in his eyes. He was no longer a shiftling, only an animal.

The bliss I'd felt was his soul coming back.

I'd actually wondered if animals had them, but now I knew.

"What a crazy mess," Death said, peering at me over the now beautiful mane. "I told you to get some sleep and we'd do this tomorrow. Don't you ever follow directions?"

Andy rushed in, completely unafraid of the beast. I scooted out from under the lion, my shoulder on fire and blood everywhere. Death grabbed hold of my good arm and helped me stand. I was woozy and I canted sideways. He caught me before I fell. "Whoa there, Grave Girl. Take it easy."

I glanced around and saw Aurora was her human self again, the falcon one hundred percent bird. The witch was attending to O'Leary and Megan, who were huddled on the floor near the open door.

I scanned the destroyed suite for Cosima's ghost, but didn't see her. "She's gone." I pointed half-heartedly at the exit. My arm felt like it weighed two tons. "Her shade escaped."

Death held a hand over my ripped up shoulder and it

began to mend itself. "Nah, Ghost crossed her, and not to the light." He winked.

When I glanced at where her body had been, only a mound of what looked like sawdust remained. I knew what that meant.

I held my throbbing arm, the pulse of my dripping blood keeping the beat with the drum in my head. "Ghost is okay?"

He was no longer wearing the suit and was back to distressed jeans and a tight t-shirt. "Of course."

"You're about to reap this girl, whether you want to or not," Aurora said. "I can't save her. She's too far gone. Unless you want me to…" She paused and sighed, glancing at O'Leary. "You know."

Use her necromancy. I shivered.

O'Leary rocked Megan in his arms, begging her in a low voice not to die. Tears streaked down his cheeks.

I glanced at Death. "Well? Save her. Her contract's not up."

"Her father's is, and you know how SMG is regarding universal balance."

A soul for a soul. Grim Manual Statute 6-32A. "I just reaped Cosima—a horrible being all the way around, and took out three shiftlings. That should count for something."

The lion and Andy flanked me, both leaning against my legs. Ghost popped in and rushed into my arms, thankfully as her puppy self and not her psychopomp. I caught her and hugged her tight as she licked my face.

"She's gone," Aurora said, and O'Leary let out a wail.

"No." I shuffled toward them, but it was too late.

Her spirit broke free from her body and she looked straight at me. "Do something," she ordered, seething. "This is your fault."

It wasn't, but... I turned on Death. "You owe me. I just stopped an apocalypse."

"Chloe, the rules are the rules."

My old friend injustice, and the anger that came with it, reared up once more, cold and icy inside me. "What do you want? I'll do it."

He gave me a sad smile. "You have to let people die."

I flung out my hand, pointing at Megan. "She's an innocent girl."

He used his reasonable tone. "Not that innocent. She was dabbling in dark, ancient magic, and that's why Cosima used her."

Megan's ghost zoomed over, and I realized she could hear and see him. "I didn't know." She reached for me, now all big eyes and a victim. "Tell him. I'm too young to die."

Death ignored her to speak to me "You didn't reap Andy, you interfered with your professor's contract, and now you want me to bring this girl back to life?"

"Yes." I stepped forward and pointed at myself. "Take me in her place."

FORTY-TWO

Death laughed. Huge guffaws that sent him reeling and he had to balance himself on the counter. More plaster fell as the echoes engulfed us and he grabbed his belly like Santa Claus. "Good one, Chloe," he said, finally. He wiped tears from the corners of his eyes.

"I'm serious." I reached for a scalpel and held it to my neck. "A soul for a soul."

Lightning fast, he grabbed my arm and squeezed, the pressure causing me to cry out and drop the weapon. "We all know you'd just come back to life," he said in a low, dangerous voice. "That's hardly a bargaining chip."

Yet, I'd seen a flicker of fear in his eyes. "There has to be a way."

"There is, if you reap her father." He lowered his face so it was an inch from mine and my body buzzed with his closeness. Nothing better than Death staring you in the face. "Stop interfering with contracts."

"No," Megan cried. "You can't kill my dad!"

The man in question was still bent over her corpse in grief. I tried to bring myself to do it, but I couldn't. There was no right answer here, and it left me in quicksand. I was unable to make a choice, drowning because of it.

Aurora stood and leaned against the wall, looking worn out. I knew the feeling. My emotions were my strength, she'd told me, but this time, I had to shut them down.

I could let her raise the girl, but Death would just kill her again, or take O'Leary or Aurora. I considered sacrificing the lion, but that wasn't right either.

I drew on what I'd experienced when the amulet had shown me the endless loop of time. I now realized it hadn't been a vampire's perspective—it had been Grim Zero's. There was no painful decisions, only strategic ones. Life and death were abstract, remote, yet each contained the seed of the other. The yin and yang of the universe.

An unaccustomed calmness stole over me. A centered, emotionless void. "I quit," I told Death and headed for the door. "I'll turn in my robes and scythe to Killion."

Killion—was he even alive? There was one more entity I was going to reap, but the rest of it? *I am done.*

"Wait." Megan trailed along beside me, floating several inches off the floor. "You can't leave me here like this."

I glanced at her on my way past her father. "I'm sorry." I knew Death would wipe O'Leary's memory, but he'd have to create a reason for Megan's demise.

Aurora pushed off the wall, Andy joining her. "We're coming with you."

"Chloe." Death's voice was more annoyed than commanding. "You're upset. I get it. But—"

Ghost barked and bolted after me. I slammed the door and started jogging down the corridor. I needed to hurry.

Aurora and the wolf followed. "Did you just quit your grim job?" she asked.

I raced down the steps, a fresh energy surfacing from somewhere. "Sure did."

Ghost and Andy took the lead, almost playful in their exuberance. Seeming to also catch a second wind, Aurora kept up with me. "That was impressive. Even I hadn't thought of resurrecting those animals to overtake the bodies." She glanced around. "Where are we going?"

"To find my..." I started to say *mentor*. That didn't begin to fit anymore. "Killion. I think he's in trouble."

On the sidewalk, we stopped and Aurora surveyed the area. "And where is he, exactly?"

I actually had no idea. Later, I knew my guilt over Megan would eat me alive, but I had to be sure Killion was okay. I glanced around and made sure the girl's ghost wasn't following. She wasn't. I turned to the shifter. "Can you track him?"

One of Andy's paws slapped the ground, and I felt immense relief. Dante's Grove was not a big city, but Killion could be anywhere.

"We need a vehicle." Aurora said, focused on the parking lot.

"Do you have your cell phone?" I called after her.

"Sure, I keep it in my panther's back pocket." She grinned. "Sorry, I didn't have it on me when Cosima showed up. I went panther on her, but she darted me." She rubbed her right buttock through her dress, then pointed at the professor's van two rows over. "We'll take that."

"Doesn't Andy have to keep his nose on the ground?"

She chuckled. "He can stick his big head out the window and catch the scent on the air."

Color me impressed. Maybe that's how he'd found me. "You're pretty cool," I said to the shifter. "You know that?"

He leaned over and licked my face. "Rixer."

Fixer. Yes, he was. I wiped off my cheek with exaggerated disgust. "Save that for your girlfriend."

"I'll pass," she said, but I saw the smile she tried to hide.

The van doors were locked and we had no keys. It also seemed wrong to steal the professor's vehicle on top of everything else. She made some sort of motion with her fingers and a *thunk* echoed through the air.

That's when I noticed a slick, black limo pulling in. "Wait," I said, running to meet it, and praying Killion was alive and well inside.

Moss stopped, his window down. "Master's in trouble, Grave Girl." He hitched a thumb over his shoulder. "Get in."

Aurora backed away. "I'll follow in the van."

I grabbed her hand. "No way. You go with us."

Vampire and witch glared at each other. Moss' upper lip curled, revealing his fangs. "Her kind don't ride in the master's—"

"She's my friend, like you." I manhandled Aurora to the back door and shoved her inside. Andy followed. "You can take it up with Killion after we save him."

Moss sighed loudly, revved the engine, and we were off.

FORTY-THREE

Real thunder boomed, the skies alive with lightning as we sped through an inky black storm. It was more suitable for early summer than late December, but the universal balance had definitely been upended. The result seemed to cause Mother Nature to lash out, as well.

It felt as though I had lost days rather than hours, fresh adrenaline warring with my already overloaded nervous system. The Grim Zero detachment was fading, and my anger at Simone took its place. "What has she done?" I asked Moss. "How bad is it?"

The limo purred as we took a side street. "She's incapacitated him. I don't know how, only the end result. She's taking over."

Cosima's bag. How could anyone do that to a master vampire? Even in the state I'd last seen him, he was still a powerful entity. He hadn't lived for centuries by being careless or vulnerable. "I knew he wasn't feeling good. I should have done something for him."

Aurora glanced my way. The shifter lay on the floor at our feet. Ghost was in my lap. "You can't save everyone."

How many times had I heard that recently? I was tired of it. "Cosima concocted an enchantment to render him weak, so Simone could get the upper hand. I should have seen that coming."

" I saw it." A concerned, pensive expression passed over her features. "Could be an actual hex bag this time, but vampires are too smart for that kind of thing. They can smell it."

"He didn't scent the one we found lodged in Jackal's throat."

"That wasn't a hex bag, remember? That was simply to animate the creature and send it to Simone's for the so called attack."

A phone rang from inside the cabinet under the seat. Moss glanced at me in the rearview. "That's yours. I found it at the penthouse."

I scrambled to remove it from its hiding place and found a message from Nita. It felt so...normal, and I nearly laughed with relief. "Speaking of, that's weird, but some-one's responded to my lost and found for Corvus." I typed out a quick response, telling my friend I'd already found the owner. "Guess someone else is missing a talking raven."

Aurora smiled and winked. "It is Dante's Grove. There are plenty of talking animals around here. Magic practition-ers, too."

Too many, in my opinion.

There was another message, this one from Dr. Maxwell, my grief counselor. I hadn't sent her my journal pages and she wanted to make sure I was going to show up for my appointment before Christmas. "Ugg." I dropped my head back on the seat. I hadn't touched my journal in two weeks. I would blow her off, but Death had made me agree to keep seeing her, and maybe, just maybe, it was actually helping me. "Christmas break is not going at all like I anticipated."

The storm raged, sheets of water coating the windows as we turned onto the street where the church sort of existed. While Killion had told me it hovered in a space between the visible and invisible worlds, right now it looked more *in*visible, and the usual magic aura I saw around it was a sickly green.

Andy whined as Moss cruised slowly into the lot in front and paused. "Where do your clothes go when you transfigure?" I asked Aurora, my pulse racing at what awaited us. "Is it like with shifters?"

"Similar. A different dimension, like limbo. It took me a while to discover how to get them back when I started out. I had a couple oopsies." She grinned, embarrassed, as she peered through the foggy windows at the scene in front of us. "Nothing like morphing back to human form completely naked, or with your underwear on your head."

The image made me chuckle through my nerves. "I would have liked to have seen that."

"Ree roo," Andy added.

She toed him in his ribs good-naturedly. "Chloe, do you want me to transfigure and go in as my panther?"

"Not sure. We're facing a vampire. What's your preference?"

She bit her bottom lip. "Witch. I can sling spells that way. If need be, I'll transfigure."

My palm tingled. "Did you find my scythe, too?" I called to Moss.

He grabbed something off the passenger seat. "Got your bag right here."

I reached for it as he held it out. "You're a lifesaver."

"Um, Grave Girl?" He pointed out the windshield.

Thick fog was rolling in. "I think we've got another problem."

I followed the direction of his finger but had to use a sleeve to wipe condensation from my window. The temperature continued to drop. "I don't understand," I said in disbelief.

Aurora leaned across me to peer out as I continued wiping, hoping that might clear my vision.

It didn't work. I'd expected vampire sentries, Simone's personal legion protecting her while she did away with Killion. If he was injured or threatened, his nest usually came to his rescue—I'd observed that firsthand. The overgrown parking lot and the old creepy, graveyard were there, just like always, but there were no vampires.

In fact, the main attraction—the church—had now disappeared as well.

FORTY-FOUR

"Okay, I may be wrong,"—I gripped the door handle so tightly my knuckles went white—"but medieval churches don't vanish into thin air."

Moss put the limo in park. "This one is no ordinary place of worship."

I explained about the church to Aurora and Andy. "Where did it go, Moss? Is it in some other realm? Did Simone do this? And where are the other vampires? When Killion was dying here at Halloween, you all descended on this place like a pack of—" I stopped myself and Andy whined. "You felt his distress, right?"

He studied the murky spot where the church should be. The wipers worked furiously to offset the pouring rain. He ramped up the defrost, but nothing could keep up with the condensation. The vehicle's lights disappeared into the fog. "I don't know how she could make the church disappear, but the place is certainly not in this reality. As far as my fellow Undead, they have not been alerted to the master's condition, or they would be here. The magic Simone is using is powerful indeed."

As I concentrated on the empty block where the formidable building normally stood, I could once more make out the sickly green glow it was emanating. "Can the church be both here and there? Like a liminal space?"

Moss considered it. "Anything's possible." He squinted. "It seems to be shifting back and forth."

A monochrome image of it appeared, shuddered, and disappeared once more. "I'm going in."

"How?" Aurora asked. "What if you end up in that in-between space?"

"After all my near-death experiences, I can walk in the ghost world, as well as this one. I'm certain that means I can hop into whatever dimension she's taken Killion to. Hopefully, I don't leave my clothes there and come back naked."

Aurora frowned at my attempt at humor. "Chloe, be serious."

"Look, the church gives off a...vibe. I can see its magic—barely—but if the place is there physically, even for a moment, I'll feel my way inside."

"And take on Simone alone?" Aurora shook her head. Moss was doing the same. "That's a stupid plan."

"Thanks for your support."

Moss put the limo in drive to get me closer to the invisible front steps, but I stopped him and opened my door. "You guys stay here. I'll be back."

Frigid rain drenched me the instant I stepped out, and I sucked in a sharp breath. The pea soup was so thick, it stuck to my clothes. This was no ordinary fog. I tucked my coat closer, even though it did no good, and blinked rapidly as I hustled for the spot where the entrance should be.

As if they sensed me, Katarina's dogs appeared, their fur soaked and muddy. Tails between their legs and ears flat, they slunk forward, their fearful whines chilling me as much as the storm.

"What's going on?" I murmured as I petted their wet heads. "Where's your master?

They both glanced at the MIA church.

Was Katarina in on this? She didn't care for me, but always seemed loyal to Killion. He'd never spoken ill of her. Had Simone kidnapped her, too?

It was one thing to stop Simone from overthrowing Killion, and I was prepared to die trying, but she'd outsmarted me. She'd taken him, and possibly the church's caretaker, to the one place she could have the ultimate control and keep me out—an invisible dimension.

Except, as I stood there, where the steps to the entrance usually were, I felt magic pulsing, pushing on my skin. Through the rain and the gloom, the building's glow brightened.

Ah ha. It was if it felt me and wanted me to help. That's all the encouragement I needed. As though I wore some kind of magic vision goggles, I could suddenly see it more clearly.

Along with that, I felt my blood warm.

Killion was here, and he was alive.

Returning to the limo, I wiped rain from my face. Killion would string me up for getting water on the expensive leather, but I would welcome it. "The church and Killion are definitely here," I said. Katarina's pets sat outside, staring at me, lost and forlorn. "Simone has glamoured the building." Giddiness rippled through me. "She doesn't have enough power to take it in to another dimension."

"Well, in that case." Aurora held out both hands toward

the church and muttered a spell. The sickly green aura again brightened and the spires came into view, poking through the fog.

"I don't need to see the whole thing," I told her. "Just reveal the doors."

She refocused and soon the ancient wooden slabs shimmered into view. I clapped and hooted. The dogs turned and saw them, too, and raced to the sidewalk.

"The stairs would be helpful," I added.

Bingo, the concrete steps to the landing appeared. The animals bounded up them and scratched at the wooden doors.

"Brilliant." I grabbed my bag and jumped out once more.

Although it was still pouring, I took a quick moment to don the robes and secure the leather holder on my back, sliding the scythe into it. Aurora, Andy, Moss, and Ghost, lined up on either side of me. I looked over the motley crew, including Katarina's pets, wanting to tell them it wasn't safe and they should stay here, but I could see the determination in their eyes.

I nodded my appreciation. It *was* too dangerous for them, but I knew it was pointless to try and talk them out of coming with me.

"Don't take foolish chances," I instructed over the din of the storm. "I'm the grim. I'll deal with Simone. Ghost, you're with me." The dog wagged furiously and then morphed into her psychopomp version. "Moss, take out any Undead in there protecting her or contriving with her against your master. Aurora, if Killion's injured, you heal him. Everyone clear?"

The witch and vampire nodded. The dogs panted. Andy smacked the ground with a paw.

"Okay, then." I drew out the death blade and rubbed my thumb over the hilt. Everything in me vibrated. I put a hand to my chest, hoping the warmth in my blood didn't go out. "Let's go get him."

FORTY-FIVE

The church doors groaned as we entered, the only light provided by candles in various holders on the stone walls.

My vision adapted rapidly, and the cemetery pets hustled to the right and a prone figure, I feared Katarina was a casualty in this coup d'état. I directed Moss to check on her.

I held up my weapon, facing the corridor that led to the nave. The perfect place for Simone to lure Killion and then overtake him. The coppery scent of fresh blood teased my nose, but my veins sang with Killion's nearness. "He's definitely here," I murmured. Ghost wagged her giant tail, nearly knocking over a candle.

"Kat's not dead yet." Moss returned to my side. "But she is catatonic."

Being the magical church's caretaker, she was probably best kept alive until Simone's task was finished. The place was connected to her in ways I didn't understand, and I wasn't sure what might happen should she expire. Would it simply cease to exist? "Can you wake her?"

He gave a bleak shake of his head. "I've never had the ability. Only the elite of my kind can put people in stasis and bring them back." It was said as though he were offering an explanation about why he was a driver.

"I might be able to help with that," Aurora volunteered. Moss and I both glanced at her. She shrugged. "If you run with shifters, you learn a few things."

Andy twitched his ears. Which begged a question I'd been meaning to ask. "Why him?"

He gave the witch a smoldering look, and she grinned. "I have a weakness for wild things."

I tipped my head at Katarina. "We could use her help, if you can."

"It's really just a matter of switching the receptors in her brain to—"

I held up a hand. "Explanation not needed, just do it. Moss and I will scout the nave. See what the situation looks like."

"Be careful." She waved a hand over us, murmuring a spell. "This might keep her from sensing you."

I suspected she already had, but so far, Simone hadn't appeared. Maybe there was some actual luck in that rabbit's foot hanging from Andy's neck. On silent feet, Moss and I stalked down the corridor, Ghost and wolf behind us. As far as I knew, it was impossible to sneak up on a vampire, and the element of surprise could mean the difference between success and sure death.

But if she ended my life, would I stay dead?

I tried not to think about it as we paused outside the massive double doors leading into the heart of the building. Carved into the ancient wood, Archangel Michael was striking down a dragon. I knew more about the angel now, and regarded his likeness differently than I had before. Religious followers would assume the engraving depicted the triumph of good over evil, but my reading had indicated there was more to it than that. The dragon represented the supernatural. The stuff of myths and magic. The angel, being the Church, was determined to snuff magic, and all supernaturals, from Earth.

Sweat trickled down my back. While I prayed—I *was* in church, after all—that Simone wasn't aware of us, I most certainly could sense and smell her. The bitter odor of vinegar mixed with the scent of blood.

The familiar warmth in my veins was waning, Killion's connection to me growing weaker by the moment. Placing one ear near the dragon on the door, I held my breath and listened. All I heard was sucking sounds.

She's draining him.

Like a wildfire, renewed rage swept through my limbs and licked up my spine. Moss must have sensed it—he drew back, as though I might explode. Ghost simply continued to wag her tail, eyes gleaming in the candlelight.

My palm heated like I held fire rather than the scythe. My arm vibrated as I adjusted my grip, the handle searing through my skin. *Kill*, it whispered. Someone's contract was up—I just hoped it wasn't mine.

While part of me wanted to kick the doors in and storm inside, logic kept me from doing so. Getting myself killed without saving Killion was reckless, and although my mentor, and even Death himself, considered me to be so, I understood the gravity of this situation beyond a shadow of a doubt. Simone was an apex predator, growing stronger with every gulp. My best play would need cunning and a bluff the size of Kansas.

So rather than shoving in and rushing her, I did the opposite—I knocked politely.

Moss' brows hit his hairline. He shook his head wildly, and I motioned for him to slide back into the shadows. I also gave Ghost the silent command to sit.

They both followed my orders, but nothing else happened.

I needed to draw her away from Killion. She had to be wondering who or what was out here. I knocked again.

I sensed her move this time, confirming that even a powerful vampire possessed enough curiosity to be drawn to the sound. "Cosima?"

Maybe I had the enchantress' scent on me, fooling her.

Third time's a charm. I hid the scythe behind my back and picked up the Madonna statue in the alcove.

Bangbangbang.

She wasn't fooled. With lightning fast speed, she threw open the doors, hissing and swinging her claws.

I dodged in the nick of time. My palm went crazy, itching like it always did when it was time to reap someone. "Hey," I said brightly. "Hate to bother you, but—" I smacked her in the stomach with the statue.

She doubled over and stumbled backwards. As I stepped into the nave, she rebounded and swung again at my face.

I sidestepped, but she got my earlobe this time. I pivoted and brought the scythe around, aiming for her neck.

The death blade sang with delight.

Simone eluded it, her supernatural abilities allowing to hinge at the hips, her upper torso falling back. She straightened once more with grace and I felt like I was in a Matrix movie.

Her claws caught my arm and I lunged and tried again to slice her with the blade. Too fast for me to track, she kicked out and caught my knee.

A loud crack sounded and I felt the pain, but adrenaline, combined with the scythe, kept me moving. It tugged me forward and took my body in a dance with hers. I yelled like a banshee and swung again and again.

She easily evaded each of my blows. She'd drank the blood of a master vampire and filled herself with it. Without it, she was a lethal weapon—with the blood, she was unbeatable.

We continued the parlay. I'd lunge, she'd swerve, then she'd attack and I'd do the same. Her face was as red as her lips and eyes. Enraged, she roared, fangs elongated.

My blood turned to ice. I saw her skin ripple with her new power, and realized she was shifting into her true vampire form.

I'd witnessed Killion's once, and it was horror movie worthy. Hers was similar, the nails becoming actual claws, the teeth, gnashing knives that could rip through me with ease.

Going head to head with her wasn't working. I needed a new tactic and I was desperate. I held out the blade. "What do you see?"

In serious fight mode, the question confounded her. Her monsterish head cocked to the side and her red gaze zoomed in on the sharp steel. Her nostrils flared and I saw it—blood.

For a moment, I thought I was seeing what she lusted for, but then realized, the blood coating the scythe, including the handle, ran between *my* fingers.

In my peripheral vision, I saw a body lying motionless on the dais. I also caught sight of a portion of my ear lying on the stone floor. She'd hacked it off. The blood was real and flowed profusely down my arm like a waterfall.

Moss and Ghost circled behind us, both sniffing the air. Simone growled at them and Moss froze, but Ghost kept going. Simone started to take a step toward the psychopomp and I cut her off by placing my body between her and the dog. I needed to distract her. "Wow, I'm woozy after the blood loss." I held out the blade as though I was handing it to her. "I surrender."

She threw her head back and loosed a spine tingling noise—a primal sound of laughter. Or possibly, success?

I felt Killion's energy respond. It was there and then gone, but it gave me hope. He wasn't dead yet.

"I'm serious," I told the creature in front of me. "I can't do this grim stuff anymore. I hate it. Just kill me and get it over with."

Her beady eyes sized me up. One distorted hand reached out and her nostrils flared as she eyed my blood with relish. Her fingers touched the steel, wrapping around the blade to take it from me.

"There's just one thing," I said, flashing my too-bright smile again. I hadn't lied about being woozy. My body trembled from shock and waves of pain. My vision was beginning to blur. "You've been reaped."

Her eyes went wide and she attempted to jerk away. Too late, I sliced the blade into her stomach, Ghost leaped and Simone's spirit exited her monstrous body.

I watched her physical form drop in a lump of skin and bones. It quickly turned to sawdust and *poof*, her spirit winked out.

Moss rushed forward, catching me as my legs crumbled. He kept me upright, making sure to avoid the blade. I was too weak to hold it and let it slide to the floor. "I can't believe it. You actually did it! You killed her."

My blood was everywhere. "No thanks to you," I mumbled.

"You said to stay out of danger."

I rolled my eyes and pointed. "Killion."

He drew my arm around his shoulders and guided me to the vampire. Killion had been secured with metal cuffs to a table, and my stomach lurched seeing him so still, so pale.

Aurora and Katarina arrived, Andy and the two dogs with them. Katarina gave me an odd nod of appreciation. "Thank you."

"You can grovel at my feet later." The room was starting to fade in and out, but I saw her sneer good-naturedly. Ghost returned. Andy whined, leaning into my thigh, as if to support me. I turned my focus back to Killion, the bloody puncture holes on his neck, his arms. She'd removed his shirt, baring his upper body and had been sucking him dry.

Vampire-on-vampire violence. "She wanted his power, his memories, his intelligence." Katarina bared her fangs, anger rolling off her. "Bring her back, so I can kill her again."

"His memories?" I questioned.

"Our blood holds all of that and more."

I let go of Moss and stroked Killion's hair. His essence was so faint, I couldn't detect it anymore. I leaned down. "We're going to get help. Hang on. For me." To Moss and Katarina, I asked, "What do we do?"

They exchanged a distressed look. "He needs blood," Moss told me. "Not synthetic, the real thing. Human."

All eyes landed on me. Aurora bit her bottom lip.

My stomach clenched. "I don't want to be...a vampire, and I've already had some of *his* blood. If I give him mine, won't that...you know?"

Katarina snarled at me. "That's not how you become one of us, idiot."

Aurora touched my ear and muttered an incantation. The pain stopped, as did the bleeding. I reached up and realized the lobe was back to normal. She really was a healer. "You can do something for him, right?"

She stroked my arm. "Vampire healing is about the blood. All he needs is enough to keep him alive until we find a more willing donor."

"You're onboard with this?"

She looked green at the thought, but nodded. "Considering the way he feels about witches, I'm sure he'd choose you, but if you won't, I guess I'll have to."

A small part of me rejected the idea of anyone else feeding him. A willing donor, indeed. Yet, I couldn't bring myself to feel happy about giving him a Chloe transfusion.

This was my life now. Vampires, shifters, witches. I swayed, grabbing onto the table.

His hand brushed my fingers. Glancing down, I found his eyes slitted open. He spoke softly, barely a whisper. I had to lean closer to hear him. "It's...okay. You don't have to...feed me."

"He'll die if you don't," Katarina stated, her glare intense, and those elongated fangs promising my end.

It wasn't her threat that made my resolve crumble. Seeing Killion's violet eyes as faded as his skin tone, feeling his weak touch, made the day's events press down on me like a three-ton weight. Megan hadn't deserved to die, and Killion didn't either. If I had to stick around and play grim, I wasn't doing it without him.

"Don't think you're getting out of being my partner that easy." Taking a deep breath, I motioned for Aurora to hand me the scythe. As she steadied my arm, I held the blade above my wrist.

Calling on all of my courage, I cut the sensitive skin and put it to his lips. "Drink," I ordered, and closed my eyes when his mouth latched on.

FORTY-SIX

In movies, a vampire's bite is portrayed as blissful and sexy. This was anything but.

First of all, I didn't expect him to sink his teeth in so deeply, since I was already bleeding. The tender skin gave easily, the piercing incisors like daggers as they sought my pulsing veins. I gasped and gripped his raven black waves with my free hand.

On the third pull, as I tried to find my voice through the loud thumping between my ears, the room dipped. My knees buckled, and I locked them in place. Aurora held my waist, steadying me.

Maybe this hadn't been the best idea.

"Stop," I managed to get out, but it was weak, sounding more like a whine than a command. I tried to yank him away, but it did no good. "Please, Killion."

Second, his transformation was nearly instant. My blood seemed to literally raise him from near-death. He sat up and gripped my arm tight with both hands, keeping me locked in place. His lips continued to draw on me, an animalistic hunger for survival raging through him that I could feel in my own body.

Definitely not a good idea.

Trying to save everyone was backfiring on me again. I trembled, blinking away the spots dancing in front of my eyes. My bad knee refused to hold and gave out. I faltered, falling against the table. Aurora and Moss grabbed on to keep me standing. "Master," Moss said, and it held an edge of warning.

Aurora joined in. "Enough. She said 'stop.' She's already lost blood. Killion!"

"Master Killion Reveux." Moss took all my weight, as my body went numb. The thrumming in my head morphed into a high-pitch hum. His hold, along with Killion's, was all that kept me upright. "You must leave her be."

Too bad that wasn't his real name. While it might still hold sway with him to an extent, only that elusive secret identity could give Moss dominance over a master vampire.

Ghost howled. Andy joined in.

Aurora said something else, but the noise in my head muffled it. She dug in my pocket where the amulet was tucked. Through my dimming vision, I watched as she slammed the stone into Killion's forehead.

His reaction was swift and downright frightening. He released me so quickly, I snapped backward, sending Moss and myself staggering. He bared his fangs at Aurora, their normally sharp, white tips dripping blood, and ripped the crystal from her. With incredible, and surprising strength, he crushed it in his hand.

The ringing in my ears cleared, and I held up my injured wrist, hoping to stem the bleeding. Aurora snarled back at Killion, her eyes turning the ice blue shade of her panther.

Oh boy.

His lips were smeared with my blood, his own eyes wild with power and lust. The two locked into a deadly glare, and I swallowed hard to clear my throat. "I'm okay," I said weakly. "We're all friends here. Everybody take a breath and—"

Killion threw the busted crystal pieces at Aurora, hard. The sharp edges sliced into her skin, drawing blood on her chin, her neck. She hit him with a spell, and his head snapped back, his already red eyes going crimson with rage.

Kill, the song of the death blade rang in my head.

Breaking free from Moss, I lurched forward and threw myself between them. "Stop." My voice was stronger than I was. "Both of you..."

Not even fear, or my abundance of adrenaline, could overcome my weakened state or my injured knee. It buckled, and I teetered. Moss wasn't quick enough to catch me this time.

For a heartbeat, I seemed suspended, then with a vicious dip, I dropped like a two-ton brick.

I whacked my head—same spot—on the table. My skull ricocheted back, my body twisting, as I hit the ground. I landed in a bloody heap.

Moss and Katarina jumped into the fray, separating the vampire and the witch by extreme force. I heard my name echo through the room, over the din of growls and cries.

Staring up at the overhead lights, the thumping in my skull vibrated like a bass drum. Darkness ghosted along the edges of my vision.

The last thing I saw was Ghost stepping through my blood, the liquid seeping from my destroyed forearm and leeching across the floor. My exhausted body was shutting down—my grim healing given to Killion. A rough tongue licked across my cheek before my vision dissolved into a black void.

FORTY-SEVEN

Eventually, I swam up from the depths of nothingness, my mind and body heavy and dull. I was lying on a soft bed, the main light in the room coming from the open double doors of a veranda.

Body aching, I shifted various parts between the satin sheets that smelled like warm caramel and old libraries. I inventoried my injuries. Knee: sore, but I could bend it without much pain. Arm: bandaged with layers and layers of gauze. Earlobe: healed, but my hearing had a fuzzy layer to it, ebbing and flowing.

Deciding it was better to not move too much, I next inventoried my surroundings: fireplace, sitting area, nightstand, armoire. A gold-framed painting of a dog—Beowulf.

While a fire simmered in the hearth, the cold, crisp air breezing in made me shiver. I was in the penthouse master bedroom, but what idiot had thought it smart to leave the veranda doors open?

I la id there for an eternity, attempting to convince myself I was warm enough. Positive thinking didn't work, and I entertained the idea of calling for Pennyworth. He was probably on high alert, waiting to spring into action. But the quiet, and my mixed feelings about tipping off Killion that I was awake, warred with my laziness.

I wanted to fall back asleep, skip the reckoning that was sure to come. The hard chills that set in, racking my body and causing my teeth to chatter, forced me to admit that wasn't going to happen.

Shifting to my side, I slowly propped myself on an elbow, glad when the shadowy room didn't tilt or spin. I felt no pain from my injured arm, but found it now tangled in intravenous tubing.

Gingerly, I sat up, blinking away the fogginess in my brain. An IV bag was nearly empty, shriveling in on itself, and a second empty bag was on the pole with it. It appeared to have held blood.

Clinging to the edge of the bed, I grit my teeth and yanked out the needle. A drop of blood at the injection site formed and I stared at it for a moment, precious stuff that it was. It's effect on reviving Killion had been riveting...and disturbing.

My weak body fighting me, I found my footing and noted I was wearing nothing but a man's royal blue pajama top. Unbelievably soft and comfortable, it was at least two sizes too big and had Killion's scent all over it.

Killion. I swallowed hard against the tightness in my throat. He was near; I could feel him. Once I finally made it to a standing position, I rubbed my upper arms against the chill and shuffled for the doors.

He was so still, so silent, I nearly didn't notice him leaning on the ivy colored railing. The sky had cleared, a crescent moon shedding light on his head and turning his hair a rich midnight blue, similar to the pajama bottoms he wore. The night breeze made his matching satin robe flutter and dance at his ankles, but the cold didn't seem to bother him, not even with his chest bared.

For half a second, I froze, instinct telling me to stay quiet. Ridiculous that. He sensed every move I made, and knew I was there. Yet, things had changed between us. The quiet of the night kept them at bay.

The cold air cleared my brain and I drew in a sustaining breath. At least I hadn't died. Neither had he.

The normal tingling of my blood felt sharper, and I knew it was because of our last exchange. I could sense mine inside him, calling to me. Was that what he experienced when I was near? I glanced between his pants and the shirt I wore. If anyone saw us, they'd assumed we'd been together.

Had we? I was naked underneath it.

"Aurora and Katarina tended to you." His voice was a soft purr. It still made me jump. "I did not touch you."

I found I was a bit relieved. A little disappointed, as well. "How are you?"

His attention stayed on the street below, the black Victorian lamps on the sidewalks glowing. They gave the fake garlands and red bows wrapping their posts a yellow tinge. "I'm indebted to you." Due to his fingers gripping the railing so tightly, his knuckles appeared as white as the moon overhead. The purr left his tone. His words became forced, stiff. "I should have not drank from you. It was a mistake, but what's done is done. I cannot correct it."

A mistake? A sharp sensation hit me between the ribs, as if I'd sucked in too much cold air.

Rubbing my arms again, I stepped closer, keeping a slight distance between us. "I didn't realize you thought so little of me. I mean, I know I'm not your usual...source, but I was trying to help. Would you have preferred the witch?"

"Of course not." A tic made his jaw, set firmly, jump. His eyes slid my way. "You misconstrued my words. I nearly killed you."

Well, there was that. "It was an emergency. You were dying. I'm still here, by the way, in case you hadn't noticed, so you didn't. From what I've learned about myself, it's doubtful you could. And if memory serves, it was only a few months ago when you saved my life by giving me your blood." This wasn't the time to void him of that notion because of Aurora's theory. "I'd say we're even."

The normally violet irises were a deep purple and sullen. They stared elsewhere. "The validity of that has been challenged. If I'm to believe your witch, you are a most unusual supernatural creature. One whose blood I now crave with an insatiable...lust."

That was...unfortunate news.

Wasn't it?

My fingers trembled and the spot between my legs caught fire. I, too, gripped the railing.

Sarcasm being my go-to when freaking out, and known to have no filter when something threw me for a loop, I asked the first thing that popped into my head. "Did you just refer to me as a creature?" He didn't respond. "We've discussed your word choices. And by the way, the 'unusual' is also a bit shady. Like calling someone *interesting* when you actually mean they're crazy, eccentric, or just plain basic. We really need to work on your social skills."

He didn't react, not even with a twitch of that jaw.

I shivered hard and shifted from one foot to the other. "Can we go back inside? It's freezing out here."

"Are you well enough to dress yourself?"

"Need your shirt back?"

He cut those sullen eyes to me again, peeling his hands

from the railing. As he faced me, I felt a wall of his energy hit me like a blast from a furnace. His gaze fell to my chest, lingering on my tattoo, then down to my bare legs. One hand shot out to grip onto the railing again, as if he had to keep himself from lunging for me.

I took a step back, heart hammering like a maniac.

His face blanched.

This is Killion. He was always in control and he would never hurt me...except he had, and we both knew it.

Yet, I wasn't a coward. Not now, anyway. I was...an *unusual creature.*

Grim Zero.

I'd taken down Cosima and her shiftlings. I'd stopped a powerful vampire, hopped up on her master's blood.

Renewed confidence trickled through me. "You can't hurt me, and you won't." My voice came out strong. I closed the distance between us and took his free hand. His nostrils flared and he sucked in air. I intertwined his fingers with mine. "We're partners and...friends. We'll figure out a way to control your craving. Aurora probably has a tea, god help you, or Death has another crystal. Maybe we'll get lucky and the desire will fade over time."

Fingers stiff and body rigid, his eyes held mine. The emotion they conveyed was raw and desperate. "It's too dangerous. I could lose control."

"Like you're about to do now?"

There was a twitch of that broody jaw muscle. "You have no idea how close I am to snapping."

I forced a smile, once again reaching for sarcasm to cover my fear. I would not show it, no matter what. "Good. Just think of how much more reserved, taciturn, self-controlled, and anti-social you'll be with me constantly testing your willpower. No vampire will ever attempt a coup again with such a powerful master at the helm."

He detached his hand from mine, removed his robe, and placed it around my shoulders. His chest was as beautiful as the rest of him, and I bit my lips before I blurted out something to that effect.

Leaning close, his breath teased my ear. "My true name is Constantin Radu—"

"Stop." I turned my ear away from his mouth. He was telling me his name—what was wrong with me? "I don't want to know." Slowly, I met his eyes. "To me, you're very much Killion Reveux. My friend, mentor, and partner."

His body relaxed slightly. "Truly?"

"Yes." I swallowed, wanting to lean into those gorgeous eyes, taste his exquisite lips. "And I don't want to be tortured in order for someone to be able to command you to do their bidding." I faked a visible shudder.

He saw through it, but the corner of his mouth quirked with a barely concealed smile. "Get inside," he ordered.

Reveling in the warmth of the robe, as well as the relief I sensed in him, I grinned and did as instructed.

TWO HOURS LATER, I had downed copious amounts of hot chocolate, Christmas cookies, and a full breakfast, complete with espresso and orange juice. Aurora watched from across the table, one perfect brow arched in astonishment. Andy and Ghost lounged near the fire. Killion sat at the head of the table, unreadable and silent.

"Does she always eat like this?" Aurora asked him.

His nod was sharp. Pennyworth's Christmas carols played softly in the background. "What is your recommendation?"

"Hide your favorite candies at Halloween," she said, sipping a cup of tea.

"I meant about…"

She waved him off. "I know what you meant. Lighten up." She glanced at me. "Is that possible?" Back to him. "I need time and a boatload of unusual resources to figure this out. Be patient. I've never encountered this type of situation before."

There was that word again. Unusual. "Why didn't Death's amulet protect me from Killion?" I asked around a bite of cookie.

Her eyes narrowed in thought and she studied her cup. "You'd have to ask him to know for sure, but I believe the amulet works—worked—in conjunction with your inner survival system. Your subconscious knows immediately when danger is imminent. It knows who you trust or don't. It tapped into that and could sense danger based on your internal radar."

I swallowed. "I trust Killion, so it didn't react when"—I hesitated to say it—"you know."

"That's my guess. Even when I slapped it against him, it read no ill intentions."

Although, it had certainly pissed him off. I glanced at him. "This is good news. See? You wouldn't have killed me, even the crystal knew it. At some point, you would have stopped."

His cool return look was unconvinced. "I do not believe that's why." He pushed a slip of paper across the table. "This fell out of your pocket when Aurora removed the amulet."

It was the slip that Death had given me—my next reaper assignment. I unfolded it. "Even if she hadn't rebelled against you, Simone was next on my—" I blinked, reading the name. Not Simone. Not Moss or Aurora, either.

The dread I had felt but hadn't had time to examine, hit me all over again. My stomach flipped, the food in it threatening to come back up. I dropped the paper and shook my head. "No, that can't be right."

Aurora reached over and grabbed it. Her face went pale as she saw why it upset me. She glanced between us. "Well, that puts a new spin on things, doesn't it?"

I shoved my chair back and stood. "There's been a mistake. I'll fix it."

Killion's eyes, those lovely violet irises that I had come to love, held deep sadness. "You cannot fix this, Chloe. The reason the amulet didn't protect you was because you were supposed to kill me. Your reaper should have surfaced and ended my life. My contract is up."

I started to argue, when, without so much as a knock, Death appeared.

FORTY-EIGHT

Aurora gasped and scooted her chair away. Raw fear slid over my skin. "Don't you have this place warded?" I mumbled. It wouldn't keep my boss out, and I knew it. He'd paid me an unexpected visit here before.

The master vampire didn't respond, his focus on our new guest.

"Ooh," Death said, helping himself to a cookie. He smiled at me as he ate it. "I'm famished. I cleaned up the mess you left at the University, by the way."

"The last name you gave me." It felt like there was a peach pit stuck in my throat. I had to swallow twice before I could continue. "That was a joke, right?"

He faked a perplexed expression and shook his head. "No joke." He grabbed another cookie and glanced at Killion. "Wow, these are excellent. You must have a great chef."

The vampire rose and I jetted around the table, placing myself between him and Death. This was going to go three shades of bad if I didn't think of something quick. "I'm not reaping Killion until I see the contract."

Death swallowed and grinned again. "That's what I like about you—you're a stickler for details. Oh, wait! That's my other three-thousand-plus grims all over the world who actually follow the rules and do their job." The smile faded and his eyes turned hard. "And you no longer get the pleasure of reaping him, nor do you get to lay eyes on his contract. You're on suspension."

"I'm *what?*"

His false good humor returned and he picked up a pinecone from the nearby sideboard's floral arrangement. "Your little love affair with undead boy, here, is over, as is your working partnership. You fed him your blood to keep him alive —a clear violation of Section 84B—and you saved him rather than reaping him—that's a violation of Section 12A. Both serious offenses. So, you are hereby suspended until a full investigation takes place and the committee decides whether to fire or relocate you. Either way, there will be disciplinary measures taken."

At the last bit, he appeared almost giddy.

Speechless, I stuttered. Killion stood at my back and I could feel his anger razing my spine. I was the only thing between him and Death, figuratively, as well as literally, and he wanted to shove me out of the way and take on my boss himself. I had to do something, and fast.

"First of all, I didn't know Killion was the assignment. Secondly—" Before I could go on, I felt the vampire in question touch the small of my back. A warning.

Aurora came to stand next to me, as did Ghost in her psychopomp form. That gave me pause—she was nuts about Death, but here she was, ready to defend me and the vampire.

Andy rose from his comfy spot in front of the fireplace and went to the witch's side, and Katarina unfolded herself from a chair near the hearth, as well. I hadn't even noticed her. She joined our wall of protection in front of Killion.

All righty then. "Secondly," I repeated with more confidence. "Simone deserved to be reaped in his place. Without her help, Cosima might not have—"

Death cut me off. "Cosima and her shiftlings are no longer an issue, and, as you may recall, weren't by the time you reached the church. Your arguments are moot. No more deals, Chloe. No more bluffing or tricks." He jutted his chin at Andy.

I expected the shifter to hide behind Aurora, but he stood unmoving, head held high.

"Andy was invaluable in my investigation. He helped me, in fact, when you didn't." I peeled away from the group, striding forward and staring up into Death's eyes. "How will SMG react when I tell them about your undercover operation? When I plant the suspicion you were not only working with Cosima, but sleeping with her, in fact."

He registered shock, then blustered. "You know that's not true. We've had this discussion."

"You changed Aurora's spell so it would deliver me to Cosima, not remove my necromantic abilities."

His brows crashed together. "We need to have your concussion checked by a doctor."

Aurora said nothing, going along with my bluff. I wondered how much of what I was piecing together might actually be correct. "You wanted me to discover my real identity and become a weapon for her and her disgusting monsters." I took another step and poked him in his hard chest. "You set me up."

"Chloe," he started, in a tone that suggested he was speaking to a small child. "You've got this all wrong."

I picked up my cell from the table. "Fine, we'll let SMG

sort it out." I tapped out a message to Mei Han. If I raised suspicions with them over this, she would open an official inquiry with the oversight board. Reading the Grim Manual was paying off after all.

"What are you doing?"

I poised my finger over the send button. "I'm alerting Ms. Han about my concerns and formally accusing you of sleeping with the enemy and letting it nearly unleash an apocalyptic storm on the human and supernatural worlds alike."

He snatched the phone from my hand. Killion bared his teeth and drew me behind him into the protection of the group.

Death stood his ground, reading my text. He deleted it and tossed the phone on the table. It clanged against the now empty cookie plate. "I *was* undercover." He insisted. "It wasn't my idea to keep you in the dark about your past —*our* past. When I discovered Cosima was looking for Grim Zero, and closing in on succeeding at making her creatures, I knew you were the only hope we had to stop her. While I couldn't be directly involved, if I hadn't triggered your abilities, she might have won and you'd all be down on your knees, bowing to her right now."

"Why didn't you just tell us that?" Katarina demanded.

He sighed. "I would have been in breach of my contract with SMG. Free will and all that. Like I said, I'm not allowed to interfere with humanity as a whole."

"They hid Chloe here in Dante's Grove, didn't they?" Aurora asked. "They thought she was safe, that Cosima would never learn where she was if she never realized *who* she was."

He suddenly looked very tired, very ancient. "The Grim Z contract was set for immortality, like mine. She was never supposed to die. When she did, it upset the balance big time, and put me in her debt. SMG had to reincarnate her at some point, and"—he waved a hand in my direction—"here we are. Cosima found her, and that was thanks to Simone." He glared at Killion.

Hiding behind the vampire wasn't an option. I stepped out but stayed at his side. "Neither she, nor Cosima, are problems now, and that's because of me." I pointedly glanced around. "Because of all of us. You withheld the truth—you and SMG—I was nearly killed again, as well as a whole lot of innocent people. Megan did, in fact, lose her life, and if that isn't injustice, I don't know what is. The scales are unbalanced whether you like it or not. Also, I'm not taking the blame for that, just because I saved her father."

"Megan is alive."

My jaw fell. "What?"

"Not because you begged me to save her, but because..." He ran a hand over his face. "You were right, and like I mentioned, I owe you. The girl was vulnerable and gullible, and Cosima used her. I made an arrangement with SMG and they agreed. I wiped her and her father's memories of what happened, but before they put her spirit back in her body, I made her promise to leave the necromancy and witchcraft alone. She'll stay on a better path now. I hope."

I was shocked. "You have a heart after all."

Ignoring my sarcasm, he continued. "I can't do anything about your suspension, but I can look the other way about him,"—his eyes flicked to Killion—"if you agree to my demands."

At this point, I would do anything to save the master vampire, but I wasn't going to throw myself on Death's mercy just yet. "They better be simple ones," I insisted.

"Easy. Otherwise I go to SMG with all of this, regardless of your claims. It's a he-said, she-said situation, so you can take your chances."

Unfazed, he held up his index finger. "One: no more whining about reaper assignments."

"I don't whine."

He barked a laugh that shook the crystal chandelier over our heads. Then he stared me down, waiting.

"Fine," I conceded. "I'll keep future complaints to myself."

He held up a second finger. "Two: no more trying to make deals and save people."

I began to object, but Killion brushed my hand. This was Death, after all. One blink and we could all be lights out. "Agreed," I mumbled, while crossing my fingers behind my back.

"Stop that."

"Stop what?"

That got me the 'Death' glare.

How did he know? I uncrossed them.

Appeased, he pointed those two fingers at my face. "This clears my debt to you. You try to wiggle out of any of it, and I'll ruin you, you understand? I'll make sure you're penniless, friendless, and sick all the time. Your dream of reopening the clinic will never happen."

My heart sank, but I nodded. "Letter of the law, that's me from now on."

"No more bringing reaped souls back from the dead," he added.

"That might be impossible since I can't control the necromancy."

He fished out a necklace from under his shirt, removed it, and handed it to me. "For now, wear this. It will do the trick. I'm working on something more permanent, but it may take a while."

I hesitated to accept it. "Is this going to track me, like the previous one?"

The glare came back, and he put his hands on his hips. "That was for your own good. I knew if Cosima kidnapped you, I might not be able to find you because of her magic."

And that *had* happened. I still didn't like the idea of wearing anything he gave me, but for now... I slipped it on and held up my own finger. "I want your promise that Killion will be protected and respected going forward."

"No."

"Yes. Your debt isn't wiped clean yet. Grim Zero died for you. You owe me this."

He looked both resigned and annoyed. "I knew you'd play that card. Fine. Whatever."

"I want it in writing."

He narrowed his eyes. "You know what that requires."

"I do."

He screwed up his face, but gave a faint nod. I held up my hand and he did the same. My skin burned with a sudden cut across my palm and drops of blood floated up from it.

"Chloe," Killion growled, "what are you doing?"

"Shut up for once," Death commanded. "She's doing this for you."

A blood contract would seal the deal. My blood floated to Death's palm and drops of his floated to mine. At the same time, both fell and vanished in to our respective hands. I felt the sickening rush of the seal and then it was done.

He glanced forlornly at the empty cookie plate and then strode for the door. "We've got grave robbers upsetting the ghosts. Hard for them to rest in peace." he glanced over his shoulder at me. "You can't reap anyone who's alive while you're suspended, but I'll get the board to give you permission to investigate the graveyard vandalism and find out who's disturbing the dead." He swung back at the threshold. "Merry Christmas."

That was directed at the group, and yet his wink at me held more than a casual good wish. He was giving me a great gift—Killion's life.

He disappeared and I turned to my friend and took his hand. Giving it a squeeze, I grinned, trying to remove the crease between his brows and the protective wall of heat rolling off of him. "See? Everything's fine."

While he gave me a return smile, I saw the doubt in his eyes.

FORTY-NINE

The next two days went by in a blur of holiday festivities. My wounds healed nicely, and I suffered no lasting effects from the concussion.

I ran on my usual cocktail of coffee and sugar to stay awake, and spent time with Vera and Velma, my aunt and uncle, Nita, and even Mason and the other Bean employees during a Christmas Eve open house at the coffee shop.

Throughout each day, I found small gifts at my back door, saw eyes watching me from alleys and bushes. Animals, shifters and non-, seemed to be drawn to me, and wanted to be friends.

After a huge late afternoon meal on Christmas Day with Aunt Camille and Uncle Morty, I decided to walk home in an attempt to aid my digestion and clear my head. Killion had kept his distance, finding excuses to decline my offers of holiday interactions. I knew he was spending more time with his nest, reestablishing his leadership and letting them know he was still concerned with their well-being. Still, I couldn't tell if his refusals to my invites were due to his usual anti-social behavior, or if he was afraid to get too close because of the blood lust.

Nita and Vera both voiced concerns that we'd "broken up," and although his boyfriend status was a ruse, I pretended everything was fine. Truth was, I wasn't sure we hadn't.

Aurora assured me she could make a potion for him that would dampen his desire, but if she'd given it to him, he hadn't mentioned it. I assumed he'd need to be near me to test it.

Light snow fell as I detoured to the south end of town, Ghost enjoying the layer of flakes as she skidded and slid in it. The shorter days and gray skies suggested sundown was around the corner. I let her meander on and off the sidewalks that grew scarcer the farther we journeyed, the scattering of houses thinning as well. A few here and there had windows lit with Christmas trees and others had a few tired decorations.

At the graveyard, the gate was unlocked and it squeaked with a familiar grating noise. Ghosts hovered around graves and various statues. They watched me with hollow eyes, but none dared get too close this time.

Inside the mausoleum, Corvus met us, and the air temperature was cooler. Aurora, dressed in a long red and green plaid skirt, with a red velvet top, greeted me with a cup of tea that smelled like grass. In her hand was a book from one of her shelves. "For you." The volume had no title, and instead sported a black skull and crossbones on the brittle cover, not unlike my grim tattoo. "It's on the subject of death."

I would have never guessed. "Aww, you shouldn't have," I teased, setting down the cup without drinking. The pages contained crude drawings and what appeared to be journal entries. "I didn't get you anything."

"It's your first assignment." She began grinding dried herbs in a marble bowl with her stone pedestal. "If you're a death dealer, you need to know everything about it, including how the human body works. There's stuff in there about supernaturals and the different types of magic. Not all of them, but the most common." She wiped her hands on a towel and went to search a shelf. Andy lay by the water-fall, letting Ghost use him to leap off his back and splash into the water. "And this one." Aurora pulled out a thick leather-bound tome with gold lettering. "Myths and legends. You'll find information about yourself in here."

My skin tingled. The title was in an archaic script. "What language is this?"

"Language. Grim," Corvus called.

Aurora placed a ringed finger on an odd symbol in the center and her lips moved with whispered words. "Go ahead," she told me, when she'd finished. "See if you under-stand it now."

The cover made a cracking noise as I opened it and flipped through the thin, fragile pages. Sure enough, wher-ever my focus landed, the odd words morphed into English. "I want to be you when I grow up."

She laughed, that tinkling sound that both Andy and I loved, echoing in the room. "Drink your tea and you might."

Begrudgingly, I took a tiny sip. My stomach clenched and I screwed up my nose. "Needs honey. Or maybe a do-over. This tastes horrible."

"If you want to control the necromancy without Death's amulet, drink it. He's right, you know."

I narrowed my eyes. "About what?"

"You whine a lot."

I stuck out my tongue, and then, holding my breath, I pressed my eyes shut and downed the awful liquid in two gulps. "There," I croaked and slammed down the cup. "Done."

Having earned my gold star for the day, I stuck my homework in my backpack. "There's something I need to talk to you about," I told her.

"There are a lot of things we need to talk about."

True. "This one isn't about me. You healed Andy, but you gave his cancer to someone who was innocent."

She flinched. "I did no such thing."

"Pretty sure you did."

"I can't heal cancer, Chloe. Wish I could."

"But someone cured him."

We both looked at the shifter and he slid his attention away, pretending not to be eavesdropping.

"Hmmm," Aurora said. "I don't know any healer who could do that. Witch, either. Are you sure he had cancer?"

At this point, it probably didn't matter. "So the woman who ended up with it, who wasn't on my reaping list and now is, isn't due to anything Andy or his healer did?"

Aurora shook her head. "Sometimes bad things just happen to people."

It sucked, but she was right. "About the ghosts in the graveyard. They need to move on. It's not healthy for them to remain earthbound."

"It's all illusion. Can't you tell?"

I shook my head, frowning. "They look real to me. I sent one to the afterlife." *I think.*

"Your blade muted the magic, is all, and it disappeared. I use the illusion to keep those stupid ghost tours away. Keeps most people away, in fact." She winked. "Just how I like it."

"I would think the tours would love to see a cemetery full of them."

"Ha!" She continued mixing up her potion, adding some mint leaves. Her Irish accent was beautiful and light. "People like to be scared a bit, but coming face to face with a ghost is actually more than most care for. Mine may be illusions, but they can be pretty terrifying, if I wish them to be." Her evil grin told me this was true. "Had to up my game with those pesky grave robbers running around."

She hummed a carol under her breath as I watched her work. I was curious why anyone would steal from the dead, but that was for next week. Right now, I wondered if she were lonely, here by herself all the time. "Do you have Christmas plans? Any family to hang out with?"

"I celebrated Yule with my coven." Her eyes flicked to me and over to Andy. "Don't you be worrying about me, now. I have a special project I'm working on today, and you best be going."

Andy made a funny noise in his throat, and waggled his furry eyebrows at her. Her tinkling laughter filled the room again.

Yep, definitely time to go. "I wish you the best with your...project."

I rounded up my wet dog and said goodbye, wondering who Death would send for the woman with cancer, and saying a prayer for her.

My next stop was the church. Outside the front entrance, I placed a set of Mardi Gras beads over the Virgin Mother's head, and looked around for the dogs. They were nowhere to be seen, which was odd. Snow had accumulated on Ghost's fur and it covered her muzzle, giving her the appearance of a beard.

I knocked on the doors and waited. Knocked again. "I know you're in there, Katarina," I called. "I come in peace."

She made me wait several more minutes before sliding open a slot in the wood to peer out at me. "What do you want?"

I held up a gift-wrapped box. While the vampire didn't like me, her loyalty to Killion made me like her. I had the feeling should I need her down the road, I'd best do what I could to make friends with her, or at the very least, keep her as an ally. "I'm sorry I upset you about your pets. And I'm grateful for your assistance with Simone and Death."

Her blood red lips curled. "I did it for the master, not you, and just so you know, it's dangerous for you to come here without him. I could kill you and dispose of your body and no one would be the wiser."

"You actually like me, don't you?"

She rolled her eyes and her painted nails flashed as she motioned for me to hand her the box through the opening. I did and took a step back, glancing around. Night was truly falling. Across the street, the bar was still open, green and red lights blinking furiously around a lighted beer sign in the lone window.

She tore open the gift and held up the comb for her hair. It was a shiny black goth thing that I'd picked up on my shopping trip with Nita. There was a tiny bat and a hairy spider dangling from one end. Her eyes lit up and she pursed her lips, trying not to smile.

I could hear the dogs on her side, panting and whining, sensing or smelling Ghost. The psychopomp stood at attention, wagging her tail and waiting for us to go in and greet her new friends.

Katarina carefully placed the comb in her upswept hair. "You're okay, Grave Girl," she said, begrudgingly. "Even

Moss likes you, and he doesn't like anybody. Just don't screw over the master, got it?"

"Same goes for you." I gave her a steady look. "If anyone tries to overthrow Killion again, I will consider them my enemy."

One side of her mouth twitched, as my message registered. The second reason I was here. "He doesn't need you to keep his status."

If it wasn't for me, Simone would now be in charge. I let it go, though. "Regardless, I'd appreciate you spreading the word."

I didn't wait for a response. Ghost and I skipped down the steps and into the growing night.

FIFTY

A few blocks from the church, my blood heated and my skin tingled. The limo slid to the curb next to me, the downtown streets quiet and nearly abandoned.

Killion emerged and I had trouble catching my breath as his gaze met mine. A long, wool coat, black as the night, covered his suit. His violet eyes sparkled under the street-light. I had one more stop planned before heading home, but seeing him wiped everything from my mind.

The tickle under my breastbone grew to a wave of desire. He had consumed my blood and we were connected on a whole different level.

"I can feel you wherever you go," he said, as quiet as the night air around us.

Had his lips moved? Everything but him seemed to disappear. "I can feel you, too, but it's muffled until you're close like this."

"I sense your emotions. I know what you're thinking."

"Okay, that's creepy, but even more so is the fact you aren't actually speaking, are you?"

Our telepathic connection is now level six.

Both Jacqueline and Cosima had tried to crawl into my mind. It had felt awful. With Killion? Melted chocolate.

I bit my bottom lip, feeling flustered. *You can read my mind? Like, all the time?*

A nod. His eyes felt as if they were burning in to me.

You poor thing. It's a mess in here. You do remember what I said about boundaries, right?

The corner of his mouth quirked. "May I walk with you?" He used his voice this time, which made me feel better, and the tunnel focus his connection had caused eased up. Ghost wagged her tail and went to sniff his pant leg.

"Of course. I'm glad you're here." I dug out a final gift. "This is for Moss."

The driver's window rolled down and Moss looked genuinely surprised. He tore open the gift with glee as Killion and I watched. One part of it was practical, and he tugged on the new leather driving gloves, flexing his fingers. "Sweet." Under those was an air freshener called Bones and Blood that I'd found in a clearance bin at Nita's favorite magic shop. He held it up, seeming confused.

"To help with the wet dog smell," I explained, even though I was sure the limo had been cleaned and sanitized repeatedly.

"You're all right," he said, gripping the steering wheel. The copper threads in the gloves glinted under the lamplight. "I won't call you Grave Girl anymore."

I gave him a thumbs-up.

"Perhaps tomorrow night," Moss said, flexing his hands in the gloves again, "we could light a candle at the church for your parents. I know it's not your typical sacred setting, but I'm decorating the altar to pay tribute to our fallen and wanted to invite you."

My heart warmed. Not only by the offer to honor my parents, but to be included in a vampire observance. "I would love that. Maybe afterwards, you can show me how I'm telegraphing my swing."

"Deal." We bumped fists.

"You're welcome to walk with me," I said to Killion as I returned to the sidewalk. Ghost led the way and we fell into step together behind her. Soft snow crunched under our feet and flakes stuck to our hair. We said nothing and I tried to keep my thoughts bland and in the background, enjoying the night. The silence was comfortable, and although I did mentally reach out to see if I could hear Killion's thoughts, I didn't succeed at it.

That was for the best. As we arrived at the veterinary clinic, I stopped. The plastic dog with the sad eyes was the same, although someone had strung Christmas lights around the display window. My heart fell as I saw as flyer taped in the corner announcing it was opening under new management in the New Year.

"Oh my god." If I could, I would have reached through the glass and tore it off. *Frosty Paws Small Animal Clinic,* the announcement read. "They can't do that." Blood rushed in my ears and my stomach turned over. "That was the name of our business!"

Killion took my hand, his fingerless gloves allowing skin to skin contact as he threaded his fingers through mine. "I'm sorry, Chloe."

Tears welled in my eyes. "I've been saving to buy it back. Now, it's too late."

He reached inside his breast pocket. "No, I meant I'm sorry I didn't do this sooner."

Handing me a manila envelope, he released my hand so I could open it. "What is this?" I drew out a set of papers and my heart stopped. I scanned the top page again. "I don't understand."

The corner of his mouth tipped and he looked almost bashful. "I own the building, and I'm leasing it to you as of January first."

"What?" Incredulous laughter bubbled up from my belly and echoed down the street. I jumped up and down in place, tears flooding my eyes. This was too good to be true. "But I'm not a vet, yet. I'm only a tech still."

"I've hired Dr. O'Leary. While he prefers to go by Professor, he's still licensed to practice. You can work as much or as little as you want. Hire others. It's all up to you."

I couldn't believe it and more tears flowed. I crinkled the papers a bit just to make sure I wasn't dreaming. "You don't have to do this," I said, and then kicked myself. "But I'm so, so grateful you did. You can't know how much this means to me."

He gave me a full smile, as rare as a diamond. "Rent is due on the first of each month and I'll expect quarterly reports and projections. We need to work on your business plan and set up an accounting system. I've scheduled a strategic planning meeting next Wednesday with my executive team, and I'm anxious to hear your ideas for making this new endeavor successful."

Always a businessman. That was good, because I wasn't. I would learn, though. "Thank you."

We stood there, staring at each other, my blood heating again at the desire I saw in his eyes. He cleared his throat. "You're welcome. It was the least I could do after you saved my Undead life."

The air went charged with something I couldn't name. It was dangerous and wild, reckless. I liked it. "Best. Gift. Ever," I said.

A raven cawed and a wing brushed the top of my head. I instinctively ducked. Corvus landed a few feet away, dusting up snow. He flopped up and down. "Jelly bean!"

Ghost barked. Running at me, Corvus threw his wings around my leg. "Kill! Kill!"

I gently tugged him off. "What are you doing here?"

Andy, in human form, emerged from a shadow, startling me. "I need a job. You hiring?" He pointed at the window.

"How are you human again?"

A shoulder shrugged. "That project Aurora mentioned? She fed me this horrible tea, and..."

"Say no more." I held up a hand. "I know all about her potions."

"Reapers keepers," the bird sang, dancing around my ankles. He did some sort of strut, flapping his wings, pulling them in, then repeating the dance.

"What in the world is he doing?" I asked the two men.

"Mating dance. Apparently, he's bonded with you." Andy made a face. "He about killed himself trying to follow you after you left. Prior to today's visit, he was moping around like he was heartbroken. Aurora says he belongs to you now."

"Oh no." I took a step back and the raven rushed for my leg again. "I don't need another pet."

"Reapers keepers," he sang.

I glanced at Killion, who was failing in his attempts not to laugh. "Perhaps the clinic could use a mascot," he offered.

The bird would not let go. "I can reap you, you know," I threatened.

It fell on deaf ears and Andy chuckled. "Is the apartment above the clinic for rent?"

"Yes," Killion said, at the same time I said, "No."

We glared at each other, and I asked, "Aren't you and

Aurora *together*? She must want you around if she managed to make you human again."

"She needs her space." I could hear his eye roll in the words, even if he didn't actually make the physical action. "Don't worry, I'll wear her down with my magic touch." He made a suggestive face and winked. "Fixer, that's me."

"TMI."

Killion typed a note into his phone. "I'll email you the rental agreement tomorrow. You start work January second."

"Awesome." Andy waved. "See you next year, grim."

I gaped at his retreating back, then at the vampire. It was all happening so fast. "I'm not sure I even like him."

He put an arm around my shoulder and steered me to the limo, idling at the curb. "We all have our cross to bear."

The raven and Ghost joined us in the backseat. Killion poured hot chocolate and added a handful of those magnificent marshmallows. "I have info on the grave robberies," he told me, "but tonight we relax." He handed me the cup and raised his own crystal glass into the air. "To our partnership."

Feeling a warm flush at the idea of working with Killion and opening the clinic after all this time, I grinned. "To us."

"Kill!" the raven shouted. At my chastising look, he added, "Ho ho ho, jelly bean."

Dirty Deeds, Witches Anonymous Step 7

Wicked Wedding, Witches Anonymous Step 8

Paranormal Romantic Suspense

Soul Survivor, Moon Water Series, Book 1

Soul Protector, Moon Water Series, Book 2

Cozy Mysteries (writing as Nyx Halliwell)

Sister Witches Of Raven Falls Mystery Series

Of Potions and Portents

Of Curses and Charms

Of Stars and Spells

Of Spirits and Superstition

Confessions of a Closet Medium Series

Pumpkins & Poltergeists

Magic & Mistletoe

Hearts & Haunts

Vows & Vengeance

Cupcakes & Corpses

Once Upon a Witch Cozy Mystery Series

If the Cursed Shoe Fits (Cinder)

Beastly Book of Spells (Belle)

Poisoned Apple Potion (Snow) - only available in the Black Cat Crossing box set which is FREE when you sign up for the Whiskered Mysteries newsletter!

Red Hot Wolfie (Ruby)

Hexed Hair Day (Rapunzel)

SEALs of Shadow Force Series

Fatal Truth

Fatal Honor

Fatal Courage

Fatal Love

Fatal Vision

Fatal Thrill

Risk

SEALS of Shadow Force Series: Spy Division

Man Hunt

Man Killer

Man Down

The SCVC Taskforce Series

Deadly Pursuit

Deadly Deception

Deadly Force

Deadly Intent

Deadly Affair, A SCVC Taskforce novella

Deadly Attraction

Deadly Secrets

Deadly Holiday, A SCVC Taskforce novella

Deadly Target

Deadly Rescue

Deadly Bounty

Deadly Betrayal

Deadly Threat

The Super Agent Series

Operation Sheba

Operation Paris

Operation Proof of Life

Operation Lost Princess

Operation Ambush

Operation Christmas Contraband

Operation Sleeping With the Enemy

The Secret Ingredient Culinary Mystery Series

The Secret Ingredient, A Culinary Romantic Mystery with Bonus Recipes

The Secret Life of Cranberry Sauce, A Secret Ingredient Holiday Novella

MEET MISTY

USA TODAY Bestselling Author Misty Evans has published over seventy-five novels and writes romantic suspense, urban fantasy, and paranormal romance. Under her pen name, Nyx Halliwell, she also writes cozy mysteries.

When not reading or writing, she embraces her inner gypsy and loves music, movies, and hanging out with her husband, twin sons, and three spoiled puppies. She's a crafter at heart and has far too many projects to finish.

Don't want to miss a single adventure? Visit www.mistyevansbooks.com to find out ALL the news!

Check out her humorous pen name Nyx Halliwell for magical mysteries https://www.nyxhalliwell.com .

www.ingramcontent.com/pod-product-compliance
Lightning Source LLC
Chambersburg PA
CBHW070830190726
48292CB00006B/2169